Ray Palmer

The Poetical Works of Ray Palmer

Ray Palmer

The Poetical Works of Ray Palmer

ISBN/EAN: 9783337275198

Printed in Europe, USA, Canada, Australia, Japan

Cover: Foto ©Andreas Hilbeck / pixelio.de

More available books at **www.hansebooks.com**

TO THE

REV. MARK HOPKINS, D.D., LL.D.,

WHOSE FAITHFUL FRIENDSHIP,

EXTENDING OVER MANY YEARS, HAS NOT ONLY CHEERED AND

ENRICHED THE PAST, BUT HAS ALSO GIVEN TO THE

PRESENT AND THE FUTURE A TREASURE

OF CHERISHED MEMORIES,

THIS VOLUME IS AFFECTIONATELY INSCRIBED BY

RAY PALMER.

PREFACE.

THE greater number of the Poems contained in this volume are already, in one form or another, before the Public. Of the hymns, nearly all those previously published, that were designed to be sung, have found their way, some of them many years ago, into the Manuals for public worship. A considerable number that have never before appeared, with others only to be found in one or two of the very latest collections, are published here. The writer has so often had requests from various persons, at home and abroad, for the correct texts of his contributions to the service of Christian song, that he has felt constrained to prepare this complete and accurate edition of them. Hymns of a certain class are intended only for private reading. Many of this class are mingled, in this arrangement, with the others. It is hoped that these may help to kindle Christian affections in the closet, and to carry comfort and cheer to depressed and troubled hearts.

The Poem entitled "Home, or the Unlost Paradise," as originally published by itself, was very kindly received, and has been circulated widely, especially as

a bridal gift. Its purpose was not to describe New England life and character, but, by presenting a general and typical picture of an intelligent and virtuous Home, to awaken the many pleasant associations that cluster around every such Home, wherever found.

Of the miscellaneous Poems, some have been published in former volumes, some in various periodicals, and some are now first printed.

The author takes leave to add that his time and strength, for more than forty years, have been almost unremittingly devoted to the absorbing duties of a Christian minister, and for more than three-fourths of this period to the manifold labors of a city Pastor. Poetry, instead of filling any prominent place in the programme of his life, has been only the occupation of the few occasional moments that could be redeemed from severer, and generally very prosaic, forms of work. It has, in this way, afforded him not a little pleasure and refreshment. But what has been written under such disadvantages must needs claim some indulgence, as compared with what, in the case of others, has been the fruit of ample literary leisure. He will be content if these leaves gathered from the wayside of life, together with those that have now been added, shall prove acceptable and useful to the lovers of pure thoughts.

R. P.

New York, September, 1875.

TABLE OF CONTENTS.

HYMNS AND SACRED LYRICS.

HYMNS AND SACRED LYRICS (*continued*).

HYMNS AND SACRED LYRICS (*continued*).

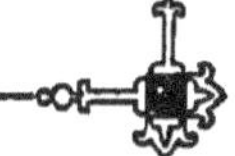

MISCELLANEOUS POEMS.

MISCELLANEOUS POEMS (*continued*).

MISCELLANEOUS POEMS *(continued).*

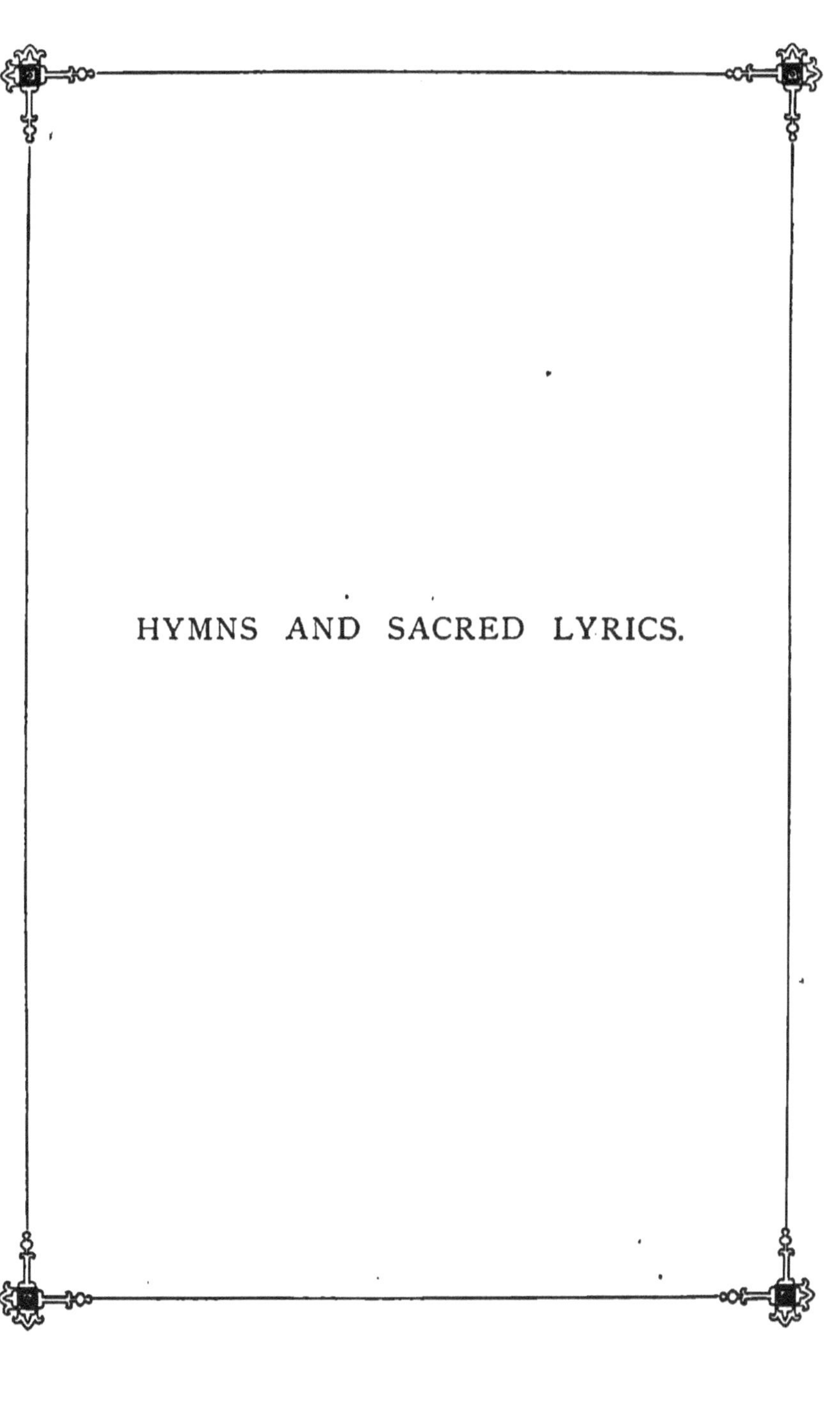

HYMNS AND SACRED LYRICS.

Τῷ Χριστῷ καὶ τῇ Εκκλησίᾳ.

Speaking to yourselves in psalms and hymns and spiritual songs, singing and making melody in your heart to the Lord. — EPH. v. 19.

Let every thing that hath breath praise the Lord. — Ps. cl. 6.

HYMNS AND SACRED LYRICS.

SALVATOR MUNDI.

THE following piece was written at the request of the Rev. PHILIP SCHAFF, D.D., as a prelude to his elegant volume, entitled "Christ in Song," in which it first appeared.

O LONG and darksome was the night
    That in dull watches wore away,
With moon and stars alone to light
    A world bewildered and astray;
        While oft thick shade and murky cloud
        Pale moon and stars did deep enshroud;
And nations looked, and hoped in vain
That over earth, of guilt and sorrow,
Of sin and hate, the sad domain,
Might dawn a bright and cheerful morrow.

'Twas not, Eternal Love, that Thou
    Hadst lost Thy care for mortal men:
No, Thou didst yearn of old, as now,
    To fold them to Thy heart again;
        Thou didst but wait till men might know
        That sin's ripe fruits were death and woe;
Till, worn and sick of fruitless grief,
Of lust's foul cup to loathing taken,
With longing they might crave relief
Ere yet of God and hope forsaken.

There were who heard with trusting heart,
  E'en then, Thy words of hope and cheer;
Who saw by faith the night depart,
  And morning break serene and clear.
    On holy prophets shone afar
    The gleam of Jacob's promised Star;
The rising of the Lord of day,
That, o'er the world his radiance throwing,
Should chase the spectral night away,
And mount to noon resplendent glowing.

When Thou, O Christ, of flesh wast born,
  To greet Thee in Thy humble bed,
Though earth Thy lowliness should scorn,
  Celestial bands with rapture sped;
    At midnight on the silent air
    Thy birth their floating strains declare:
The shepherds catch the thrilling lay,
In harmonies their senses steeping;
Then to Thy manger take their way,
And gaze on Thee, an infant sleeping!

While Thou didst dwell with men below,
  'Twas morning twilight's early blush;
Thy light yet veiled, 'twas Thine to know
  Sweet childhood's dream, youth's joyous flush;
    Then manhood's burdens, cares, and fears,
    Its toils and weariness and tears;
Tears shed for human grief and woes
Mark Thee, of all, the Man of Sorrows;
And through Thy life the grandeur grows
That manhood from the Godhead borrows!

When, all forsaken of Thine own,
  Robed in mock purple Thou didst stand,
Thou wast a King — without a throne;
  A sovereign Lord — without command;
    'Neath purple robe and thorns concealed,
    Divinity its light revealed;
Upon the Roman's heart it fell,
And its keen flash, his conscience waking,
Wrought in him like some mighty spell,
The pride of his strong spirit breaking.

When came at last Thy darkest hour,
  On which the sun refused to look,
Though hell seemed armed with conquering power,
  And earth, as seized with terror, shook;
    Though from Thy lips the dying cry,
    By anguish wrung, went up on high;
Still, 'mid the darkness and the fear,
O Son of God, Thy life resigning,
Thou didst to those that saw appear
The Light of men, — eclipsed, yet shining!

E'en the dark tomb of chiselled rock
  Thy glory could not all repress:
A moment hid, with earthquake shock
  Abroad it streamed again to bless;
    Angels first caught the vision bright,
    Then broke its beams on mortal sight;
The Conqueror of Death and Hell,
Thou stoodst, Thine own each word attending,
Till on their wistful eyes there fell
Splendors divine from Thee ascending!

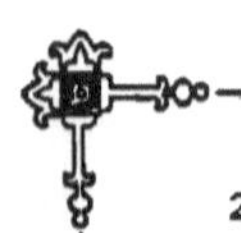

For ever on the unveiled throne,
  O Lamb divine! enrobed in light,
Thou life and love, and joy unknown,
   Dost shed while ages wing their flight;
    The cherubim before Thee bow;
    The fulness of the Godhead Thou!
Thy uncreated beauty greets
The longing eyes that, upward gazing,
Feast on Thy smile, that ever meets
Thy saints that wait before Thee praising.

Head over all! 'tis Thine to reign;
  The groaning earth with joy shall see
What ages sought, but sought in vain,
   The balm for all its woes in Thee;
    Eyes fixed on Thee shall dry their tears;
    Hearts stayed on Thee shall lose their fears;
Fair innocence and love shall breathe
Their fragrant breath o'er vale and mountain,
And Faith pure altars shall enwreathe,
And nations bathe in Calvary's fountain.

Crowned Lord of lords, Thy power shall bring
  All Thine Thy glory to partake;
Thyself enthroned Eternal King,
   Of them Thy love shall Princes make;
    And Priests, that in the Holy Place
    Shall serve, adorned and full of grace;
The Church, Thy queenly Bride, shall stand
In vesture like Thy brightness shining,
Content to clasp Thy royal hand,
All other love for Thine resigning.

O Love beyond all mortal thought!
  Unquenchable by flood or sea!
Love that, through death, to man hath brought
  The life of Immortality!
    Thou. dost enkindle Heaven's own fire
    In hearts all dead to high desire.
Let love for love our souls inflame,
The perfect love that faileth never;
And sweet Hosannas to Thy Name
Through heaven's vast dome go up for ever!

1868.

FAITH.

THE writer has given in the Appendix a brief statement in relation to the origin
of this hymn, wh'ch, as embodying the simple act of faith in the crucified Redeemer,
has so widely commended itself to Christian hearts. It has been translated into as
many as seven or eight languages. See Appendix, Note A.

"Behold the Lamb of God!" — JOHN i. 29.

MY faith looks up to Thee,
  .Thou Lamb of Calvary,
    Saviour divine:
Now hear me while I pray,
Take all my guilt away,
O let me from this day
    Be wholly Thine.

May Thy rich grace impart
.Strength to my fainting heart,
    My zeal inspire;
As Thou hast died for me,
O may my love to Thee
Pure, warm, and changeless be, —
    A living fire.

While life's dark maze I tread,
And griefs around me spread,
    Be Thou my guide;
Bid darkness turn to day,
Wipe sorrow's tears away,
Nor let me ever stray
    From Thee aside.

When ends life's transient dream,
When death's cold, sullen stream
    Shall o'er me roll;
Blest Saviour, then, in love,
Fear and distrust remove;
O bear me safe above, —
    A ransomed soul.

1830.

A HYMN OF PRAISE.

" Let every thing that hath breath praise the Lord." — Ps. cl. 6.

ETERNAL Father, mighty Lord,
    We join to celebrate Thy praise;
Let earth and heaven, in full accord,
    To Thee one song of gladness raise.

Thrice Holy! cry the cherubim;
    Thrice Holy! we responsive cry;
Well-pleasing to Thine ear the hymn,
    When mortal voices reach the sky.

Our lips would magnify Thy name,
  Exhaustless Source of life and joy!
'Twas from Thy breath our being came;
  Thy praise shall our best thoughts employ.

Thy power hath fashioned sea and land,
  Hath filled with worlds the eternal deep;
And suns and stars, by Thy command,
  On their unmeasured courses sweep.

Thou hast redeemed a world from death,
  The ransom Thine eternal Son!
He, by His cross and dying breath,
  Immortal life for man hath won.

We cannot touch angelic lyres,
  Nor wake the strains that seraphs sing;
Yet, Lord, our souls Thy love inspires,
  And, with all heaven, we praise our King!

1874.

CHRISTUS VICTOR.

" That at the name of Jesus every knee should bow." — PHIL. ii. 10.

PRAISE Him! Praise the conquering King!
  Christ our Lord is Lord of all;
Nations, joyful tribute bring!
  Princes, low before Him fall!
See unfurled His royal banner!
  On He cometh to subdue;

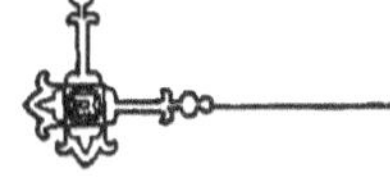

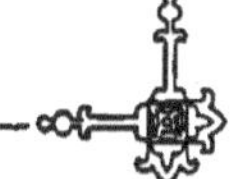

Earth's long wail becomes hosanna,
  Lo! He maketh all things new.
      Hallelujah!
Reign, O Christ, Thou just and true!

Praise Him!   Praise the Prince of Peace!
  Angels, wake your strain again;
Chant His triumphs, ne'er to cease
  Till our God shall dwell with men.
Christ hath heard the ages sighing;
  Christ hath pitied mortal grief;
At His coming tears are drying,
  Millions hail the glad relief.
      Hallelujah!
Hell, thy reign shall now be brief.

Praise Him!   Praise the Lord of Life!
  Him that liveth and was dead;
Past the cross and dying strife,
  Vanquished Death He captive led.
Ever-living, life-bestowing,
  In Thee all the holy live;
Fount exhaustless, overflowing,
  Health and gladness Thou dost give.
      Hallelujah!
Earth and heaven from Thee receive.

Praise Him!   Praise the Lamb enthroned,
  Radiant at His Father's side;
Him who by His blood atoned,
  Him who names the church His Bride!

Thou, O Lamb of God, for ever,
  Where eternal noontide glows,
Thine own flock wilt feed, and never
  Cease to guard their sweet repose.
     Hallelujah!
Thou hast crushed their mighty foes.

Praise Him! Praise Incarnate Love!
  Ranks seraphic, legions bright,
Souls redeemed, who, fixed above,
  Glow in His eternal light;
All on earth who, upward gazing,
  See His beauty and adore,
One far-sounding chorus raising,
  Speak that name forevermore.
     Hallelujah!
Crown Him! Once the cross He bore.

1871.

PRAISE TO CHRIST.

" King of kings, and Lord of lords." — REV. xix. 16.

O CHRIST, the Lord of heaven, to Thee,
  Clothed with all majesty divine,
Eternal power and glory be,
  Eternal praise of right is Thine!

Reign, Prince of Life, that once Thy brow
  Didst yield to wear the wounding thorn;
Reign, throned beside the Father now,
  Adored the Son of God first-born!

From angel hosts that round Thee stand,
  With forms more pure than spotless snow,
From the bright, burning seraph band,
  Let praise in loftiest numbers flow!

To Thee, the Lamb, our mortal songs,
  Born of deep, fervent love shall rise;
All honor to Thy name belongs,
  Our lips would sound it to the skies.

Jesus! all earth shall speak the word;
  Jesus! all heaven resound it still;
Immanuel, Saviour, Conqueror, Lord,
  Thy praise the universe shall fill.

1867.

THE LOVE THAT STOOPETH.

"What is man, that Thou art mindful of him?" — Ps. viii. 4.

MY God, though far above my thought
    The wonders of Thy being rise;
Though earth itself appears but naught,
  And all the orbs in yonder skies
Seem trifles while I think of Thee,
Yet Thou dost deign to visit me!

Lord, what is man?   Ah! not to him
  Is due Thy coming down to dwell;
Thou whose high praise the seraphim
  Touch their entrancing lyres to tell;
Thou comest for no worth of mine,
'Tis all of grace and love divine!

And I may speak, as speaks a child
  That gazes on a father's face
Suffused with love, serenely mild,
  And fair with tenderness and grace;
May lift my eyes without a fear,
And know that, speaking, Thou wilt hear.

Thou wouldst not that my needy soul,
  For what might ease its inward pain,
From clime to clime, from pole to pole,
  O'er the wide world should seek in vain;
Should burn with deep, intense desires,
As one consumed with hidden fires.

Thou bidst me come my thirst to slake
  At the full fountains of Thy love;
And Thou my soul dost fill and make
  Content and glad like those above;
For with Thy gifts enriched and blest,
My search is o'er, and found my rest.

1867.

SUBMISSION.

" Thy will be done !" — MATT. xxvi. 42.

THY holy will, my God, be mine;
  I yield my all to Thee;
No more shall thought or wish repine,
  Whate'er my lot shall be.

Thy wisdom is a mighty deep,
  Beyond my thought Thy grace;
My soul shall lay her fears asleep,
  Secure in Thine embrace.

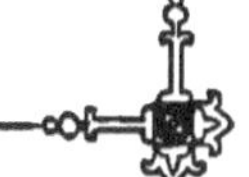

When clouds and darkness rule the hour,
 Thy bow on high I see;
And e'en the rending tempest's power
 Shall work but good for me.

At every step mine eyes shall turn
 To watch Thy guiding hand;
My dearest wish shall be to learn
 And do Thy pure command.

On Thee I rest my trusting soul,
 Thou wilt not let me fall;
Though surging billows o'er me roll,
 I shall be safe through all.

Grant me, my God, at last to hear,
 Well pleased, the call to die,
And 'mid the shades, with vision clear,
 To see my Saviour nigh.

Then when Thy glory breaks on me,
 All radiant as the sun;
Be this the joy of heaven, — to see
 Thy will for ever done!

1867.

UNSEEN, NOT UNKNOWN.

"Whom having not seen ye love." — 1 PETER i. 8.

JESUS, these eyes have never seen
   That radiant form of Thine;
The veil of sense hangs dark between
   Thy blessed face and mine.

I see Thee not, I hear Thee not,
   Yet art Thou oft with me;
And earth hath ne'er so dear a spot
   As where I meet with Thee.

Like some bright dream that comes unsought,
   When slumbers o'er me roll,
Thine image ever fills my thought,
   And charms my ravished soul.

Yet though I have not seen, and still
   Must rest in faith alone,
I love Thee, dearest Lord, and will,
   Unseen, but not unknown.

When death these mortal eyes shall seal,
   And still this throbbing heart,
The rending veil shall Thee reveal,
   All glorious as Thou art.

1858.

       A PRESENT GOD.

A PRESENT GOD.

" In Thy presence is fulness of joy." — Ps. xvi. 11.

SMILE, O my God, on me ;
    Thy presence let me feel ;
My soul Thy glory longs to see,
    Thyself in me reveal.

I would not wait for heaven,
    Heaven may begin below ;
To every new-born soul 'tis given
    A present God to know.

The vision of Thy face
    Fresh life and joy inspires,
While o'er my spirit flows the grace
    That kindles all her fires.

Though on my saddened heart
    The gloom of night should lie,
Faith shall not fail nor hope depart,
    If I but feel Thee nigh.

When earth's fleet years are past,
    And I no more shall roam,
Give me, my God, to find at last
    With Thee my changeless home.

Then shall my blessed soul,
    At fountains gushing o'er,
While circling ages ceaseless roll,
    Drink pleasures evermore.

1867.

THE SOUL'S CRY.

"I cry unto Thee daily." — Ps. lxxxvi. 3.

O EVER from the deeps
    Within my soul, oft as I muse alone,
Comes forth a voice that pleads in tender tone;
    As when one long unblest
    Sighs ever after rest;
Or as the wind perpetual murmuring keeps.

    I hear it when the day
Fades o'er the hills, or 'cross the shimmering sea;
In the soft twilight, it is wont to be,
    Without my wish or will,
    While all is hushed and still,
Like a sad, plaintive cry heard far away.

    Not even the noisy crowd,
That like some mighty torrent rushing down
Sweeps clamoring on, this cry of want can drown;
    But ever in my heart
    Afresh the echoes start;
I hear them still amidst the tumult loud.

    Each waking morn anew
The sense of many a need returns again;
I feel myself a child, helpless as when
    I watched my mother's eye,
    As the slow hours went by,
And from her glance my being took its hue.

I cannot shape my way
Where nameless perils ever may betide,
O'er slippery steeps whereon my feet may slide;
Some mighty hand I crave,
To hold and help and save,
And guide me ever when my steps would stray.

There is but One, I know,
That all my hourly, endless wants can meet;
Can shield from harm, recall my wandering feet;
My God, Thy hand can feed,
And day by day can lead
Where the sweet streams of peace and safety flow.

1867.

ABIDE WITH ME.

"I will not leave you comfortless : I will come to you." — JOHN xiv. 18.

COME, Jesus, Redeemer, abide Thou with me;
Come gladden my spirit that waiteth for Thee;
Thy smile every shadow shall chase from my heart,
And soothe every sorrow, though keen be the smart.

Without Thee but weakness, with Thee I am strong;
By day Thou shalt lead me, by night be my song;
Though dangers surround me, I still every fear,
Since Thou, the Most Mighty, my helper art near.

Thy love, O how faithful! so tender, so pure;
Thy promise, faith's anchor, how steadfast and sure!
That love, like sweet sunshine, my cold heart can warm,
That promise make steady my soul in the storm.

Breathe, breathe on my spirit, oft ruffled, Thy peace;
From restless, vain wishes, bid Thou my heart cease;
In Thee all its longings henceforward shall end,
Till glad to Thy presence my soul shall ascend.

O then, blessed Jesus, who once for me died,
Made clean in the fountain that gushed from Thy side,
I shall see Thy full glory, Thy face shall behold,
And praise Thee for ever with raptures untold!

1867.

UNFALTERING TRUST.

" How unsearchable are His judgments ! " — ROM. xi. 33.

L ORD, my weak thought in vain would climb
    To search the starry vault profound;
In vain would wing her flight sublime,
    To find creation's outmost bound.

But weaker yet that thought must prove
    To search Thy great eternal plan, —
Thy sovereign counsels, born of love,
    Long ages ere the world began.

When my dim reason would demand
    Why that, or this, Thou dost ordain,
By some vast deep I seem to stand,
    Whose secrets I must ask in vain.

When doubts disturb my troubled breast,
 And all is dark as night to me,
Here as on solid rock I rest,
 That so it seemeth good to Thee.

Be this my joy, that evermore
 Thou rulest all things at Thy will;
Thy sovereign wisdom I adore,
 And calmly, sweetly, trust Thee still.

1858.

THE COMFORTER.

*" The Comforter, which is the Holy Ghost, whom the Father will send in
my name." —* JOHN xiv. 26.

O HOLY Comforter,
  I hear
Thy blessed name with throbbing heart,
Pressed oft with sorrow, sin, and fear,
And pierced with many a venomed dart;
 Come, Messenger divine,
 Come, cheer this heart of mine!

O Holy Comforter,
  I know
Thou art not to dull sense revealed,
Thou com'st unseen as the sweet flow
Of the soft wind that wooes the field;
 Breathe, Messenger divine,
 Breathe on this soul of mine!

O Holy Comforter,
    Thy light
Is light eternal and serene;
Shine Thou, and on my ravished sight
Visions shall break of things unseen;
    Come, Messenger divine,
    Make these bright glimpses mine!

O Holy Comforter,
    Thy love
O'erfloweth as the flooding sea;
Give me its tenderness to prove,
Then shall my heart o'erflow to Thee;
    Come, Messenger divine,
    Fill Thou this breast of mine!

O Holy Comforter,
    Thy grace
Is life and health and hope and power;
By this I can each cross embrace,
Can triumph in the darkest hour;
    Come, Messenger divine,
    The strength of grace be mine!

O Holy Comforter,
    Thy peace,
The peace of God, impart and keep
Unruffled till life's tumults cease,
And all its angry tempests sleep;
    Come, Messenger divine,
    Thy perfect peace be mine!

1867.

THE HOUR OF JOY.

" Thou hast put gladness in my heart." — Ps. iv. 7.

ALL things to mine eyes are bright;
Throbs my heart with deep delight;
Birds pour forth delicious notes,
Fragrance on the still air floats,
Earth and heaven seem full of gladness,
And my soul forgets all sadness,
Glows and quivers with the thrill
Of the joy that doth it fill.

Swift-winged thought exults to range,
Fancy, as with magic change,
Makes e'en ugliness look fair,
Finds fresh beauty everywhere;
Life itself is one pure pleasure,
Tasted without mete or measure;
Of whate'er could make her blest,
My glad soul seems now possest.

Upward, upward, strong and free,
Borne on wings I seem to be;
Unconfined by earthly bars,
Soars my spirit to the stars;
E'en beyond the starry regions,
Filled with orbs in countless legions,
Mounts she with untiring wings,
Mounts and evermore she sings.

Whence this ecstasy divine?
Why so rapt this soul of mine?
O my God, with warm desire
Thou didst set my heart on fire;
Then Thy love and goodness showing,
And Thy light around me throwing,
Thou didst give Thyself to me,
Thou hast made me glad in Thee.

Thou art of all joy the crown;
Thou with joy canst sorrow drown;
Let me drink for evermore
At the well-spring running o'er;
In Thy smile is sadness never,
In Thy smile is gladness ever;
To Thy child, O Father, give
Ever in Thy love to live!

1867.

THE COMING GLORY.

"And there shall be no night there." — REV. xxii. 5.

LORD, Thou wilt bring the joyful day!
   Beyond earth's weariness and pains,
Thou hast a mansion far away,
   Where for Thine own a rest remains.

No sun there climbs the morning sky,
   There never falls the shade of night,
God and the Lamb, for ever nigh,
   O'er all shed everlasting light.

The bow of mercy spans the throne,
    Emblem of love and goodness there;
While notes to mortals all unknown
    Float on the calm, celestial air.

Around the throne bright legions stand,
    Redeemed by blood from sin and hell;
And shining forms, an angel band,
    The mighty chorus join to swell.

There, Lord, Thy way-worn saints shall find
    The bliss for which they longed before;
And holiest sympathies shall bind
    Thine own to Thee for evermore.

O Jesus, bring us to that rest,
    Where all the ransomed shall be found,
In Thine eternal fulness blest,
    While ages roll their cycles round.

1858.

DE PROFUNDIS.

" Out of the depths have I cried unto Thee, O Lord." — Ps. cxxx. 1.

IN the dark days of grief,
    When the dull hours drag wearily and slow,
When from the brimming eyes hot tears do flow,
    Where, where to find relief,
    Shall the bruised spirit go?

I see the world rush on;
Each, passion-stirred, intent to reach his end;
All, nerved for life's high prizes to contend,
    Glide by me and are gone;
    No healing can they lend.

    Voices of mirth I hear;
But these chase not the gloom thick brooding o'er,
Nor calm the billows that about me roar;
    They jar upon mine ear,
    And wound me but the more.

    I look on Nature's face,
The groves and summer fields and lawns and streams,
All beautiful as visions seen in dreams;
    But Nature's smile and grace
    To mock my anguish seems.

    The silent woods I tread,
Where aisles invite with oak and beech o'erhung,
And sweet wild notes by many a bird are sung;
    The still, cool paths I thread,
    But yet my heart is wrung.

    To friendship's breast I fly;
Of its deep tenderness I own the power,
More gently throbs my brow for one short hour,
    But, ere my tears are dry,
    Falls a returning shower.

O Jesus, Thou hast wept;
When faithful hearts mourned o'er a brother dead,
For mortal griefs Thine own pure tears were shed;
        And ever Thou hast kept
        Kind watch o'er hearts that bled.

Since Thou art Love divine,
And deep compassions in Thy bosom glow,
This heart, whose anguish Thou alone canst know,
        Would all to Thee resign,
        And trust Thee though laid low.

My spirit Thou canst heal,
Canst give me patience while I wait for light,
Bid cheerful day smile on my starless night,
        And peace canst make me feel,
        While yet tears dim my sight.

On Thee, O let me lean;
As if on Thine own bosom let me weep,
Till restless sorrow there is lulled to sleep, —
        Sleep, gentle and serene
        If Thou my slumber keep.

To joy then shall I wake,
And, taught new trust, with constant, loving heart,
To Thee shall cling, nor bear again to part,
        Till heaven's bright dawn shall break
        And bring me where Thou art.

                                        1867.

THE ROCK OF AGES.

"In the Lord Jehovah is the Rock of Ages." — ISA. xxvi. 4.

O ROCK of Ages, since on Thee
    By grace my feet are planted,
'Tis mine, in tranquil faith, to see
    The rising storm, undaunted;
When angry billows round me rave,
    And tempests fierce assail me,
To Thee I cling, the terrors brave,
    For Thou canst never fail me;
Though rends the globe with earthquake shock,
Unmoved Thou stand'st, Eternal Rock!

Within Thy clefts I love to hide,
    When darkness o'er me closes;
There peace and light serene abide,
    And my stilled heart reposes;
My soul exults to dwell secure,
    Thy strong munitions round her;
She dares to count her triumph sure,
    Nor fears lest hell confound her;
Though tumults startle earth and sea,
Thou changeless Rock, they shake not Thee!

From Thee, O Rock once smitten, flow
    Life-giving streams for ever;
And whoso doth their sweetness know,
    He thenceforth thirsteth never;

My lips have touched the crystal tide,
   And feel no more returning
The fever, that so long I tried
   To cool, yet felt still burning;
Ah, wondrous Well-Spring, brimming o'er
With living waters evermore!

On that dread day, when they that sleep
   Shall hear the trumpet sounding,
And wake to praise, or wake to weep,
   The judgment-throne surrounding;
When wrapt in all-devouring flame,
   The solid globe is wasting,
And what at first from nothing came
   Is back to nothing hasting;
E'en then my soul shall calmly rest,
O Rock of Ages, on Thy breast.

1869.

PRIVATE WORSHIP.

*" Ye have received the spirit of adoption, whereby we cry, Abba,
Father."* — ROM. viii. 15.

I KNOW, my God, that Thou art near,
   For o'er my trusting, waiting soul,
While starts the silent, grateful tear,
   Full tides of sweet emotion roll,
     My blessed God!

Thou dost to faith Thyself reveal;
  I see Thy face serene and mild;
By Christ's dear cross, while here I kneel,
  I know that I am made a child,
    My blessed God!

I need not speak, for Thou dost see
  All that I feel, but cannot tell;
The longings to be filled with Thee
  That stir my heart, Thou knowest well, .
    My blessed God!

In Thee, when sorrows rend my breast,
  Love's tenderest sympathy I find,
As to a Father's bosom prest,
  As by a Father's arms entwined,
    My blessed God!

As if in ocean's darkest deep,
  Thy grace hath buried all my sins,
And o'er me faithful watch shall keep,
  Till heaven's eternal joy begins,
    My blessed God!

That grace, with pure, divine delight,
  My joyous, thankful soul shall own,
When bursts upon my ravished sight
  The splendor of Thy burning throne,
    My blessed God!

1864.

MORNING WORSHIP.

"My voice shalt Thou hear in the morning, O Lord." — Ps. v. 3.

FATHER, while the shades of night
　Fly before the crimson dawn,
Heavenward speeds my soul her flight,
　Gladdened by the day new born.

Nature, fresh enrobed and fair,
　Greets me with her kindly smile,
And I breathe the fragrant air,
　Drinking in Thy love the while.

All Thy works are full of Thee!
　Glows my heart with living praise;
Lowly bends the reverent knee,
　Upward waiting eyes I raise.

While from garden, field, and grove,
　Morning carols wake around,
Swift my thoughts ascend and rove
　Where eternal songs resound.

With the wide creation's choir,
　My rapt soul would chant her hymn,
Kindling with the holy fire
　Of the burning seraphim.

Light of men, when forth shall break
　Thy full splendor, dimmed so long,
Earth one hymn of praise shall wake,
　Ages the glad strain prolong.

Son of God, Redeemer, Lord,
   All Thy goodness none can tell;
When Thy gifts I would record,
   High as heaven the numbers swell.

Through all labors of this day,
   Let Thy hand sustain me still;
Through all perils guard my way,
   Make me strong to do Thy will.

Let my day dawn calm and bright,
   Where no eye for ever weeps;
Where for ever comes no night,
   Where eternal sunshine sleeps.

1866.

EVENING WORSHIP.

" At evening time it shall be light." — ZECH. xiv. 7.

COME, Jesus, with the coming night,
   Refresh and cheer my weary heart;
At evening-time it shall be light,
   If Thou art near, though day depart.

Welcome this shade that brings release
   From hurrying labor's noise and strife;
That calls from restless thought to cease,
   And calms the throbbing pulse of life.

From tedious toil, from anxious care,
   Dear Lord, I turn again to Thee;
Thy presence and Thy smile to share
   Makes every burden light to me.

With Thee, of all sad thoughts beguiled,
   Peace nestles in my tranquil breast ;
And, like a pleased and happy child,
   In Thy kind arms I sink to rest.

Till night's dark watches all are gone,
   O faithful Shepherd, guard my sleep,
And, when yon mountains greet the dawn,
   Give strength my heavenward way to keep.

1866.

MIDNIGHT WORSHIP.

" At midnight I will rise to give thanks unto Thee." — Ps. cxix. 62.

" O UNSLEEPING ! ever keeping
   Faithful watch about my bed,
O'er me bending, and defending
   From all ill my weary head ;
Now each restless thought composing,
And in peace these eyelids closing,
   Father, keep my soul," I said.

Thou didst hear me, Thou art near me,
   Waking at this midnight hour ;
Changing never, loving ever,
   Thou art my defence, my tower ;
Thoughts of Thee dispel all sadness,
Thoughts of Thee give strength and gladness,
   And I rest upon Thy power.

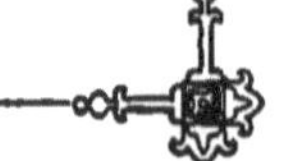

Purely glowing, stars are throwing
  Glad rays through the solemn night,
Ever gleaming, as if beaming
  With Thy glory on my sight;
By their order and their beauty,
Thou dost teach me love and duty,
  Bid me shine with virtue's light.

Praises bringing, upward springing,
  Mounts my quickened soul to Thee;
Hope fulfilling, passion stilling,
  Thou dost come, my God, to me!
And in holy, sweet communing,
All my noblest powers attuning,
  Thou dost teach me Thine to be.

Nightly waking, from me shaking
  Slumbers soft, I will arise;
Bowing lowly, O Most Holy,
  I will lift to Thee mine eyes;
So shall speed my warm devotion,
Winged by tender, pure emotion,
  Upward through the midnight skies.

Ever living, ever giving
  Life and joy to all Thine own;
Interceding, as once bleeding,
  Priest and Lamb before the throne;
Thou my prayer presentest ever,
Thou my praise refusest never,
  Christ, I trust in Thee alone!

So while praying, calmly saying,
  "Father, bless me from above!"
So believing and receiving
  Gifts of grace and smiles of love,
I again mine eyelids closing,
And till dawn in peace reposing,
  All Thy faithfulness shall prove.

1866.

THE BREAD OF LIFE.

"If any man eat of this bread, he shall live for ever." — JOHN vi. 51.

AWAY from earth my spirit turns,
  Away from every transient good:
With strong desire my bosom burns
  To feast on heaven's diviner food.

Thou, Saviour, art the living bread;
  Thou wilt my every want supply;
By Thee sustained and cheered and led,
  I'll press through dangers to the sky.

What though temptations oft distress,
  And sin assails, and breaks my peace;
Thou wilt uphold and save and bless,
  And bid the storms of passion cease.

Then let me take Thy gracious hand,
  And walk beside Thee onward still;
Till my glad feet shall safely stand
  For ever firm on Zion's hill.

1833.

THE CROWN.

" There is laid up for me a crown." — 2 TIM. iv. 8.

THE crowns of earth are jewelled dust,
  Or weights, the wearer's brow to press;
But Thou, O Christ, dost give the just
  A nobler crown of righteousness.

That crown, of Thine own love the seal,
  On Thine a gift of love bestowed,
Diviner splendors shall reveal
  Than e'er on princely head hath glowed.

Ten thousand faithful souls and true
  Now wear the crown that wore Thy shame;
That many a wasting anguish knew,
  And as through fires to glory came.

We yet must wage the long-drawn strife,
  And oft with prayers our groans ascend;
We battle for immortal life,
  Give strength and courage to the end.

Then be it ours to hear Thee say,
  When we shall lay our armor down, —
" The faith ye kept!   Ye won the day!
  Come, take and wear the matchless crown!"

1866.

HYMN TO THE HOLY GHOST.

" The promise of the Father." — ACTS i. 4.

HOLY Ghost, that promised came
With the pentecostal flame,
Comforter! we hail Thy name!

For Thy mighty help we call;
On our waiting spirits fall;
Fill us, cheer us, rule us all.

When returns the vernal glow,
Bud and blossom wake and grow;
All things the sweet influence know.

'Neath Thy breath our graces bloom;
Flee our wintry shades and gloom;
Come! our hearts prepare Thee room.

If Thou but within us move,
We shall mount on wings of love,
Joyous as the hosts above.

O what raptures may we feel,
If but Thou our eyes unseal,
And the things of Christ reveal!

Blessed Helper! by Thee led,
On our willing feet shall tread,
Till we see our glorious Head!

Then, immortal years begun,
While the eternal circuits run,
Praise, all Heaven, the Three in One!

1873.

GLORIA CHRISTI.

*" That they may behold my glory which Thou hast given
me." —* JOHN xvii. 24.

THAT glory I would see
    Where Thou, my Saviour, art, —
Thy Father's glory and Thine own,
O Lamb divine, amidst the throne !
    One of that host to be
    I pray with longing heart,
Who evermore Thy unveiled face behold,
And, like Thee, wear celestial beauty's mould.

    Thou art adored, I know,
    By all the shining train, —
Archangels, seraphs, spirits fair,
Whose robes no spot did ever bear ;
    But Thou, who once below
    For mortal guilt wast slain,
Wilt sweetest count the strain Thy ransomed sing,
When to Thy bleeding love they wake the string.

    O Christ, Thy rich reward
    'Twill be, when Thine at last,
Made white — strange mystery — in blood,
Shall faultless stand, the sons of God,
    With Thee, their risen Lord ;
    And, all earth's sorrows past,

Shall want no more, safe gathered round Thy seat,
Than their bright crowns to cast before Thy feet!

    On earth, dear Lord, to Thine
    'Tis given the cross to bear;
As Thou wast once to Calvary led,
Through death, to live our glorious Head,
    And with the Father shine;
    All who would rise to share
Thy life, Thy joy, Thy triumph all sublime,
Must learn by pangs the arduous height to climb.

    'Tis thus with faithful care
    Thou makest glad through pain;
Dost prove Thine own with fires, as gold;
Dost make them, by long wrestlings, bold
    For Thee all things to dare;
    That hell may rage in vain,
While they with steadfast love unfaltering stand,
And share Thy glory, set at Thy right hand.

    Thy glory! How my thought
    In conscious weakness tries
Up to that sky serene to soar,
Which night shall darken nevermore!
    My soul, divinely taught,
    On Faith's strong wing would rise,
And, as the eagle mounts with sunward gaze,
Would lose herself in the full Godhead's blaze!

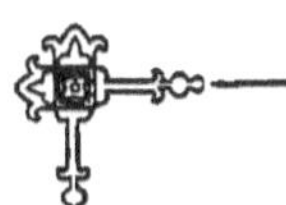

Nor shall that blaze confound
My spirit with its glow;
Not like the enchanted moth that flies
Into the scorching flame, and dies,
She in fresh life new found
Her bliss complete shall know;
Made like to Thee, and in Thy lustre bright,
Unharmed she shall behold the dazzling light!

As from the kindly earth,
Where broods the noontide heat,
Start forth, born of the vernal ray,
Sweet flowers that with the glad winds play;
So 'neath those beams the birth,
Thou, O my soul, shalt greet
Of graces in thyself unknown before,
That live and bloom to wither thence no more.

With Thee! With Thee, my Lord,
Where falls Thy smile benign!
That will be bliss beyond compare,
To see Thee, who the thorn didst wear,
To heaven's high seat restored,
And feel Thy glory mine:
Thou whom unseen I loved! O that shall fill
My blessed soul and all its longings still!

With Thee, yet not alone;
All Thine in Thee made one,
The fellowship of perfect love
To holiest sympathies shall move;

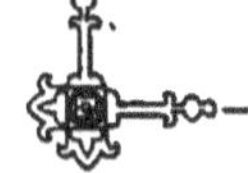

With joy to earth unknown,
Thy saints, their wrestlings done,
Dear friendships shall renew once rent in tears,
And in that bliss forget their painful years.

Ne'er shall the splendors wane
That gather round Thy brow;
Though suns and stars that burn on high
Shall perish from the midnight sky,
Thy glory shall remain, —
The same for ever Thou!
And while eternal days are told,
Thine own that glory shall behold.

1866.

STAND FOR CHRIST.

*" Take unto you the whole armor of God, that ye may be able to withstand
in the evil day, and having done all to stand." —* EPH. vi. 13.

STAND for Christ, bravely stand! thee, thee He
    calleth;
Stand for Christ, toil for Christ, till the night falleth;
Falter not, win the crown, ere day declineth, —
The crown never fading, — behold, how it shineth!

Follow Christ! take the cross, all uncomplaining;
'Mid the strife thou shalt find strong arms sustaining;
When the foe onward sweeps, like a flood swelling,
Thy Lord shall defend thee, His madness all quelling.

Watch and pray, faithful one, hell would confound thee;
Shafts of death ever fly thick all around thee;
Christ in love evermore o'er thee is bending,
And thou shalt go safely, His might thee defending.

Be thy heart warm with love, faithfully beating;
Be thy heart dead to joys empty and fleeting;
Up to yon city fair always be climbing,
Where hymns of the holy for ever are chiming.

1869.

CONSECRATION AND WORK.

" Thou knowest that I love Thee. Feed my sheep." — JOHN xxi. 16.

LORD, Thou hast taught our hearts to glow
    With love's undying flame;
But more of Thee we long to know,
    And more would love Thy name.
Chorus.   All Thy dear will
        Would we fulfil,
      Till life's last toil is o'er;
        And when we rise
        Beyond the skies,
    We'll serve Thee evermore.

Thy life, Thy death, inspire our song,
    Thy Spirit breathes through all;
And here our feet would linger long,
    But we obey Thy call.

Thou bid'st us go, with Thee to stand
 Against hell's marshalled powers ;
And, heart to heart and hand to hand,
 To make Thine honor ours.

With Thine own pity, Saviour, see
 The thronged and dark'ning way !
We go to win the lost to Thee :
 O help us, Lord, we pray !

Teach Thou our lips of Thee to speak,
 Of Thy sweet love to tell ;
Till they who wander far shall seek,
 And find and serve Thee well.

O'er all the world Thy Spirit send,
 And make Thy goodness known,
Till earth and heaven together blend
 Their praises at Thy throne !

1865.

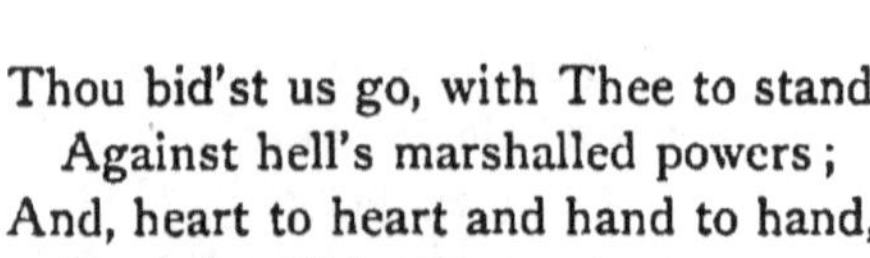

AT THE CROSS.

*" I am crucified with Christ, . . . who loved me, and gave Himself
for me."* — GAL. ii. 20.

O JESUS, sweet the tears I shed,
 While at Thy cross I kneel,
Gaze on Thy wounded, fainting head,
 And all Thy sorrows feel.

My heart dissolves to see Thee bleed,
 This heart so hard before ;
I hear Thee for the guilty plead,
 And grief o'erflows the more.

'Twas for the sinful Thou didst die,
 And I a sinner stand;
What love speaks from Thy dying eye,
 And from each piercéd hand!

I know this cleansing blood of Thine,
 Was shed, dear Lord, for me;
For me, for all — O grace divine! —
 Who look by faith on Thee.

O Christ of God! O spotless Lamb!
 By love my soul is drawn;
Henceforth for ever Thine I am,
 Here life and peace are born.

In patient hope the cross I'll bear,
 Thine arm shall be my stay;
And Thou, enthroned, my soul shalt spare,
 On Thy great judgment-day.

1867.

THE THORN.

"I besought the Lord thrice, that it might depart from me. And He said unto me, My grace is sufficient for thee." — 2 COR. xii. 8, 9.

EACH pang I feel is known to Thee,
 Dear Lord, for Thou hast sent the thorn
  That pierceth me;
Hast fixed it festering in this breast,
That with new anguish wakes each morn,
  And finds no rest.

Though oft with burning tears I've prayed
That Thou wouldst take this grief away,
      Thou hast delayed ;
Yet Thou hast pledged Thy word to keep,
To succor in the sorrowing day
      Thine own who weep.

Why tarriest Thou ?   Long must I plead,
With hope deferred, that Thou wilt send
      The help I need ?
Hast Thou Thy words of love forgot,
That, when o'erwhelmed I lowly bend,
      Thou answerest not ?

Be still, my soul, and meekly bear
Thy pain, nor yield one doubt a place,
      Lest dark despair
Prevail thy steadfast trust to shake ;
Though in thick shades He hides His face,
      The dawn shall break !

Ah ! now, at last, He speaks.   A thrill
Sweeps through my soul, and tides of love
      My being fill : —
" Canst thou not bear the cross with me ?
I may not yet the thorn remove
      That woundeth Thee ;

But thou shalt lean upon my breast,
My strength shall make thy weakness strong ;
      When most oppressed,
Then most my grace shalt thou partake ;
And from thy burdened heart a song
      Of joy shall break ! "

1864.

SELF-SURRENDER.

" I will arise and go to my Father." — LUKE xv. 18.

TAKE me, O my Father, take me, —
    Take me, save me, through Thy Son ;
That which Thou wouldst have me, make me,
    Let Thy will in me be done.

Long from Thee my footsteps straying,
    Thorny proved the way I trod ;
Weary come I now, and praying,
    Take me to Thy love, my God !

Fruitless years with grief recalling,
    Humbly I confess my sin !
At Thy feet, O Father, falling,
    To Thy household take me in.

Freely now to Thee I proffer
    This relenting heart of mine ;
Freely life and soul I offer,
    Gift unworthy love like Thine.

Once the world's Redeemer, dying,
    Bore our sins upon the tree ;
On that sacrifice relying,
    Now I look in hope to Thee.

Father, take me ! all forgiving,
    Fold me to Thy loving breast ;
In Thy love for ever living,
    I must be for ever blest.

1864.

SELF-QUESTIONING.

"One of you shall betray me." — MATT. xxvi. 21.

O TELL me, Jesus, to my heart —
    My troubled heart — the secret tell;
May I from Thee and Thine depart,
    As Judas, when he falsely fell?
Is it not love, — this kindling flame
That warms my breast oft as Thy name
        Falls on my willing ear?
Is it not faith that oft hath brought
My trembling soul the peace it sought,
        And stilled each restless fear?

This quiet joy that hidden flows
    Deep in my soul, and makes me glad,
Though many a rude wind round me blows,
    And many a sorrow makes me sad;
Can this calm joy that ever lives
Be aught but that Thy presence gives,
        To faithful souls revealed?
The presence and the loving smile
That gladdens all Thine own, — the while
        From unbelief concealed?

The tears that oft these eyes have wept,
    When I before Thy feet have knelt,
Or watch about Thy cross have kept,
    And all Thy pangs have keenly felt, —

Came they not from that holy grief
That brings the broken heart relief,
    And softens it to love?
Was not the hope that wakened there
Hope that shall triumph o'er despair
    And bear the soul above?

Speak, Thou that knowest well, decide;
    If I am Thine, O clasp this hand,
And when my feet would stray or slide,
    Then firmly hold and bid me stand.
Go forth from Thee?   Give me to bear
Thy bitter cross, Thy thorns to wear;
    But let me not depart!
No, Lord, afresh to Thee I bring,
A free, a cheerful offering,
    This trusting, grateful heart.

1863.

GOD REVEALED.

"All my springs are in Thee." — Ps. lxxxvii. 7.

L IGHT, light upon my soul!
    Downward it streams from its celestial
      fountains;
About me glows like sunrise on the mountains;
    It bringeth gladsome cheer,
    Farewell, my night of fear!

Life, life I feel within!
Fresh from its rich, immortal source descending,
It lends me power divine, for ever ending
          The weakness felt before;
          I now can faint no more.

Love, love my bosom fills!
From Him whose name is Love, it comes, inspiring
Deep, warm, responsive love, my spirit firing
          With holy, rapturous glow,
          Such as pure seraphs know.

Joy, joy within my heart!
From its bright home above divinely flowing,
Like perfume from some orient garden blowing,
          Or like the fragrant air
          Wafted o'er meadows fair.

God, God the great and good!
That from the sense His glory all concealing,
To lowly faith delighteth in revealing
          Himself, the Highest, Best, —
          All being's bliss and rest!

1864.

THE JUBILEE.

This Hymn was written for the fiftieth Anniversary of the American Board of Commissioners for Foreign Missions, and sung at the Jubilee Celebration, held in the Tremont Temple at Boston, Oct. 3–5, 1860.

ETERNAL Father! Thou hast said
   That Christ all glory shall obtain;
That He who once, a sufferer, bled,
   Shall o'er the world, a conqueror, reign.

We wait Thy triumph, Saviour, King!
   Long ages have prepared the way;
Now all abroad Thy banner fling,
   Set Time's great battle in array.

Thy hosts are mustered to the field,
   "The Cross! the Cross!" their battle-call;
The old grim towers of darkness yield,
   And soon shall totter to their fall.

On mountain tops the watch-fires glow,
   Where scattered wide the watchmen stand;
Voice echoes voice, and onward flow
   The joyous shouts from land to land.

Thou hast our humble service blest,
   While fifty years have rolled their round;
Weary and worn the fathers rest,
   But in their stead the sons are found.

O fill Thy church with faith and power!
  Bid her long night of weeping cease;
To groaning nations haste the hour
  Of life and freedom, light and peace.

Come, Spirit, make Thy wonders known!
  Fulfil the Father's high decree;
Then earth — the might of hell o'erthrown —
  Shall keep her last great jubilee.

1860.

MISSIONARY PARTING HYMN.

" Go ye into all the world, and preach the gospel to every creature." —
MARK xvi. 15.

ETERNAL Lord, whose power
  Can 'calm the heaving ocean,
    Exalted Thou,
    Yet gracious bow;
Accept our warm devotion.

For Thee our all we leave,
Nor drop a tear of sadness;
    As on we glide,
    Be Thou our guide,
And fill our hearts with gladness.

We go 'mid pagan gloom
To spread the truth victorious;
    Thy Spirit send,
    Thy word attend,
And make its triumph glorious.

And, when our toils are done,
Smooth Thou the dying pillow,
　　O bring us blest
　　To endless rest,
Safe o'er death's troubled billow!

1834.

REPENTANCE AT THE CROSS.

*" This is my blood of the New Testament, which is shed for many for
the remission of sins."* — MATT. xxvi. 28.

JESUS, Lamb of God, for me
　　Thou, the Lord of life, didst die;
Whither, whither but to Thee,
　　Can a trembling sinner fly?
Death's dark waters o'er me roll,
Save, O save, my sinking soul!

Never bowed a martyred head,
　　Weighed with equal sorrow down;
Never blood so rich was shed,
　　Never king wore such a crown!
To Thy cross and sacrifice
Faith now lifts her tearful eyes.

All my soul, by love subdued,
　　Melts in deep contrition there;
By Thy mighty grace renewed,
　　New-born hope forbids despair;
Lord, Thou canst my guilt forgive,
Thou hast bid me look and live.

5

While with broken heart I kneel,
 Sinks the inward storm to rest;
Life, immortal life, I feel
 Kindled in my throbbing breast;
Thine, for ever Thine, I am,
Glory to the bleeding Lamb!

1863.

GOD'S HIDDEN ONES.

" In the time of trouble He shall hide me in His pavilion." — Ps. xxvii 5.
*" He that dwelleth in the secret place of the Most High shall abide under
the shadow of the Almighty."* — Ps. xci 1.

M Y God, within Thy secret place
 Thou all Thine own dost hide;
There, sheltered by Thy power and grace,
 They in Thy peace abide.

Beneath Thy wing and near Thy heart,
 Eternal Love, they rest;
No foe they fear, no venomed dart,
 With Thee secure and blest.

Thanks, thanks that Thou my wandering feet
 Hast led, and made me Thine;
That, safe within this dear retreat,
 Thou bidst me call Thee mine!

No·more I yield to boding fears,
 Since in Thine arms I lie;
When grief would drown mine eyes in tears,
 Those tears Thy hand shall dry.

Let thunders shake the solid ground,
  Serene my soul shall be;
Let gloom and darkness close me round,
  'Tis ever light with Thee!

O more and more my soul possess,
  Make heart and will Thine own;
Enrobe me with Thy righteousness,
  And in me reign alone.

1874.

SABBATH MORNING.

"A day in Thy courts is better than a thousand." — Ps. lxxxiv. 10.

THINE holy day's returning
  Our hearts exult to see,
And, with devotion burning,
  Ascend, our God, to Thee.

To-day with purest pleasure,
  Our thoughts from earth withdraw;
We search for sacred treasure,
  We learn Thy holy law.

We join to sing Thy praises,
  God of the Sabbath day!
Each voice in gladness raises
  Its loudest, sweetest lay.

Thy richest mercies sharing,
  O fill us with Thy love!
By grace our souls preparing
  For nobler praise above.

1834.

THE DAY OF JOY.

*" The Lord shall be thine everlasting light, and the days of thy mourning
shall be ended." — *Isa. lx. 20.

WAKE thee, O Zion, thy mourning is ended;
　　God, thine own God, hath regarded thy prayer;
Wake thee, and hail Him, in glory descended,
Thy darkness to scatter, thy wastes to repair.

Wake thee, O Zion, His spirit of power
To newness of life is awaking the dead;
Array thee in beauty, and greet the glad hour
That brings thee salvation through Jesus who bled.

Saviour, we gladly, with voices resounding,
Loud as the thunder our chorus would swell;
Till from rock, wood, and mountain its echoes re-
　　bounding,
To all the wide world of salvation shall tell.

1834.

THE TRANQUIL HOUR.

" Return unto thy rest, O my soul." — Ps. cxvi. 7.

THOU, Saviour, from Thy throne on high,
　　Enrobed in light and girt with power,
Dost note the thought, the prayer, the sigh
　　Of hearts that love the tranquil hour.

Oft Thou Thyself didst steal away,
　　At eventide, from labor done,
In some still, peaceful shade to pray,
　　Till morning watches were begun.

Thou hast not, dearest Lord, forgot
  Thy wrestlings on Judea's hills;
And still Thou lov'st the quiet spot
  Where praise the lowly spirit fills.

Now to our souls, withdrawn awhile
  From earth's rude noise, Thy face reveal;
And, as we worship, kindly smile,
  And for Thine own our spirits seal.

To Thee we bring each grief and care,
  To Thee we fly while tempests lower;
Thou wilt the weary burdens bear
  Of hearts that love the tranquil hour.

1864.

EVENING WORSHIP.

"In Thy light shall we see light." — Ps. xxxvi. 9.

STEALING from the world away,
  We are come to seek Thy face;
Kindly meet us, Lord, we pray,
  Grant us Thy reviving grace.

Yonder stars that gild the sky
  Shine but with a borrowed light;
We, unless Thy light be nigh,
  Wander, wrapt in gloomy night.

Sun of Righteousness, dispel
  All our darkness, doubts, and fears;
May Thy light within us dwell,
  Till eternal day appears.

Warm our hearts in prayer and praise,
Lift our every thought above;
Hear the grateful songs we raise,
Fill us with Thy perfect love.

1834.

THE UNITY OF LOVE.

*" Having loved His own which were in the world, He loved them unto
the end."* — JOHN xiii. 1.

" That they all may be one." — JOHN xvii. 21.

LORD, Thou on earth didst love Thine own,
   Didst love them to the end;
O still from Thy celestial throne,
   Let gifts of love descend.

The love the Father bears to Thee,
   His own eternal Son,
Fill all Thy saints, till all shall be
   In pure affection one.

As Thou for us didst stoop so low,
   Warmed by love's holy flame,
So let our deeds of kindness flow
   To all who bear Thy name.

One blessed fellowship of love,
   Thy living Church should stand,
Till, faultless, she at last above
   Shall shine at Thy right hand.

O glorious day when she, the Bride,
With her dear Lord appears!
When robed in beauty at His side,
She shall forget her tears.

1804.

THE DAYSPRING.

" Through the tender mercy of our God; whereby the dayspring from on high hath visited us." — LUKE i. 78.

BEFORE Thy throne with tearful eyes,
My gracious Lord, I humbly fall;
To Thee my weary spirit flies,
For Thy forgiving love I call.

I know Thy mercy overflows,
When sinners on Thy grace rely;
Thy tender love no limit knows;
O save me, — justly doomed to die!

Yes, Thou wilt save; my soul is free!
The gloom of sin is fled away;
My tongue breaks forth in praise to Thee,
And all my powers Thy word obey.

Hence, while I wrestle with my foes, —
The world, the flesh, the hosts of hell, —
Sustain Thou me till conflicts close,
Then endless songs my thanks shall tell.

1834.

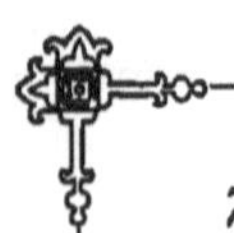

ALONE WITH CHRIST.

"I will not leave you comfortless : I will come to you." — JOHN xiv. 18.

ALONE with Thee! Alone with Thee!
    O Friend divine!
Thou Friend of friends to me most dear,
Though all unseen I feel Thee near,
And with the love that knows no fear,
    I call Thee mine.

Alone with Thee! Alone with Thee!
    Now through my breast
There steals a breath like breath of balm,
That healing brings and holy calm,
That soothes like chanted song or psalm,
    And makes me blest.

Alone with Thee! Alone with Thee!
    Thy grace more sweet
Than music in the twilight still,
Than airs that groves of spices fill,
More fresh than dews on Hermon's hill,
    My soul doth greet.

Alone with Thee! Alone with Thee!
    In Thy pure light
The splendid pomps and shows of time,
The tempting steeps that pride would climb,
The peaks where glory rests sublime,
    Pale on my sight.

Alone with Thee!   Alone with Thee!
My softened heart
Floats on the flood of love divine,
Feels all its wishes drowned in Thine,
Content that every good is mine
Thou canst impart.

Alone with Thee!   Alone with Thee!
I want no more
To make my earthly bliss complete,
Than oft my Lord unseen to meet;
For sight I wait till tread my feet
Yon glistering shore.

Alone with Thee!   Alone with Thee!
There not alone,
But with all saints, the mighty throng,
My soul unfettered, pure and strong,
Her high communings shall prolong,
Before Thy throne.

1867.

THE HEAVENLY REST.

*" For the Lamb which is in the midst of the throne shall feed them, and shall
lead them unto living fountains of waters : and God shall wipe away
all tears from their eyes."* — REV. vii. 17.

AND is there, Lord, a rest,
For weary souls designed,
Where not a care shall stir the breast,
Or sorrow entrance find ?

Is there a blissful home,
   Where kindred minds shall meet,
And live and love, nor ever roam
   From that serene retreat?

Are there bright, happy fields,
   Where nought that blooms shall die;
Where each new scene fresh pleasure yields,
   And healthful breezes sigh?

Are there celestial streams,
   Where living waters glide,
With murmurs sweet as angel dreams,
   And flowery banks beside?

For ever blessed they,
   Whose joyful feet shall stand,
While endless ages waste away,
   Amid that glorious land!

My soul would thither tend,
   While toilsome years are given;
Then let me, gracious God, ascend
   To sweet repose in heaven!

1843.

THE RESURRECTION.

" Jesus said, . . . I am the resurrection and the life." — JOHN xi. 25.

WHEN downward to the darksome tomb
  I thoughtful turn my eyes,
Frail nature trembles at the gloom,
  And anxious fears arise.

Why shrinks my soul?   In death's embrace
  Once Jesus captive slept ;
And angels, hovering o'er the place,
  His lowly pillow kept.

Thus shall they guard my sleeping dust,
  And, as the Saviour rose,
The grave again shall yield her trust,
  And end my deep repose.

My Lord, before to glory gone,
  Shall bid me come away ; .
And calm and bright shall break the dawn
  Of heaven's eternal day.

Then let my faith each fear dispel,
  And gild with light the grave ;
To Him my loftiest praises swell,
  Who died from death to save.

1842.

THE FATHER'S HOUSE.

" In my Father's house are many mansions. . . . I go to prepare a place
for you." — JOHN xiv. 2.

THY Father's house! Thine own bright home!
    And Thou hast there a place for me!
Though yet an exile here I roam,
    That distant home by faith I see.

I see its domes resplendent glow,
    Where beams of God's own glory fall;
And trees of life immortal grow,
    Whose fruits o'erhang the sapphire wall.

I know that Thou, who on the tree
    Didst deign our mortal guilt to bear,
Wilt bring Thine own to dwell with Thee,
    And waitest to receive me there.

Thy love will there array my soul
    In Thine own robe of spotless hue;
And I shall gaze while ages roll,
    On Thee, with raptures ever new.

O welcome day! when Thou my feet
    Shalt bring the shining threshold o'er;
A Father's warm embrace to meet,
    And dwell at home forevermore.

1864.

JESUS THE ALL IN ALL.

" Looking unto Jesus the author and finisher of our faith." — HEB. xii. 2.

WHEN inward turns my searching gaze,
  And stains of sin deep fixed I see,
When doubt and fear my soul amaze,
  O Jesus, come to comfort me.

When heavenward, o'er the flinty way,
  I tread with faltering feet and sore,
And need some arm of strength to stay,
  O Jesus, help me evermore.

When faded, like autumnal leaves,
  My heart's best hopes all withered lie,
And o'er the lost for earth it grieves,
  O Jesus, wipe the tearful eye.

When in the still retreat I kneel,
  To tell Thee all I hope or fear,
Let no thick cloud Thy face conceal:
  O Jesus, lend a listening ear.

When glows with joy my throbbing heart,
  And light and gladness round me fall,
The sunshine of Thy smile impart,
  O Jesus, brightest, best of all !

When springs my glad, unfettered soul,
To seek her home beyond the spheres,
Thee will I praise while ages roll,
O Jesus, mine to endless years.

1868.

THE PLACE OF PRAYER.

*" Enter into thy closet, and when thou hast shut thy door, pray to thy
Father which is in secret."* — MATT. vi. 6.

O EVER sacred spot,
Where clamor cometh not,
Where earth may be forgot,
And peaceful stillness undisturbed may reign;
I joy that I may know
Such holy calm below,
Nor feel life's restless flow,
When Thy sweet solitude well pleased I gain.

While lowly here I kneel,
My God, Thy love reveal,
And give Thy child to feel
A Father's blessing falling on his head;
I see Thy smile benign,
I hear Thee call me Thine,
For Thee I all resign,
And evermore would by Thy will be led.

Hither, O Christ, I flee,
That I by faith may see
Thy face unveiled to me,

And all the secrets of my heart may tell;
    May lean upon Thy breast,
    Lull all my fears to rest,
    And — joy of joys the best —
Hear Thy loved voice known to my soul so well.

    Tell Thou my longing heart,
    Dear Lord, that mine Thou art;
    Then all afresh shall start
The tears of grateful tenderness and love;
    Give me that precious stone
    That bears a name unknown,
    The pledge that Thou wilt own,
And make me to behold Thy face above.

    Oft as I enter here,
    Great Comforter, be near,
    My wrestling soul to cheer,
Let Thy best gifts and graces all be mine;
    In Thine own perfect light,
    O give me visions bright
    Of things beyond my sight;
Fill my whole being with the life divine!

1866.

SPIRITUAL REFRESHING.

" I will pour my Spirit upon thy seed, and my blessing upon thine offspring." — ISA. xliv. 3.

FOUNT of everlasting love,
    Rich thy streams of mercy are;
Flowing purely from above,
    Beauty marks their course afar.

Lo ! Thy church, athirst and faint,
   Drinks the full, refreshing tide ;
Thou hast heard her sad complaint,
   Floods of grace are sweeping wide.

God of mercy, to Thy throne,
   Now our fervent thanks we bring ;
Thine the glory, Thine alone,
   Joyous praise to Thee we sing.

While we lift our grateful song,
   Let the Spirit still descend ;
Roll the tide of grace along,
   Widening, deepening, to the end.

1831.

LIFE FROM THE DYING CHRIST.

" I live by the faith of the Son of God, who loved me, and gave Himself for me." — GAL. ii. 20.

WOULDST thou eternal life obtain,
   Now to the cross repair ;
There stand and gaze, and weep and pray,
Where Jesus breathes His life away ;
   Eternal life is there.

Go, — 'tis the Son of God expires !
   Approach the shameful tree ;
See quivering there the mortal dart,
In the Redeemer's loving heart,
   O sinful soul, for thee !

Go, — there from every streaming wound
  Flows rich atoning blood :
That blood can cleanse the deepest stain,
Bid frowning justice smile again,
  And seal thy peace with God.

Go ! at that cross thy heart subdued,
  With thankful love shall glow ;
By wondrous grace thy soul set free,
Eternal life from Christ to thee
  A vital stream shall flow !

1864.

CHRIST IN THE STORM.

*" And He arose, and rebuked the wind, and said unto the sea, Peace, be
still."* — MARK iv. 39.

AMID the darkness, when the storm
  Swept fierce and wild o'er Galilee,
Was seen of old, dear Lord, Thy form,
  All calmly walking on the sea ;
And raging elements were still,
Obedient to Thy sovereign will.

So on life's restless, heaving wave,
  When night and storm my sky o'ercast,
Oft hast Thou come to cheer and save,
  Hast changed my fear to joy at last ;
Thy voice hath bid the tumult cease,
And soothed my throbbing heart to peace.

But, ah! too soon my fears return,
 And dark mistrust disturbs anew;
What smothered fires within yet burn!
 My days of peace, alas, how few!
These heart-throes, — shall they ne'er be past?
These strifes, — shall they for ever last?

I heed not danger, toil, nor pain,
 Care not how hard the storm may beat,
If in my heart Thy peace may reign,
 And faith and patience keep their seat;
If strength divine may nerve my soul,
And love my every thought control.

O may that voice that quelled the sea,
 And laid the surging waves to rest,
Speak in my spirit, set me free
 From passions that disturb my breast;
Jesus, I yield me to Thy will,
And wait to hear Thy " Peace, be still!"

1867.

———◆———

FATHER, LEAD ON.

" O my Father, if this cup may not pass away from me, except I drink it,
Thy will be done." — MATT. xxvi. 42.

MY Father God, lead on!
 Calmly I follow where Thy guiding hand
Directs my steps. I would not trembling stand.
  Though all before the way
  Is dark as night, I stay
  My soul on Thee, and say —
Father, I trust Thy love; lead on.

Just as Thou wilt: lead on!
For I am as a child, and know not how
To tread the starless path whose windings now
      Lie hid from mortal ken.
      Although I know not when
      Sweet day will dawn again,
Father, I wait Thy will; lead on.

I ask not why: lead on!
Mislead Thou canst not. Though through days of
    grief
And nights of anguish, pangs without relief,
      Or fears that would o'erthrow
      My faith, Thou bidst me go,
      Thy changeless love, I know,
Father, my soul will keep: lead on.

With Thee is light: lead on!
When dank and chill at eve the night-mists fall,
O'erhanging all things like a dismal pall,
      The gloom, with dawn, hath fled;
      So, though 'mid shades I tread,
      The dayspring o'er my head,
Father, from Thee shall break : lead on.

Thy way is peace: lead on!
Made heir of all things, I were yet unblest
Didst Thou not dwell with me and make me rest
    Beneath the brooding wing
      That Thou dost o'er me fling,
      Till Thou Thyself shalt bring,
Father, my spirit home: lead on.

Thou givest strength : lead on !
I cannot sink while Thy right hand upholds,
Nor comfort lack while Thy kind arm enfolds.
Through all my soul I feel
A healing influence steal,
While at Thy feet I kneel,
Father, in lowly trust : lead on.

'Twill soon be o'er : lead on !
Left all behind, earth's heart-aches then shall seem
E'en as the memories of a vanished dream ;
And when of griefs and tears
The golden fruit appears,
Amid the eternal years,
Father, all thanks be Thine !   Lead on !

1873.

MY BELOVED IS MINE.

" I am my Beloved's and my Beloved is mine." — SONG OF SOL. vi. 3.

JESUS, this heart within me burns
To tell Thee all its conscious love ;
And from earth's low delights it turns,
To taste a joy like that above.

When Thou to meet me dost descend,
In love divine, thou blessèd One,
The moments that with Thee I spend
Seem e'en as heaven itself begun.

Though oft these lips my love have told,
  They still the story would repeat ;
To me the rapture ne'er grows old
  That thrills me, bending at Thy feet.

I breathe my words into Thine ear ;
  I seem to fix my eyes on Thine ;
·And sure that Thou dost wait to hear,
  I dare in faith to call Thee mine.

Reign thou sole Sovereign of my heart !
  My all I yield to Thy control ;
O let me never from Thee part,
  Thou best Belovéd of my soul !

1863.

THE VICTORY OF FAITH.

*"Thanks be to God, which giveth us the victory, through our Lord Jesus
Christ."* — 1 COR. xv. 57.

WHY should these eyes be tearful
    For years too swiftly fled ?
And why these feet be fearful
  The onward path to tread ?
Why should a chill come o'er me
  At thoughts of death as near ?
Or when I see before me
  The silent gates appear ?

Behold my Saviour dying!
  I hear his parting breath;
Entombed I see Him lying,
  A captive held of death;
Yet peacefully He sleepeth,
  No foe disturbs Him now,
And love divine still keepeth
  Its impress on His brow.

But lo! the seal is broken!
  Rolled back the mighty stone;
In·vain was set the token
  That friend and foe should own;
The weeping Mary bending,
  Sees not her Saviour there;
But sons of light attending,
  A joyful message bear.

The Lord is risen! He liveth,
  The first-born from the dead;
To Him the Father giveth
  To be creation's head;
O'er all for ever reigning,
  Of death He holds the keys,
And hell, His might constraining,
  Obeys His high decrees.

Flies now the gloom that shaded
  The vale of death to me;
The terrors that invaded
  Are lost, O Christ, in Thee!

The grave, no more appalling,
  Invites me to repose ;
Asleep in Jesus falling,
  To rise as Jesus rose.

O when to life awaking,
  The night for ever gone,
My soul, this dust forsaking,
  Puts incorruption on ;
Lord, in Thy lustre shining,
  In Thine own beauty drest,
My sun no more declining,
  Thy service be my rest !

1867.

THE CONSENTING HEART.

" Come unto me, all ye that labor and are heavy laden, and I will give you rest." — MATT. xi. 28.

YES, kind Saviour, grieving
    O'er the sad past,
All my vain hopes leaving,
  Come I at last ;
    Thine, Thine I am,
    O bleeding Lamb !
To Thy heart receiving,
  Hold Thou me fast.

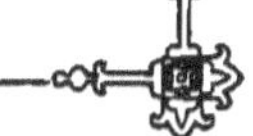

On Thy word relying,
  Safe let me rest,
All my tears now drying
  On Thy dear breast;
    Dawns the sweet day,
    Bright o'er my way,
Foes and fears all flying,
  Here I am blest.

All my footsteps heeding,
  Shield me from ill,
In green pastures feeding,
  By waters still;
    Always with Thee,
    Lord, let me be;
Thou all kindly leading,
  Thine be my will.

When — life's last day ending —
  Dark death is nigh,
Jesus, o'er me bending,
  Note my last sigh;
    In that dread hour,
    Strong in Thy power,
On swift wing ascending,
  Home let me fly!

1867.

THE VISION OF CHRIST.

" Now we see through a glass, darkly ; but then face to face." —
1 COR. xiii. 12.

O CHRIST, I long to know Thee
  As Thou art known above ;
Long, face to face, to show Thee,
  In faultless praise, my love ;
But Thou Thyself now hidest
  Beyond my feeble sense,
Though all my steps Thou guidest,
  Thine arm my sure defence.

O'erpowering is the splendor
  About the unveiled throne ;
Where bright archangels render
  A service all their own ;
That glory sight confounding,
  Those wonders rich and rare,
The anthems high resounding,
  This mortal could not bear.

Yet, Lord, to see Thee, pining,
  In thought I oft ascend,
And where Thy hosts are shining,
  I, too, before Thee bend ;
As one in rapture dreaming,
  Celestial bliss I feel,
And in that moment's seeming
  Glow with a seraph's zeal.

When from this dream awaking,
  A weary pilgrim still,
Sloth from my spirit shaking,
  With fixed, unfaltering will,
My soul, in courage stronger,
  Holds on her toilsome way,
Content to watch yet longer,
  Till dawns the wished-for day.

1867.

THE PILGRIM FATHERS.

This hymn was written, by request, for the service commemorative of the two hundred and fiftieth anniversary of the landing of the Pilgrims at Plymouth. The meeting was held in the Tremont Temple, Boston, on the evening of Dec. 22, 1870; and the hymn was sung to original music furnished by Mr. S. M. Downs of that city.

" The Lord saith, . . . them that honor me I will honor." — 1 SAM. ii. 30.

FIRM as the rock beneath their feet,
  The saintly Pilgrims stood;
On Thee, O God, their trust was stayed,
Thy voice their steadfast souls obeyed,
And Thou didst answer when they prayed
  Beside the wintry flood;
Didst give them strength, in faith sublime,
To work the noblest work of time.

To-day by centuries we count
  The slowly measured years:
And, lo! wide o'er a smiling land,
Fair homes and sacred temples stand;

Where frowned rude wastes and forests grand,
  A peopled realm appears;
O'er hills and plains, from sea to sea,
Sweep thronging millions of the free!

Tears for the days of deadly strife, —
  Tears for the young and brave,
Who, fired by Freedom's battle-cry,
Flung broad her banner to the sky,
Content on gory fields to lie,
  That they her home might save;
That chains from every hand might fall,
And Love's wide arms encircle all.

As Thou didst hear, O faithful God,
  The prayer our Fathers said;
So hear us while, like them, to Thee,
We for our children bend the knee;
Let them to distant ages be
  As if the Pilgrims, dead,
In them did wake and live again,
Their shields the shields of mighty men!

O Christ, be Thine the Pilgrims' land!
  Reign Thou from shore to shore;
Here let Thy church beneath Thy sway,
Grow fairer till her bridal day,
When Thou shalt come in glad array,
  Her Lord, — as mountains o'er,
In splendors robed, the morning sun
Ascends his flaming course to run.

Praise God! praise Him who changeth not!
　　Our Fathers' God, and ours;
To Thee our thankful praise we bring,
Ancient of Days!　Our glorious King!
Let earth and heaven together sing
　　With all their raptured powers;
Till listening stars shall catch the strain,
And shout the chorus back amain!

1872.

THE DEDICATION OF A CHURCH.

" And above the firmament that was over their heads was the likeness of a throne, as the appearance of a sapphire stone; and upon the likeness of the throne was the likeness as the appearance of a man above upon it." — EZEK. i. 26.

COME, Jesus, from the sapphire throne,
　　Where Thy redeemed behold Thy face,
Enter this temple, now Thine own,
　　And let Thy glory fill the place.

We praise Thee that to-day we see
　　Its sacred walls before Thee stand;
'Tis Thine for us, — 'tis ours for Thee;
　　Reared by Thy kind, assisting hand.

Oft as returns the day of rest,
　　Let heartfelt worship here ascend;
With Thine own joy fill every breast,
　　With Thine own power Thy word attend.

Here, in the dark and sorrowing day,
  Bid Thou the throbbing heart be still;
O wipe the mourner's tears away,
  And give new strength to meet Thy will.

When round this board Thine own shall meet,
  And keep the feast of dying love,
Be our communion ever sweet,
  With Thee, and with Thy church above.

Come, faithful Shepherd, feed Thy sheep;
  In Thine own arms the lambs enfold;
Give help to climb the heavenward steep,
  Till Thy full glory we behold.

1875.

INFANT BAPTISM.

"And they brought unto Him also infants." — LUKE xviii. 15.

WE praise Thee, Saviour, for the grace
  That bids us with our infants come;
That gives them in Thy heart a place,
  And in Thy kingdom grants them room.

We bring them to Thine altar, Lord,
  And here the holy seal apply;
O make them clean, — their names record
  In Thine own Book of Life on high.

When storms shall beat, or gathering foes
  Beset the path their feet must tread,
Dear Shepherd, let Thine arms enclose,
  Or o'er them for defence be spread.

If Thou hast marked them for the tomb,
 Ere morning brightens into day,
As in Thy bosom bear them home,
 And gently wipe our tears away.

Or if when gathered to Thy rest,
 'Tis ours to leave them pilgrims still,
Guide Thou their steps till with us blest,
 They reach Thine Everlasting Hill.

1864.

THE LAMB ENTHRONED.

"And lo, in the midst of the throne . . . stood a Lamb as it had been slain." — Rev. v. 6.

SON of God, who 'midst the throne
 Standest as the Lamb once slain,
Never in their need Thine own
 Lift their eyes to Thee in vain.

Thou hast set our spirits free,
 While before Thy cross we knelt;
Thou hast drawn our hearts to Thee,
 While Thy wondrous love we felt.

Now with fervent thanks we come,
 All to Thee our Lord we give;
From Thee never would we roam,
 With Thee ever would we live.

When our hearts with gladness beat,
 When our paths with sunshine glow,
Be Thy love than all more sweet,
 Be Thy smile as heaven below.

Should we strive 'mid doubts and fears,
  Be Thy help not long delayed;
From our eyes, when dimmed with tears,
  Chase away grief's darksome shade.

Lead us daily by Thy grace,
  Till these years of earth are sped;
Then unveil to us Thy face,
  Thou that livest and wast dead!

DOXOLOGY.

Praise to God the Father give,
  Praise the Lamb that once was slain,
Praise the Spirit, all that live,
  Triune God, for ever reign!

1875.

THE INSPIRING SPIRIT.

" Holy men of God spake as they were moved by the Holy Ghost." —
2 PETER i. 21.

O SPIRIT of the living God,
  Effulgence of the Eternal One,
Where'er Thy splendor streams abroad,
  It cheers and gladdens like the sun.

Thine was the light in days of old,
  When raptured prophets saw and spoke;
What wonders did their eyes behold!
  What glories on their vision broke!

They were but ministers of Thine,
  When glowed their lips with sacred fire;
And Thou through them on us didst shine,
  When Thou didst all their thoughts inspire.

Theirs was the voice, the truth Thine own,
  When love's great mystery, long concealed,
To unborn ages was made known
  In their illumined souls revealed.

'Twas taught of Thee that holy men
  Wrote the full page of Jesus' grace;
And Thou didst guide each faithful pen,
  The record of His love to trace.

O blessed Book!   O Word divine!
  'Tis God the Spirit speaks in Thee;
And I will make Thy wisdom mine,
  Till in heaven's perfect day I see.

1874.

THE CLOSING YEAR.

" Thou crownest the year with Thy goodness." — Ps. lxv. 11.

THOU who roll'st the year around,
  Crowned with mercies large and free,
Rich Thy gifts to us abound,
  Warm our thanks shall rise to Thee:
Kindly to our worship bow,
  While our grateful praises swell,
That, sustained by Thee, we now
  Bid the parting year farewell.

All its numbered days are sped,
  All its busy scenes are o'er,
All its joys for ever fled,
  All its sorrows felt no more:
Mingled with th' eternal past,
  Its remembrance shall decay,
Yet to be revived at last,
  At the solemn judgment day.

All our follies, Lord, forgive;
  Cleanse each heart and make us Thine;
Let Thy grace within us live,
  As our future suns decline;
Then when life's last eve shall come,
  Happy spirits let us fly
To our everlasting home,
  To our Father's house on high.

1832.

THE REST OF FAITH.

"Happy is he that hath the God of Jacob for his help." — Ps. cxlvi. 5.

LORD, I would heavenward ever press,
  In Thee alone, my Helper, strong;
Through blooming vale and wilderness
  Alike, be Thou my joy and song.

When tempests darken o'er my way,
  And winds are raging fierce and wild,
In humble trust my soul shall say:
  O God, my Father, keep Thy child!

Why should I e'er distrust Thy care,
 Though troubles all my steps beset?
Why with sad heart my burdens bear,
 And all Thy faithful love forget?

That love through many a year hath led
 From scene to scene my pilgrim feet;
Hath daily, as with manna, fed,
 And shown me fountains pure and sweet.

A thousand sacred memories rise
 Of mercies that the days have crowned,
When o'er me spread unclouded skies,
 And light and gladness smiled around.

My faith shall on Thy promise rest,
 That Thou my stay and strength wilt be;
If Thou but fold me to Thy breast,
 No foe shall rend my soul from Thee.

Forgiveness, peace, and life divine,
 Through Christ's dear cross Thy grace hath
  given;
And Thou, I know, wilt call me Thine,
 When breaks the blessed morn of heaven!

1874.

———◦◦◦———

GETHSEMANE.

" Then cometh Jesus with them unto a place called Gethsemane." —
MATT. xxvi. 36.

WHERE climbs thy steep, fair Olivet,
 There is a spot most dear to me:
The spot with tears of sorrow wet,
 When Jesus knelt in agony.

I love in thought to linger there,
  To tread the hallowed ground alone,
Where, on the silent midnight air,
  Rose heavenward, Lord, Thy plaintive moan.

I fondly seek the olive shade
  That veiled Thee when Thy soul was wrung;
When angels came to bring Thee aid,
  That oft to Thee their harps had strung.

There on the sacred turf I kneel,
  And breathe my heart's deep love to Thee,
While tender memories o'er me steal,
  Of all Thou didst endure for me.

O mystery of anguish, when
  The sinless felt sin's heavy woe!
Hell madly dreamed of triumph then,
  While Thy dear head was bending low.

Vain dream!   No grief shall evermore
  Stain, as with bloody sweat, Thy brow;
Robed in all glory — thine before —
  The seraphim surround Thee now.

Yet, Lord, from off the burning throne,
  Above yon stars that softly gleam,
Thou com'st to meet me here alone,
  By Kedron's old, familiar stream.

1864.

VIA DOLOROSA.

"And He bearing His cross went forth." — JOHN xix. 17.

I SEE my Lord, the pure, the meek, the lowly,
    Along the mournful way in sadness tread;
The thorns are on His brow, and He, the Holy,
    Bearing His cross, to Calvary is led!

Silent He moveth on, all uncomplaining,
    Though wearily His grief and burden press;
And foes — nor shame nor pity now restraining —
    With scoff and jeering mock His deep distress.

'Tis hell's dark hour; yet calm Himself resigning,
    Even as a lamb that goeth to be slain,
The wine-press lone He treadeth unrepining,
    And falling blood-drops all His raiment stain.

In mortal weakness 'neath His burden sinking,
    The Son of God accepts a mortal's aid!
Then passes on to Golgotha unshrinking,
    Where love's divinest sacrifice is made.

Dear Lord! what though my path be set with sorrow,
    And oft beneath some heavy cross I groan?
My soul, weighed down, shall strength and courage
      borrow,
    At thoughts of sharper griefs which Thou hast
    known.

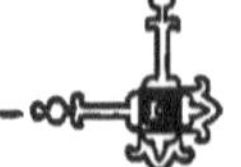

And I, in tears, will yet look up with gladness,
  And hope when troubles most my hope would drown;
The mournful way which Thou didst tread with sadness
  Was but Thy way to glory and Thy crown!

1864.

BURDENS.

" Cast thy burden upon the Lord." — Ps. lv. 22.

EVER as I onward go
  Through the mazy round of life,
  Days and years with struggles rife,
Wearily I tread and slow;
Oft my spirit falters, faints,
Oft breathes out her sad complaints.

Guilt's huge burden weighs me down,
  Pressing heavily and sore;
  Till Thy face, dear Lord, no more
Glows with smiles; Thou seem'st to frown,
Though I long Thy grace to prove,
Though I know that Thou art Love!

Oft thou chafest, haggard Care!
  Wearing, wasting, day by day,
  Thou each rising joy dost slay
That my soul would upward bear;
Thou dost clog my heavenward flight,
Spoil my spirit of her might.

Leaden Grief, thou pressest hard,
   When have sped the shafts of fate,
   When my heart bleeds, desolate,
And by many an arrow scarred ;
When on sorrow's sea long tost,
All the lights of hope are lost.

Dark thou broodest o'er my soul,
   Gloomy Doubt, when hidden lie,
   Locked in awful mystery,
God's deep counsels, and the scroll
Sleeps unopened till the time
When goes forth His word sublime.

Thou, O spectre-loving Fear,
   All too oft hast o'er me flung
   Terrors that like rocks have hung,
Sinking every thought of cheer ;
Till a ship I seemed to be,
Foundering in the far-off sea.

Yet I hear a Father's voice :
   " I, Jehovah, am thy strength ;
   All thy burdens bring, at length,
Cast on me, — then go, rejoice !
Make thy days with songs resound,
Rest in holy peace profound !"
   Yes, my God ; away, away
      Haunting unbelief and gloom !
      Vanish, and for joy give room,

Joy of faith, while now I pray;
Henceforth sweetly on Thy breast,
Love Eternal, will I rest!

1868.

TWILIGHT WORSHIP.

*" Surely goodness and mercy shall follow me all the days of my life ; and
I will dwell in the house of the Lord for ever." —* Ps. xxiii. 6.

WELCOME the sweet evening-tide!
 While its peaceful moments glide,
Jesus, in the twilight dim,
Thou shalt hear my grateful hymn;
Nightly let this hour be given,
Lord, to thoughts of Thee and heaven.

Thou through all the day hast led,
Poured glad sunshine o'er my head;
Thou hast been my guard and guide,
Turned each deadly shaft aside,
Made e'en care and labor blest,
Laid each rising fear to rest.

In this stillness, Saviour dear,
Be Thou to my spirit near;
Shed Thy grace like heavenly balm,
This my care-chafed soul shall calm;
Though Thy form I may not see,
Let me draw fresh life from Thee.

When shall set my latest sun,
All life's years of labor done,
Let me gently sink to rest,
As reposing on Thy breast;
Sleeping till the shadows flee,
And I wake, my Lord, with Thee.

1875.

THE SABBATH BELL.

"*For a day in Thy courts is better than a thousand.*" — Ps. lxxxiv. 10.

I DO not know who is the author of the first of the following stanzas. It was set to a piece of music by Neukomm, and was placed in my hands by Dr. LOWELL MASON, with the request that another stanza might be added.

"THE sabbath bell so full and swelling,
　Whose rich vibrations greet the ear,
To me in solemn note seems telling
　Of faith, of hope, of heaven near;
My heart with holy joy is bounding,
　From earth my thoughts are on the wing,
Whene'er the welcome call is sounding
　That bids me join the choir and sing."

And while I hear the organ pealing,
　And raptured voices shouting praise,
While, at God's holy altar kneeling,
　The tranquil eye of prayer I raise,
Sweet dews of heaven seem o'er me falling,
　Subduing all my soul to love;
I seem to hear some seraph calling,
　To bid me join the choir above.

1834.

REPOSE IN GOD.

*" The Lord is my strength, and my shield ; my heart trusted in Him, and
I am helped."* — Ps. xxviii. 7.

THEE would I trust, my God,
   And still each anxious fear ;
Thy hand can feed and clothe and keep,
Uphold when, as through waters deep,
   Borne on, I find no helper near.
Since led by Thee, without alarm
   Life's devious way I tread, unheeding
   Death's noiseless shafts around me speeding ;
Without Thy leave no power can harm.
Thy love hath made me safely dwell ;
Thy mercies, more than words can tell,
Have made my cup to overflow :
Henceforth, since all to Thee I owe,
   My joy shall be to give Thee all ;
To banish fear, to trust Thee still,
   In every need on Thee to call ;
Most blest that Thou shouldst work Thy will :
So through the round of mortal days
This heart and tongue shall give Thee praise.

1874.

CONQUERING AND TO CONQUER.

" That at the name of Jesus every knee should bow." — PHIL. ii. 10.

O CHRIST, the same through changing years,
　　Thou hast Thy church in safety kept;
Thy love hath calmed her rising fears,
　　Hath heard her when she prayed and wept.

Her faithful sons, for love of Thee,
　　Have dared opposing powers to brave;
Resolved from every bond to free
　　The soul that Thou alone canst save.

Still for the honor of Thy name,
　　O give Thy servants strength to stand
Unmoved by foe, reproach, or shame,
　　A loving, trusting, dauntless band.

O gather to Thy peaceful fold
　　The lost that on dark mountains stray;
Let sinful souls that Cross behold
　　Whose blood can take their guilt away.

Let triumph crown Thy holy cause,
　　The last strongholds of darkness fall;
The nations learn and keep Thy laws,
　　And own Thee, Jesus, Lord of all!

1875.

THE SECOND COMING.

" Behold, He cometh with clouds, and every eye shall see Him, and they
also which pierced Him." — REV. i. 7.

"BEHOLD, I come!"   O Son of God,
   Of old that word of Thine was spoken ;
And since by Thee this earth was trod,
   No word of Thine hath e'er been broken.
When from the crown of Olivet
Homeward Thy face divine was set,
    And blessings fell from Thee ascending,
    Angels proclaimed, Thy guard attending :
"In yonder skies, this Jesus so
Shall come as ye have seen Him go!"

"Behold I come!"   So didst Thou speak ;
   The hour Thou didst Thyself declare
Hid with the Father ; none may seek
   To read the awful secret there !
But that great day shall come when Thou,
Who didst mount up from Olive's brow,
    Shalt yet once more be seen descending,
    Heaven's countless legions Thee attending ;
And robed in splendors Thou alone
Shalt fill the flaming judgment throne !

O day of days !   When Thou, again
   In power and majesty appearing,
Shalt call to judgment mortal men,
    The quick and dead the summons hearing ;

When that dread Book Thou shalt unfold
That hath been kept from ages old,
　The record of each life unsealing,
　The secrets of each heart revealing;
When they that pierced Thee mourn too late,
And, speechless, their just sentence wait!

E'en so, Lord Jesus, come!　All Thine
　Shall hear Thy voice with transport thrilling,
When Thou, in grandeur all divine,
　As when of old the tempest stilling,
Aloud shalt call: " Ye blessed, come!
Inherit now your destined home!"
　O then — the eternal gates unfolding —
　Thy saints, the Throne of Love beholding,
With Thee in triumph shall ascend
To share Thy glory without end.

1875.

THE GOOD SHEPHERD.

*" My sheep hear my voice, and I know them, and they follow me : and I
give unto them eternal life." —* JOHN x. 27, 28.

L ET no terrors haunt thee,
　　Let no foe alarm,
E'en death shall not daunt thee,
　Nor hell do thee harm;
Thy Lord, ever living,
　New strength for each hour
In thy need ever giving,
　Shall gird thee with power.

What though He may try thee
　　As gold in the fire ;
He will not deny thee
　　Thy fondest desire ;
Thy yearning He heedeth,
　　Thy love knoweth well,
And where He His flock feedeth,
　　Will bring thee to dwell.

Let gladness possess thee,
　　Let hope cheer thee still ;
He reigneth to bless thee,
　　Thy cup He shall fill ;
Let faith, never failing,
　　All peacefully rest,
Till, His dear face unveiling,
　　He maketh thee blest !

1875.

SABBATH MORNING WORSHIP.

" This is the day which the Lord hath made ; we will rejoice and be glad in it." — Ps. cxviii. 24.

WITH the Sabbath's holy dawning
　　Let us, Lord, Thy glory see ;
Upward, on the wings of morning,
　　Our glad souls would mount to Thee ;
　　　　Let our praises
Joined with heaven's grand. chorus be !

Let our thoughts from earth ascending
  Hold communion with the skies ;
While before Thee lowly bending,
  Lord, we lift our waiting eyes,
      Pure and fervent,
Let our prayers like incense rise.

While we seek Thee, draw Thou near us,
  Let each heart Thy presence feel ;
Let Thy grace refresh and cheer us,
  And each wounded spirit heal ;
      Lead us ever,
Till before Thy throne we kneel.

1875.

NOCTURN.

" Enter into thy closet, and . . . shut thy door." — MATT. vi. 6

I SIT in my silent chamber,
    And my spirit mounts in thought ;
Dear hour of divine communion,
    That oft a deep joy hath wrought !
And lo! as in holy vision,
    The heavens unfold above,
And there fall bright beams of glory,
    There is breathed the breath of love.

I see, through the amber portal,
    The angels of God descend ;
"God's Host," — they are swift of pinion,
    And ever His saints attend ;

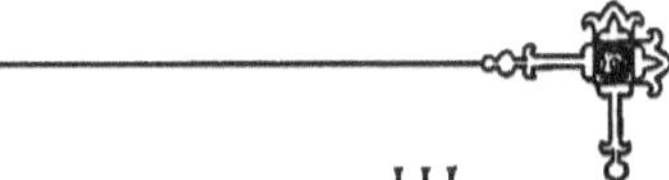

I hear the celestial chorus,
   Harps touched with divinest skill,
Tones sweeter than breathing zephyrs,
   That on my hushed soul distil.

The praise of the Holiest hymning,
   The skies with the song resound;
The stars seem to join their voices,
   As they float in the dark profound;
And the loving Father of spirits,
   Though ruling all worlds the while,
To the " Sons of God " doth hearken,
   And sheddeth on them His smile !

Ay, Lord, Thou bendest yet lower;
   The voices of earth dost hear;
Dost catch each sigh of contrition,
   Dost note each glistening tear;
My praise is to Thee as incense,
   For prayer Thou returnest grace;
Not now may these eyes behold Thee,
   But I feel Thy blest embrace.

Why, why should I envy seraphs,
   That they stand so near the throne,
If here Thou dost deign to meet me,
   If here dost Thyself make known ?
If now in these evening shadows,
   This stillness of dying day,
My soul may drink of Thy fulness
   Till won from her griefs away ?

My God, Thy secret is with me,
   A secret I ne'er can tell;
'Tis life, 'tis peace, 'tis a rapture,
   When with me Thou com'st to dwell;
While the twilight shades grow deeper,
   As spreadeth her wings the night,
On me there falleth Thy splendor,
   And all is serenely bright.

My finite and feeble spirit
   With Thine the Infinite blends,
Till with heaven's own bliss o'erflowing,
   Her weary, vain quest she ends;
As if on Thy bosom lying,
   She findeth her wished-for rest,
By Eternal Arms enfolded:
   Have ye more than this, ye blest?

Ah, yes! ye spirits immortal,
   Ye are not to sense confined;
No law in your faultless being,
   When ye long to soar, doth bind;
And I, too, at length ascending,
   From sense for ever set free,
Shall God-ward cleave the bright azure,
   As glad and as pure as ye!

My feet shall tread the fair city
   Adorned as a beautiful bride;
Shall come to the living fountains,
   And walk by the crystal tide;

To the loved again united,
  Once lost amidst tears and pain,
I shall know the full affection
  For which I have yearned in vain.

I shall then, with undimmed vision,
  See what had been hid before ;
From wonder onward to wonder,
  For ever mount up and adore;
If on earth Thy works have charmed me,
  What raptures shall fill me there,
When I gaze on spotless beauty,
  Than all I had dreamed more fair !

O, then on the throne whose brightness
  Outshineth yon blazing sun,
The Head of the whole creation,
  I shall see the Crucified One !
Where night spreads no more her shadow,
  I, amidst the ineffable glow,
Shall live on His smile for ever,
  And ALL THAT HE IS SHALL KNOW !

1867.

DOXOLOGY.

GOD our Father, God of grace,
  Saviour, born of mortal race,
Comforter, our life and light,
One in essence, love, and might ;
Thee whom all in heaven adore,
We would worship evermore.

1875.

# TRANSLATIONS.

TRANSLATIONS.

ADVENT HYMN.

" Veni Redemptor gentium."

This hymn, attributed to St. Ambrose, Bishop of Milan, who died near the close of the fourth century, 397, was translated at the request of Dr. Philip Schaff, for his " Christ in Song," in which it originally appeared.

O THOU Redeemer of our race,
   Come, show the Virgin's Son to earth ;
Let every age admire the grace ;
   Worthy a God Thy human birth !

'Twas by no mortal will or aid,
   But by the Holy Spirit's might,
That flesh the Word of God was made,
   A babe yet waiting for the light.

Spotless remains the Virgin's name,
   Although the Holy Child she bears ;
And virtue's banners round her flame,
   While God a temple so prepares.

As if from honor's royal hall,
   Comes forth at length the Mighty One,
Whom Son of God and Man they call,
   Eager His destined course to run.

Forth from the Father's bosom sent,
   To Him returned, He claimed His own ;
Down to the realms of death He went,
   Then rose to share the eternal throne.

An equal at the Father's side,
   Thou wear'st the trophy of Thy flesh ;
In Thee our nature shall abide
   In strength complete, in beauty fresh.

With light divine Thy manger streams,
   .That kindles darkness into day ;
Dimmed by no night henceforth, its beams
   Shine through all time with changeless ray.

1868.

JESUS THE BELOVED.

" Jesu, Dulcedo cordium."

FROM ST. BERNARD of Clairvaux, obt. 1153. The stanzas here translated were
selected from the much larger number' of the Latin text. The hymn has become a
favorite with both the English and American churches.

JESUS, Thou Joy of loving hearts !
   Thou Fount of Life ! Thou Light of men !
From the best bliss that earth imparts,
   We turn unfilled to Thee again.

Thy truth unchanged hath ever stood ;
   Thou savest those that on Thee call ;
To them that seek Thee, Thou art good ;
   To them that find Thee, All in All !

We taste Thee, O Thou Living Bread,
  And long to feast upon Thee still ;
We drink of Thee, the Fountain Head,
  And thirst our souls from Thee to fill.

Our restless spirits yearn for Thee,
  Where'er our changeful lot is cast ;
Glad, when Thy gracious smile we see,
  Blest, when our faith can hold Thee fast.

O Jesus, ever with us stay !
  Make all our moments calm and bright ;
Chase the dark night of sin away,
  Shed o'er the world Thy holy light !

1858.

THE LORDSHIP OF CHRIST.

" Rex Christe, Factor omnium."

Ascribed to Gregory the Great, who was elected pope in the year 590 ; obt. 604. He was a voluminous writer.

O CHRIST, our King, Creator, Lord !
  Saviour of all who trust Thy word !
To them who seek Thee ever near,
Now to our praises bend Thine ear.

In Thy dear cross a grace is found, —
It flows from every streaming wound, —
Whose power our inbred sin controls,
Breaks the firm bond, and frees our souls !

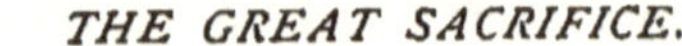

Thou didst create the stars of night,
Yet Thou hast veiled in flesh Thy light ;
Hast deigned a mortal form to wear,
A mortal's painful lot to bear.

When Thou didst hang upon the tree,
The quaking earth acknowledged Thee ;
When Thou didst there yield up Thy breath,
The world grew dark as shades of death.

Now in the Father's glory high,
Great Conqu'ror, never more to die,
Us by Thy mighty power defend,
And reign through ages without end !

1858.

THE GREAT SACRIFICE.

" Pange, lingua, gloriosi."

From Thomas Aquinas, obt. 1274.

SACRAMENTAL HYMN.

SING, and the mystery declare ;
　　Sing of the glorious Body slain ;
And of the Blood beyond compare, —
　　Price of the world, — that not in vain
He, sole of men pure born, hath shed ;
He, of the nations King and Head.

To us was born the Christ of God ;
　　A Virgin's Son to us was given ;
And, while the earth His footsteps trod,
　　Abroad He sowed the seed of heaven ;

Then, when drew near His destined hour,
Ordained this rite of wondrous power.

'Twas on the last night of the feast,
  Reclining with His faithful few,
Of ancient laws, e'en to the least,
  Each word obeyed with service true;
Himself He gave with His own hand
The Bread of Life to all the band.

The incarnate Word, in broken bread,
  His body broken there did show;
And in the wine His blood, once shed
  From guilt to cleanse, to save from woe;
Where falters sense, faith trusts His word,
And souls sincere receive the Lord.

Before this noblest sacrifice,
  In reverent love we lowly bow;
No more the appointed victim dies,
  But shadow yields to substance now;
While Faith, that want of sight supplies,
Lifts to the cross her trustful eyes.

Now to the Father and the Son,
  And Spirit sent by each, shall be
All worship, honor, homage done,
  By all that live, eternally;
Unto the Three in One be given
An equal praise, in earth and heaven.

1868.

SACRAMENTAL HYMN.

"O Esca viatorum."

THIS hymn has by some been attributed to THOMAS AQUINAS; Dr. SCHAFF thinks erroneously. He regards it as belonging to the fourteenth century, the author unknown.

O BREAD to pilgrims given,
  O Food that angels eat,
O Manna sent from heaven,
  For heaven-born natures meet!
Give us, for Thee long pining,
  To eat till richly filled;
Till, earth's delights resigning,
  Our every wish is stilled!

O Water, life-bestowing,
  From out the Saviour's heart,
A fountain purely flowing,
  A fount of love Thou art!
O, let us, freely tasting,
  Our burning thirst assuage!
Thy sweetness, never wasting,
  Avails from age to age.

Jesus, this feast receiving,
  We Thee unseen adore;
Thy faithful word believing,
  We take, and doubt no more;
Give us, Thou true and loving,
  On earth to live in Thee;
Then, death the veil removing,
  Thy glorious face to see.

1858.

I GIVE MY HEART.

" Cor meum Tibi dedo, Jesu dulcissime."

THIS beautiful hymn is found in Daniel's Thesaurus, the author and the date
both unknown.   The Latin is characterized by great simplicity and tenderness.

I GIVE my heart to Thee,
　　O Jesus most desired !
And heart for heart the gift shall be,
　　For Thou my soul hast fired :
　　Thou hearts alone would'st move ;
　　Thou only hearts dost love.
I would love Thee as Thou lov'st me,
　　O Jesus most desired !

What offering can I make,
　　Dear Lord, to love like Thine ?
That Thou, the God, didst stoop to take
　　A human form like mine !
　　" Give me thy heart, my son : "
　　Behold my heart, — 'tis done !
I would love Thee as Thou lov'st me,
　　O Jesus most desired !

Thy heart is opened wide,
　　Its offered love most free,
That heart to heart I may abide,
　　And hide myself in Thee :
　　Ah, how Thy love doth burn,
　　Till I that love return !
I would love Thee as Thou lov'st me,
　　O Jesus most desired !

Here finds my heart its rest,
Repose that knows no shock,
The strength of love that keeps it blest.
In Thee, the riven Rock,
My soul, as girt around,
Her citadel hath found.
I would love Thee as Thou lov'st me,
O Jesus most desired!

1868.

COME, HOLY GHOST.

" Veni, Sancte Spiritus."

OF this hymn TRENCH says: "The loveliest of all the hymns in the whole circle
of Latin sacred poetry has a king for its author. ROBERT the Second, son of HUGH
CAPET, succeeded his father on the throne of France, in the year 997. He was sin-
gularly addicted to church music, which he enriched, as well as the hymnology, with
compositions of his own." Obt. 1031.

COME, Holy Ghost, in love
Shed on us from above
Thine own bright ray!
Divinely good Thou art;
Thy sacred gifts impart
To gladden each sad heart:
O, come to-day!

Come, tend'rest Friend, and best,
Our most delightful guest,
With soothing power:
Rest, which the weary know,
Shade, 'mid the noontide glow,
Peace, when deep griefs o'erflow,—
Cheer us this hour!

Come, Light serene, and still
Our inmost bosoms fill;
  Dwell in each breast :
We know no dawn but Thine;
Send forth Thy beams divine,
On our dark souls to shine,
  And make us blest!

Exalt our low desires;
Extinguish passion's fires;
  Heal every wound :
Our stubborn spirits bend,
Our icy coldness end,
Our devious steps attend,
  While heavenward bound.

Come, all the faithful bless;
Let all, who Christ confess,
  His praise employ :
Give virtue's rich reward,
Victorious death accord,
And, with our glorious Lord,
  Eternal joy!

1858.

PASCHAL HYMN.

" Vita sanctorum, decus angelorum."

THIS is an ancient hymn of unknown date and authorship, probably written somewhere from the tenth to the thirteenth century. and widely used in public worship.

CHRIST, of heaven the life and grace,
  Life and grace of all below,
Yielding once to death's embrace,
  Thou didst crush the mighty foe!

By the trophy Thou didst rear,
  Keep Thy servants joyful still,
Till the promised day appear,
  When Thy name the earth shall fill.

Paschal Lamb, who from the dead
  Didst with wakened saints arise,
Then our nature, in our Head,
  Rose beyond the starry skies.

Thence, exalted, glorious Lord,
  God o'er all, yet man still known,
Thou shalt come, fulfilled Thy word,
  Seated on the judgment throne.

Lift our hearts Thy joy to share,
  Thou that shar'st the Father's seat;
Plunge us not to deep despair,
  When we rise our judge to meet.

Doxology.

This may the Father grant, with Thee,
And with the Spirit, — Holy Three, —
One reigning God, whose throne shall last
While glide eternal ages past!

1874.

LAUDES AD MATUTINUM.

" Ecce jam noctis tenuatur umbra."

By Gregory the Great, obt. 604.

BEHOLD, the shade of night is now receding!
  Kindling with splendors, fair the dawn is glowing;
With fervent hearts, O let us all implore Him,
          Ruler Almighty!

That He, our God, will look on us in pity,
Send strength for weakness, grant us His salvation.
And with a Father's pure affection give us
                    Glory eternal.

This grace O grant us, God-head ever blesséd,
Of Father, Son, and Holy Ghost in union,
Whose praises be through earth's most distant regions
                    Ever resounding.

1869.

LAUDES AD NOCTURNUM.

" Nocte surgente vigilemus omnes."

By GREGORY the Great, obt. 604.

'MID evening shadows let us all be watching,
    Ever in psalms our deep devotion waking,
And with one voice hymns to the Lord, the Saviour,
                    Sweetly be singing.

That to the holy King our songs ascending,
We worthily with all His saints may enter
The heavenly Temple, joyfully partaking
                    Life everlasting.

This grace O grant us, God-head ever-blesséd,
Of Father, Son, and Holy Ghost in union,
Whose praises be through earth's most distant regions
                    Ever resounding!

1869.

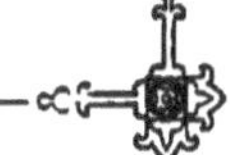

PENITENTIAL HYMN.

(From the German.)

THIS hymn is a very free translation of a German hymn, made many years since,
from an author whose name was not noted, and has been forgotten.   It has kept its
place in the manuals for public worship.

WE stand in deep repentance,
   Before Thy throne of love;
O God of grace, forgive us,
   The stain of guilt remove;
Behold us while with weeping
   We lift our eyes to Thee;
And all our sins subduing,
   Our Father, set us free!

O, shouldst Thou from us fallen
   Withhold Thy grace to guide,
For ever we should wander,
   From Thee, and peace, aside:
But Thou to spirits contrite
   Dost light and life impart,
That man may learn to serve Thee
   With thankful, joyous heart.

Our souls, — on Thee we cast them,
   Our only refuge Thou!
Thy cheering words revive us,
   When pressed with grief we bow:
Thou bear'st the trusting spirit
   Upon Thy loving breast,
And givest all Thy ransomed
   A sweet, unending rest.

1834.

HOME.

PART I.

9

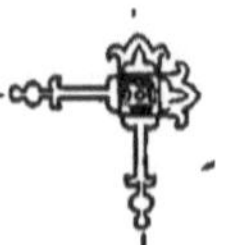

PREFACE.

THE writer has desired to present such a picture of Home as not only may be, but actually has been, substantially realized in instances almost without number. The sketch is supposed to have had its original in New England, — not because such homes are not now widely found beyond her boundaries, but because, historically, our American Homes there first exhibited their highest moral power and beauty; so that it may be fairly claimed that from her, as its source, has flowed the purest and best social life of our country. The early settlers laid the foundations of society in learning and religion; and it may reasonably be doubted whether there has ever been another spot of equal extent on the globe, in which so great a number of intelligent and virtuous Homes could have been counted. The healthful influence of New England domestic life now reaches the newly rising States to the very shores of the Pacific.

To those who have known the joys and permanent benefits of well-ordered and happy Homes, the writer trusts that the reading of these pages may afford a tranquil pleasure. It is well to revive and cherish the sweet recollections of childhood and youth, to recall the vicissitudes of after years, and to bring back the dear faces of

the loved and honored who have passed away from earth. Such reminiscences tend to make the heart better.

If what has here been written shall help, even in the least degree, to elevate in the minds of young men and women the ideal of the family and Home, and to deepen in the hearts of any a conviction of the sacredness and beauty of a pure domestic life and the peril to every interest of humanity involved in the desecration of household sanctities, the author will thankfully recognize the accomplishment of his highest purpose.

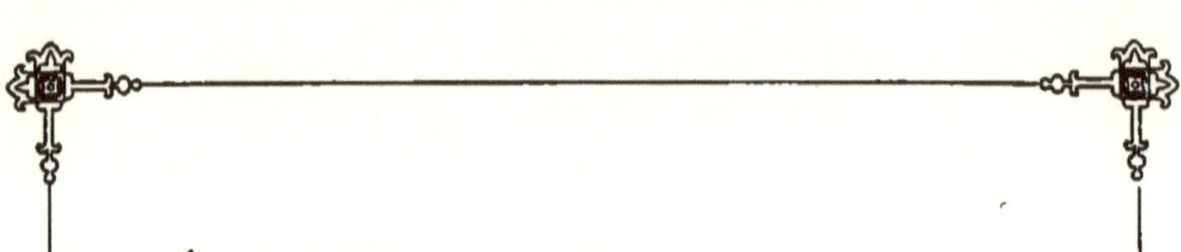

Domestic happiness, thou only bliss
Of Paradise, that has survived the fall!

COWPER.

Love is life's end : an end but never ending;
All joys, all sweets, all happiness awarding;
Love is life's wealth, ne'er spent but ever spending,
More rich by giving, taking by discarding ;
Love's life's reward, rewarded in rewarding.

SPENSER.

H O M E.

PART I.

COME, gentle lyre! sequestered from the world,
    Tired of its tumults and its pomps and pride,
Thee, wonted solace of my care-worn heart,
Glad I resume: intent not now to strike
With hurried hand thy strings, nor thee to make
Loud resonant of numbers strange or wild ;
But, with such mood serene and airy touch
As best befit soft-breathing harmonics,
To wake thy tones on a familiar theme.

As whom necessity ordains to tread
The arid waste where trackless Libyan sands
Reflect the sun, seek not in vain to find,
At distant intervals, some friendly spots
Where gurgling waters 'neath o'ershadowing palms
Invite repose ; so, o'er the wastes of life
While sent to roam, where pines full oft unfilled
Intense desire, and nameless ills beset

Us hapless wanderers on an unknown way,
We seek and find oases bright and fair.

Most fair, most bright art thou, dear peaceful Home,
Of all best earthly gifts by Heaven bestowed
Man's pilgrim path to cheer.   Ever thou art
A refuge from the storm ; from the rough wind
A covert.   All who may, in each dark hour
When sorrows bow the soul, or when of care
The lighter burden wearily doth press,
Fly to thy bosom, and secluded find
In thy sweet influence solace and repose.
Who know thee not — alas, that such should be ! —
Pine for thee, and still hope, though hope deferred
Hath oft made sick the heart, that yet for them
Some spot shall bear thy well-beloved name.
The wanderer thinks of thee.   With him he bears
A thousand hallowed memories, fondly kept,
That waken oft afresh.   E'en while he treads,
With heedful musings, old historic ground,
Rich with the spoils of Time, where crumbling stand
The hoary monuments of glories dead ;
Or climbs 'mid Alpine wonders, and surveys
Rude wilds where Nature all untamed abides ;
In search of thee his truant thought will stray.
Or, if he tempt the main, far, far away
Swept by the breeze across the heaving deep,
Fixed on his lonely watch at midnight hour,
The watery waste around, the stars above,

Back o'er the flood he roams to visit thee.
For thee the captive sighs in the still gloom
Of his dim cell.   The warrior grim, what time
He treads the battle-field where marshalled hosts
Await the bloody fray — pride on his brow
And glory on his crest — lets fall a tear,
While o'er him steal, like flute-notes faintly heard,
Remembrances thick-coming of thy joys.
Dear rest and centre thou of faithful hearts,
Where'er thy seat ; as well 'neath tropic suns
As where Arcadian realms boast genial skies,
Or arctic winter spreads eternal snows ;
O'er the wide world thy magic spell enchains.

Not many years have rolled since, where now smile
New England's happy Homes, the forest stood,
A mighty wilderness.   O'er hills and vales
Spread virgin groves, where never yet had rung
The stroke of woodman's axe, and tangled brakes
And thickets dark, that many a covert wove.
There prowled the cruel wolf.   There undisturbed
The bear reared her fierce progeny.   The owl
Hooted from his lone seat upon the pine,
And echo answered back.   The eagle soared
And screamed, or, pouncing on his quivering prey,
Perched on some naked cliff and fed secure.
Along the river, gliding broad and slow,
Or up the rapid brook, that babbling loud
Rushed from the mountain headlong to the plain,

The trout and salmon darted unensnared.
Of human kind sole tenant of the wild,
The lordly savage reigned, and urged the chase,
Of useful toil impatient ; or, when war
Roused his dark passions, from his ambuscade
Treacherous he darted, and, with horrid yell,
Vengeful and unrelenting scalped his foe.
No peaceful Home was then.   The dingy squaw,
The menial of her lord, now left to guard
The smoky wigwam, now with blows compelled
Him vagrant to attend with weary load,
Dragged out, a semi-brute, her wretched life.

For man, for woman, God all-good ordained
A worthier destiny.   By sacred ties,
In household life and harmony of love
He formed them to be joined ; society
Made sure by nature's law ; and so decreed
That states and kingdoms should successive rise ;
That mind with mind in sympathy should wake
New energies, the needs of men impel
To foster arts, and search creation through
For knowledge of his own eternal thoughts.
He meant not the prolific earth should lie
Incultivate, but, tilled with patient care,
Should smile with flowers as erst an Eden smiled,
And yield the culturing hand a rich reward.
'Twas His behest that bade the forest bow,

The savage beast retire, and savage men
Give place to cultivation, order, laws.

A lonely bark came o'er the stormy sea ;
Not freighted deep with pelf ; it richer bore,
What famed Golconda's treasures could not buy,
A band of noble hearts.   Men trod that deck
Who knew that they were men, and freely gave
For liberty and truth what else was dear.
No factious spirits, who, through spleen or pride,
Contemned their country's laws and roamed to find
What earth's circumference within, for them,
Was nowhere to be found, content and peace.
Of England's best, to her they fondly clung,
Proud of her glorious names and old renown ;
And as her loyal sons their lives had spent,
And with her honored dead had peaceful slept
'Neath hallowed aisles in storied chapels dim,
Less had they loved what most ennobles man —
Freedom of soul, pure faith, and peace with Heaven.
Hatred hath called them stern ; their sturdy strength
Of principle hath bigotry misnamed ;
And levity, with leer and gibe profane,
Blasphemed their sanctity and saintly zeal.
'Tis rather bigotry that dares deny
Their nobleness, their glory that would stain.
Warm were their hearts ; none warmer e'er did beat
In manly breasts ; and humble though their Homes,
By wealth unblest, yet love and beauty there

Found place for sweet unfolding, nor was mirth
A stranger at those hearths where nightly blazed
The fires that made a fireside worth the name.
Knowledge, religion, virtue, — wheresoe'er
These dwell together, dwell earth's best delights.
Not faultless were they, else were they not men ;
Yet less their own the faults than of their time ;
Of times long past, when many an error reigned
As yet unchallenged, blinding all alike
To truths since seen as in the midday blaze.
Beyond their fellows, keenly had they pierced
Error's thick-veiling mists, and Truth discerned
In her diviner forms ; aside had flung
Falsehoods long honored, maxims cherished long
That mighty ills had wrought ; the good, the right,
In their great hearts they worshipped ; these they
　　sought,
As misers search for gold, with deathless love ;
Clung to them found, as with the grasp of fate !
What if perchance from ardor so intense
Of quenchless earnestness, their zeal o'erglowed
At times, and they — their vision not yet clear —
There erred where all the world had erred till then ?
Ah ! ye who meanly seek to tear away
The honors thickly clustered round their brows,
Yours, yours the lack of heavenly charity
Ye charge on them ; yours with far less defence !
On you returned at last shall rest the shame ;
And as the sun from the clear mirror wipes

The envious vapor that its lustre dimmed,
Just Time their names to honor shall restore.[1]

Such were thy sires, New England ; such the men
That tamed thy wilds ; thy slopes and valleys robed
With waving fields ; made e'en thy rugged hills
Look kind ; thy teeming cities with their marts,
Their industries and commerce, rise and thrive.
Rich among lands art thou in sweet content,
In health and plenty, born of patient toil.
Rich in thy stalwart sons and daughters fair,
That o'er the world, where'er their feet may tread,
Bear with them blessing.   Known of all are they,
Of keen intelligence and purpose firm.
About their footsteps truth and freedom spring,
And law's firm voice is heard, — her word obeyed ;
Wide sown are wisdom's seeds, and useful arts,
With many a curious, many a rare device,
Lend force to labor, or embellish life.
Their Mother they forget not ; but from far,
Where, ocean-like, the boundless prairie spreads,
Where rock-ribbed mountains lift their frowning forms,
And sunset regions kiss the western wave,
Their hearts with many a yearning backward turn,
True to her still ; and all her scenes recalled
Look fairer seen in memory's mellow light.
A Holy Land she seems, where God abides ;
Nor seems alone.   Holy well named a land

1 See Appendix, note B.

Where lives a faith divine ; where graceful rise
Religion's hallowed domes, and close at hand
The school-house, fit ally, within whose walls
Kind culture early moulds the plastic mind
To virtue and to truth ; where stand embowered
The mantled cottage and the tasteful Home.
Dear tranquil scenes !   Home, o'er the world a name
That like a talisman calls to the soul
All images of bliss, hath here a spell
Of mightiest working.[1]   Other lands may boast
More friendly soils ; and blander airs may breathe
Upon their spicy beds that odors yield
More fragrant far ; and birds of rarer note
Among their groves pour richer melodies ;
And lordlier dwellings rise.   But where hath earth
A soil more free, a clime that ministers
More vigor to the frame, or fosters more
True energy of soul ?   Where Nature's face
A nobler aspect — mountain crests that climb
In their blue dimness, reverend forests tall
Crowning the hills with majesty and grace,
And waterfalls that, with sonorous voice
Softened by distance, charm the listening ear ?
Where doth the rustic dwelling more bespeak
Substantial comfort, or with happier art
Where Luxury convenience blend with taste ?

[1] Appendix, note C.

In yon sweet vale that — mingling field and grove
In fair confusion — fills the roving eye
With images of beauty ; on a slope
Gently declining toward the midday sun,
A modest mansion stands, — a rural home ;
But one of thousands that New England boasts —
The jewels of her crown — her pride and joy.
Nor rude, nor splendid, it hath yet a charm,
A quiet loveliness.   Come, ye who dream
That Peace, an exile, dwells with men no more ;
Ye who in vain pursue her through the maze
Where witching pleasure lures, and oft deceived
As oft the eager chase again renew ;
Ye who would seek her but in princely halls,
With fretted ceiling arched and draperies hung
In gorgeous richness, where luxurious couch
And orient ottoman invite repose,
With harp, or lute, by snowy fingers touched,
That soothes and lulls in soft voluptuous strain —
Come hither, mark, and muse and grow more wise.

Lo, where the hand of taste hath graced the scene !
The charms of nature by judicious skill
Are heightened here ; their absence there supplied
By quaint device.   The grassy plat that spreads
In neat simplicity before the door,
Majestic elms, by some ancestral hand
Long years ago transplanted, overhang ;
Their arching boughs affording grateful shade

To childhood's laughing groups, that gather there
In merry mood, on the bright summer day,
And with their harmless pastimes fill the hours.
The tasteful garden, with neat fence enclosed,
Bespeaks attentive culture.   Clustering trees,
The apple, cherry, pear, the tempting peach
And the delicious plum, are set to please ·
The order-loving eye ; and 'mid the shades
Of their dark foliage half conceal the bower,
Round which the woodbine creeps and roses twine.
Here, thickly set, the grateful currant grows,
And the sweet raspberry.   The vine there climbs
O'er the arched trellis ; and, when Autumn claims
Her offering of fruits, hangs richly out
Her purple clusters ; while yon beds of flowers,
Of many a name and hue, their incense pay
To genial Summer, when they drink her smiles.
Here oft at twilight of a summer's eve,
While linger yet, along the glowing west,
Clouds, that like golden islands seem to float
Upon an azure sea, or spread afar
Like some imperial pavement wrought with art
Divine, of precious stones, agate and amethyst,
Sapphire and emerald — come, arm in arm,
The beautiful and young.   The peaceful hour
Sheds its sweet influence o'er them.   Slowly now,
As best befits such converse as they hold,
They thread the winding paths, or seek the bower ;
And now, as with some sudden transport seized,

Burst forth in merry laugh, and glide along,
Like tripping fairies, in pursuit and flight
Alternate, as capricious impulse moves.
But gay or grave, alike they waken here,
'Mid outward loveliness, pure thoughts, and feel
Quick-kindling sympathies their hearts unite.
Here, as in earth's first garden, dwells sweet Peace,
With joys of innocence and social love ;
A home is here, with all its histories,
Its storied past, its present, and to come.
O'er it have passed the changing lights and shades,
Or will as years shall run their circles round,
Which, since was lost the primal Paradise,
Have checkered all the mortal lot of men.

Home ! 'tis to Heaven's wise law we mortals owe
Thee and all thine.   In the first home was placed
Not Adam sole ; with him the gentler Eve,
Woman, man's other self, in whom alone
His complement he finds.   God called, 'tis said,
Not his, but their name, Adam, in the day
When He humanity complete had made.
E'er since, in thee, O wedded love, are laid
The deep foundations of domestic bliss ;
With thee, through all the cycles, have been hid
Sweet springs of joy whence, like full streams, have
      flowed
Earth's pleasures that are likest those of heaven.
For what is heaven save innocence and love

Inseparable — in mystic life combined ? —
The sympathy of hearts that throb and glow
With love's quick impulse ; and harmonious beat,
Each vibrating to each, as in the harp
To one touched string according strings respond ?
Eternal Love, intent to make earth blest
With all best joys, nor man nor woman made
For unrelated life, but each for each ;
Each only in the other without lack
Of somewhat that, unfound, the restless heart
Yearns ever, nor can know a full content.
O subtile instinct !   Hidden law deep wrought
Into the soul's own texture, by His will
Who, Love Himself, man in His likeness framed
To dwell in love ; his native element,
The vital air, in which to live and move !
God and thy kind both loved with one pure flame,
O mortal, thou most like to God shalt be,
Blessing and blessed ; and by thy stony paths
Shall spring such flowers as Paradise did yield
Ere with the reign of love her all she lost.

Yon mansion long ago, one summer morn,
A morn bright, dewy, fresh with balmy breath
Of myriad blossoms laughing o'er the fields,
Received a youthful pair.   Late at God's shrine,
In holy rite made one, hand joined to hand
As heart before to heart, here they begin,
Rich in fair hopes and visions, and yet more

In fresh affections, for themselves and theirs
A Home to found and consecrate.   Henceforth,
Holy the place shall be through opening years,
In all their·thoughts ; sacred to wedded love,
To tranquil joys, to purity, to peace ;
To healthful pleasures with each other shared ;
To useful tasks together daily wrought ;
To books and culture, and congenial friends ;
To piety, and prayer, and heavenward steps ;
To all that earth yet yields to faithful hearts
Demonstrative that once an Eden was,
And proof, by foretaste, that a heaven shall be.
Edward and Mary, — these the names they bore ;
Names, like their story, neither new nor strange.
Nor name nor story such as one might choose
Who with romantic tale, or legend old,
Or startling horror, would the listless rouse ;
But suiting well the simple and the true.

O happy man !   To whom of God 'tis given
To lead, a joyous bride, one who has taught
Thy heart — that as in fevered restlessness,
Far roving, stayed not till her gentle eye
Seized it and fast a willing captive held —
To end its rovings and in her to rest !
How like an angel in the robes of heaven
She stands beside thee — thine own angel now !
How beats with manly pride thy heart, the while
Thou lead'st her from the altar to the seat,

Her fitting throne, at Home's dear centre placed ;
Where, as a queen, ruling without command,
She, radiant as the morning star, shall shine,
Mighty in gentleness, in sweetness strong.
It is but meet that on her maiden brow,
And in the eyes that kindle at thy glance,
Thou shouldst enraptured gaze ; and gazing find
Thy soul with nobler manliness inspired,
And high ambitions all unfelt before.
Henceforth, for thee shall each returning dawn
Wake worthiest thoughts. Not for thyself alone,
Thou shalt go forth life's battle-fields to try ;
But, with chivalric tread and lance in rest,
For her, to death if need, in gallant strife
Thou shalt defend all honor, truth, and right ;
Win all that may on her true lustre shed ;
And shield her from all ills that courage firm,
And strength of love, and patience can avert.
For God and her ! What impulse canst thou lack
To wrestle with all dangers, to withstand
Pleasure's seductive call, and Duty's voice
With quenchless ardor ever to obey !

Thou too, O woman, of thy kind most blest,
Who in thy spring of beauty standest glad
Beside thy well-beloved and call'st him now
Thy husband ! Name so rich to thy fond heart,
In promise of best joys that earth can know.
To thee no music like the bridegroom's voice ;

To that thy tremulous heart instant responds,
As to the soft west wind the swelling strain
Waked on the harp-string breathes its sweetness back.
In him thy strength thou seest.   The sturdy arm
To which thou cling'st confiding, thine shall be
In danger's hour for succor and defence;
For kind support when on the toilsome way
Thy steps would falter, or thy heart grow faint.
His wisdom, courage, manhood, to thy soul
More nicely strung, with quicker, keener sense
By God endowed, shall healthful reverence wake
And restful confidence; shall teach thy thought
In generous rivalry to tempt the heights
Of intellectual grandeur and to grasp
What best and highest mortal powers may reach,
Of knowledge that exalts and gifts that charm.
Will he repress thee?   Ay, as summer suns
Repress the morning rosebud, opening wide
Its bosom to the day and calling forth
Its sweetest odors and its loveliest hues!
Edward and Mary, each in each complete!
Husband and wife, but one Humanity —
One conscious life full-flowing — with one heart,
One will, one end supreme, one blessedness!
'Twas so that God ordained domestic bliss.

   Now, with exultant step, from room to room
They wander, and well pleased each trait survey
Of this their new abode — their HOME, when time

And love and joys the place hath sanctified,
When sorrow's shade, perchance, has overhung
And hallowed it, baptized with holy tears,
Till tenderest memories, gathered one by one,
Thick clustering, link each object to the heart.
Like children, whom new toys or pleasures fill
With gushing raptures, they with quick survey
Scan each apartment; try each chair and lounge;
Look from each window on the prospect fair;
Each picture on the garnished walls observe
With keenest glance, as if with critic's eye
In Angelo, or Raphael, they sought
Some touch of grace unnoted e'er before.
But in each other, chiefly, pleased they see
The graces most transcendent; and the light
Of love within suffuses each dear face,
And glows, as when through some fair vase or globe
Translucent, softly shines the embosomed flame.

So passed with silent feet the jocund Hours.
Then while this first day of their wedded life
Closed over them serene, and twilight fell,
Hand clasped in hand they sat, till daylight died
And set love's favorite star; too full their hearts
For words; their silent bliss like some sweet dream.
Thus for a time.   But when the deepened shade
Their faces veiled, it was as if each tongue
Gained freedom, and each heart, unlocked,
Revealed its hidden treasures; and they talked

As ne'er before of all the vanished past,
Of present pleasures and of dawning hopes;
Of all that each to each aspired to be
In the great life-work.   Then at last they kneeled
With hearts in true accord before the throne,
Their Father's throne of pure eternal love,
And in His name who bore the bitter cross
Forgiveness sought and breathed their praise to heaven.
Angels! to whom of God the task is given
With loving ministries, though all unseen, to watch
And keep, with care unwearied, every hour,
The heirs of life, whose souls in love abide;
Ye at that hour were nigh.   Ye saw them bow
And worship; heard those fervid lips declare
That God should be their God; heard them entreat
That He whom heaven itself, the heaven of heavens,
Could not contain, would with them deign to dwell,
Gladdening their Home and hearts with that same
    smile
That gladdens all above; would own them His,
Them and their household, and in trouble's day,
Or when thick perils should beset them round,
Such as must come to all, comfort and rest
Beneath the shadow of his wings would give.
Ye saw — for ye have spiritual vision clear —
How rose their warm affections to the throne,
As when of old the smoke of incense, cast
On glowing altars, rose in circling wreaths,
And He who dwelt between the cherubim

Smelled a sweet savor.   Thou thyself didst hear,
Thou without whom not e'en the sparrow falls ;
The trust Thou didst accept, and didst command
Thy blessing ; charge to all good angels Thou
Didst give, by night and day, with ceaseless guard
All evils to forefend, save such as needs
Must be for Virtue's sake, that ever best
Thrives while she wrestles, by thy grace made strong.
Henceforth, thrice happy pair, although for you
Each day new cares may spring and duty set
New tasks, with these shall come celestial Peace,
And, where God dwells and dear domestic love,
Shall nestle and abide.   Earth's purest joys,
Unsating because pure, there fresh shall spring
As o'er you swiftly pass the fleeting years ;
Till from this earthly Home ye pass to heaven.

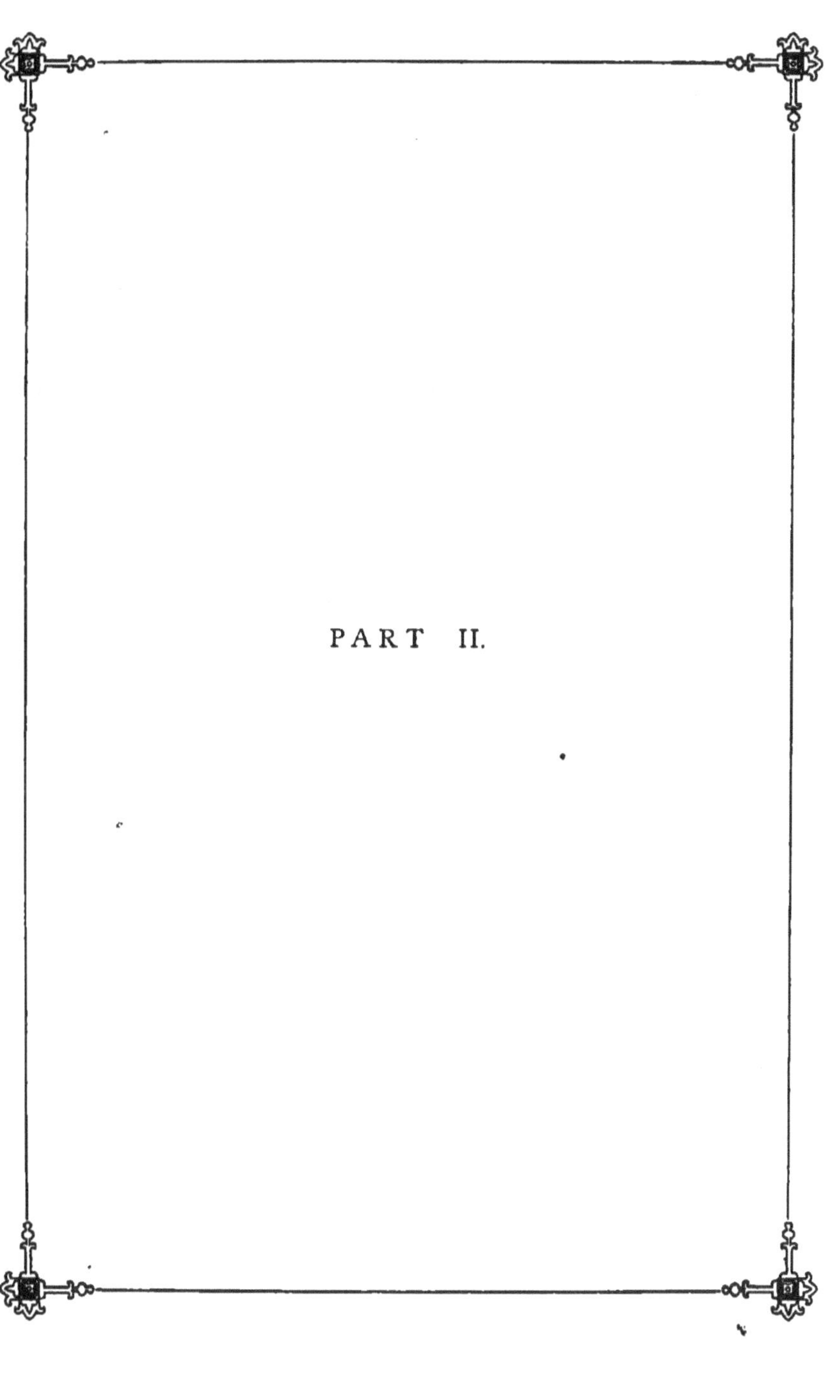

PART II.

I saw her, upon nearer view,
A Spirit, yet a Woman too!
Her household motions light and free,
And steps of virgin liberty;
A countenance in which did meet
Sweet records, promises as sweet;
A creature not too bright or good
For human nature's daily food;
For transient sorrows, simple wiles,
Praise, blame, love, kisses, tears, and smiles.

WORDSWORTH.

There are smiles and tears in the mother's eyes,
For her new-born babe beside her lies;
O heaven of bliss! when the heart o'erflows
With the rapture a *mother only* knows!

HENRY WARE, Jr.

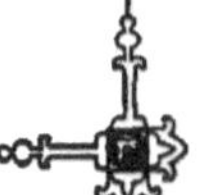

PART II.

O JOY of joys! the joy of wedded hearts,
    That at God's shrine in youthful freshness joined,
Are one for ever — mystery of love!
Thenceforth, like two clear fountains side by side,
That pour their waters into one bright stream,
They blend their free affections, till the tide,
In one deep channel, floweth ever on.
As in green meadows by some river's side,
Spring 'neath the sun daisy and violet,
With many a peer, of many a name and tinge,
And blossom numberless to grace the scene;
So where that sacred current affluent glides
Through the charmed valley of domestic bliss,
Shoot forth all virtues that humanity
Do most adorn and beauty lend to life.
Here sheltered, they may bud and bloom secure
From beasts that raven the wide world abroad;
In rich luxuriance grow, and crown thee, Home,
With graces that most charm the pure in heart.
No cynic eye thy secrecy invades,

To note, and noting check, love's language true,
That half unconsciously, with artless art,
And simplest act, some secret meaning tells.
. A gentle word; a glance; perchance a kiss;
Or whate'er slightest ministry may prove
Expressive of the fulness that o'erflows
Each happy heart — so hours as minutes fly!
In this, his fortress, Love in freedom reigns;
Commands, obeys, nor to distinguish knows
Duty and pleasure, since they here are one.

Now wakes the morn, Nature's great miracle,
Repeated ever, yet for ever new, —
When start afresh the busy wheels of life,
That through night's silent reign awhile stood still.
Listen! what mingled sounds swell on the ear,
While kindle Nature's slumbers into smiles!
The groves, but now so still, grow vocal, and pour
      forth
From thousand tuneful throats such melodies
As might e'en Dulness, drowsy maid, herself
Awake to ecstasy.   June's unmown fields
Stand tremulous, all wet with silvery dew,
Night's grateful benison.   The clouds that hung
Like parting curtains when the day awoke,
Transfigured, glow as dipped in Tyrian dyes
Of hue celestial, — ruby, jasper, gold.
The chariot of the King of Day they seem,
In which, with pomp ascending o'er the heights,

He climbs the noonward path.   The wreathing mists
That hide, and yet reveal, the stream that winds
Along the quiet valley, slowly lift,
Like beauty's veil, and show the grace beneath.
The voice of flocks and herds that hasten forth
Eager to taste the pasture blend confused,
Yet please the listening ear.   The flowery train,
With which bright Summer loves at early dawn
Her retinue to fill, spread o'er the fields,
Entincturing with their breath the roving wind
That wooes them in their sweetness, while they seem,
As if in conscious life, to glow with joy.
These, Morning, are thy charms ; and ever new,
From bounding childhood down to tottering age,
To hearts with inborn tenderness endowed,
And natures finely tuned, they yield delight.

Yet 'tis when hearts most leap with gladsome life,
And passion's impulses ; with eager hopes,
Imaginations, fancies, visions, dreams,
And, born of these, emotions, like pent fires
That will not be repressed, but force their way ;
'Tis when youth's throbbing pulses send their blood
Swift coursing through the veins, and every sense
And sensibility is quick and keen ;
'Tis most of all when love, pure, happy love,
So permeates with its subtile force the breast,
That thought and purpose, sympathy and will,
Delighted own its sway ; O yes ! 'tis then

That most the world enrobes itself in light,
With beauty all suffused ; that morn and eve,
Sun, moon, and stars, and ocean, lake, and stream,
'Woods, hills, and fields, and all earth's features fair,
Seem as incarnadined with roseate hues,
And through the liquid air there seems to float
A glory, that intoxicates the soul
With dreamy bliss, and to the softened heart
Makes Nature's simplest, lowliest work divine.

'Twas thus exultant and elate, that morn,
That Edward stood, with Mary at his side,
And from the casement gazed, with open heart
Drinking all sweetness from the radiant scene,
Through every sense ; while in her beaming face
He saw reflected his own tranquil joy.
To both, on this their wedded life's first day,
With omens kind begun, ne'er looked before
The world so beautiful ; ne'er God himself,
The Infinite Creator, seemed so good.
And while, with the ascending sun, went up
From off the dewy earth the morning mists,
Rising like incense, from their tuneful lips
And hearts o'erflowing, rose their hymn of praise
With fervent orisons to listening Heaven,
Whither no voice of love ascends in vain.

Is then the goal attained ?   Is this retreat —
The dream of many a year at last fulfilled —

A bower of ease, in which, with lotus charm,
The past may be forgot; the future, veiled
In golden haze, be all unquestioned left,
And purpose high in pleasure's cup be drowned?
No! In the blissful shades where primal man
Walked innocent with God, 'twas given to dress
And keep the garden — toil no natural ill.
For use, O mortal, God thy powers hath given,
And made their use a joy. In labors meet,
Pursued for virtue's ends, in good achieved
And triumphs won by sacrifice, by love
Enlarged and with all generous yearnings filled,
Thou shalt such pleasures find as most exalt
Thy being and thy restless soul compose.
Not by ignoble ease, but noble deeds,
Thou dost reveal the spirit all divine
That in thee lives and makes thee like to God,
And brother of the angels, who, as winds
And flames of fire, are swift to work His will;
For thee, as them, to serve is to be blest.

Home hath its tasks. Each day demands anew
The thoughtful purpose and the skilful hand.
Thou, Mary, now crowned queen of this fair realm,
Must wield thy sceptre and with gentle grace,
Grace that to thee is power, shouldst wield it well.
'Tis thine this Home to fashion as thou wilt;
To give it thine own impress, till it seems
Pervaded by thy spirit — full of thee!

'Tis thine to guard its order, beauty, health;
To keep it ever free from passion's jar
And discord's grating tones, nor e'er permit
The clamors of the rude and noisy world
Its quiet to invade. Here thou hast power,
By thine own magic arts, o'er all to shed
The living air of joy, that whoso breathes
Shall seem, as by enchantment, warmed and filled
With genial gladness. Here, by thee beguiled,
The troubled brow shall lose its furrows, deep
By cares inwrought; the heavy heart grow light
And gather strength and courage for new toils.
Music with sounding string and richest strain,
And Poesy with all her visions rare,
And kindred arts whose simplest gifts may please,
Shall blend their charms to grace thy queenly state,
Obedient to thy summons. Nor shall Mirth
Withhold her ringing laugh when thou shalt call;
But, with all innocent pleasures in her train,
Shall come to visit thee and lend her aid
To make thy court earth's fairest, happiest spot.

 Yet not to listless ease, nor pleasure's round,
The life inane that pampered luxury
Elsewhere delights to lead, thy realm be given.
This is thy pride, New England, that thy homes
With healthful industries did e'er abound.
Thy matrons, in the halcyon days of yore,
Lived not alone to order well their house

And ply the needle, but with vigorous grasp
Wielded the loom ; and from the distaff drew
With busy hand and foot the flaxen thread ;
Carded the wool and twirled the humming wheel.
O days of sweet content !   No need was then
That commerce rifle every foreign strand
From India to Peru, with raiment meet
Brought from afar, the houschold to attire.
If of this glory thou no more canst boast
As thou wast wont, — so times and manners change, —
Yet are thy dwellings Industry's abode ;
Her name is honored there.   So let it be,
Till Plymouth Rock itself shall waste with years !

    Yes, Mary !   If a queen thou hast been crowned,
Forget not that with crowns there needs must come
Duty and care.   Life opens now to thee
Its long perspective, and arrayed thou seest,
Far stretching on before, its years of toil ;
Pleasing, not terrible, the vision seems.
Thou wouldst not live a cipher.   Thy young heart
Throbs with its eagerness a part to bear,
Some worthy part, among the good and brave
Who live to conquer ill, and love the strifes
Whose prize is gladness and whose fruits are Peace.
No weak ambition thine to send thy name
Resounding, like an echo, through the world ;
Made common on all lips, sullied perchance
By its rude contacts, and its fragrance lost !

Wiser, thou choosest in the tranquil sphere
Of dear, domestic peace, by duty done
To grave thine image on the loving hearts
That gather round thee, to thine influence sweet
Opening, as lilies on the placid stream
Bare their fair bosoms to the grateful sun.
Nobler thou deem'st the task, that manly heart
Now knit to thine, beyond all chance to hold
Loyal to thee and restful in thy truth;
To make thyself his ever conscious want,
His life's chief joy; nor, striving, shalt thou fail
O'er him to throw thy spells.   Thy morning smile
Will sweetly haunt him through the livelong hours.
E'en 'mid the din of business, on his ear
Will steal thy tones.   As thou each day for him,
So he for thee, shall think and plan and toil.
Wealth, honor, fame — whate'er of either crowns
His patient strivings, most of all for thee
His thought will prize; and nightly at thy feet,
With noble pride, he will exulting lay
The trophies he has won.   Or if perchance,
In the rough contacts of a restless world,
Where thickly, oft, keen shafts of malice fly,
He hath been wounded sore; if on him fall
Misfortune's lowering shade, with doubt and dread
That tire the soul with watching, and his heart,
Firm though it be, half faints; he then to thee
Shall turn for strength and healing; and thy voice,
Thy cheering glance, thy counsels, and thy prayer,

Shall nerve him all anew; with ardor fired,
Shall send him to the battle's front again,
New triumphs in heroic strife to win.

Thou too shalt own his power.   As he to thee
Shall turn for love's deep tenderness, and warm
Each day anew his heart at the pure flame
That, as on vestal altars, ever glows
Within thy breast; so thou, when burdens press
Or dangers gather thick, in him shall see
Thy helper strong ; and ever by his side
More surely thou shalt scale the rugged steeps
And passes perilous that wait thy feet.
In his life thou shalt live, and so become
Worthy of high companionship and meet,
Sharing his struggles, with him to be crowned.
Each year shall thus thy being's measure fill,
The treasures hidden in thy soul unlock,
And make thee rich in dignity and grace,
And all that most exalts; till thou, the wife,
Shalt stand confessed the glory of the man
Thy husband, made his peer ; by trial each
Proved to the other equal, helper, friend.

O lightly dance the hours, and swift the day
Speeds round its circuit, if the heart be glad !
When with the frequent task and press of care
Come many a kindly impulse, born of love,
And many a fantasy, that warm the soul

With ever fresh delight; when sympathies
Seem e'en, like odors that exhale, to rise
Spontaneous, and to breathe themselves abroad
As if from sheer exuberance; and there flits
Before affection's eye the image fair
Of a dear face that absence cannot hide; —
Then, Time, thou turn'st in vain thy flowing glass,
To mark thy flight; no note the sand receives!
'Tis so that in that Home days seem but hours,
And weeks but days, and months as weeks go by.
The blithesome wife guides all with patient skill,
And taste that seems an instinct; fain to make
Parlor and library, each several room,
Each mantel, niche, and arch, or deep recess,
Fair with chaste beauty, grateful to his eye,
Whose look approving, oft as he returns,
For her illuminates and gladdens all.
Soon gorgeous Summer with light tread has passed;
And Autumn, laden with his sheaves and fruits,
Enrobed and garlanded with dying leaves,
That dolphin-like grow beautiful in death,
Has hasted by, and seems a vision gone;
Winter, with hoary head and frosty breath,
Hath let loose all his storms, and the free streams
And yielding earth hath fixed as adamant.
Fled swiftly all; yet, in their passing, rich
In pleasures innocent and duties done;
In memories that, as treasures of the soul,
Shall live unfading down to distant years,

When, in life's twilight dim, quiescent age
Backward shall turn to wander o'er the past.
Then trod again shall be those evening strolls
In the still gloaming, or when climbed the moon,
While Nature's kindliest influence softly stole
O'er each fond heart; lived o'er again shall be
Those fireside hours when each by turns or read,
Or eager listened to the thrilling tale,
To some old poet's lay, or ballad wild,
Or History's roll of deeds and men renowned.

But, blessed Home, these are not all thy joys;
Yet undiscovered are thy purest springs,
The streams untasted yet of holiest bliss
From wedded love by God ordained to flow.
Though now, ye favored pair, your cup seem full,
A gladder hour is nigh; a brighter star
Than e'er before your watchful eyes did greet
Now rises, o'er your path to shed its ray.
Hark! a new sound arrests the quickened ear!
A voice! a cry! — the cry of infancy!
Through every room it thrills; the very walls
That echo it, with sympathy seem touched.
A babe is born!   Mother — O hallowed name!
Mary, that name is thine! close to thy heart,
Quick beating with a rapture all unknown
Till this blest moment, thou dost fold and press
Thy first-born son!   Thine anguish all forgot,
A joy so deep, so pure, so brimming o'er,

Possesses thy whole being, that to thee
It seems a new existence; ay, so strange
Thou almost deem'st it but a blissful dream
From which thou may'st awake.   No — no!
Thou art a mother to eternal years!
Life of thy life, that helpless one is born
Immortal as the angels; by thy side
It shall still live when, as old seers have sung,
The ancient heavens have been together rolled,
And earth hath perished by devouring fire.
'Tis thine, for immortality, to guard and keep
The priceless treasure.   Unto thee 'tis given —
No work of earth more sacred, more sublime —
That trembling spirit to insphere in love,
To fashion it by love's sweet ministries,
Till faculties yet hidden, full revealed,
Declare it fellow of the hosts of heaven!
No marvel if thy heart, at thoughts like these,
Doth falter, burdened with the mighty trust.

　　But not alone thou bear'st it.   There is yet
Another holy name.   Thou, Edward, art
A Father! — name like God's! a changeless name.
Thy manly soul, warmed with paternal love,
Calm, deep, and steady as a river's tide,
By this new life shall feel its own enlarged,
More joyous made and richer.   Thou shalt find
In this, thy son, what seems another self;
Another centre, round which may revolve

Thy best affections and thy busy thought.
E'en while his infant prattle wakes the smile
Of fatherly delight, within thy breast
Grave questionings shall rise, with hopes and fears.
"How with thee shall it fare, unconscious child —
How wilt thou bear thyself, upon life's field
Where foe meets foe and wile encounters wile;
Where hapless thousands fall, or, wounded sore,
Survive but wrecks, unfit for noble tasks?
What destinies are thine?   Wait there for thee
The shouts of triumph? or the pang and shame
Of final, sad defeat?"   So wilt thou ask;
And then, with impulse new, thy soul will rise
To the firm purpose that in thee thy child
Shall find a model true, a wisdom pure;
Shall see a life well lived, and with thee walk
As one that breathes in virtue's bracing air;
As one divinely led, a child of heaven!

Father and Mother! holiest names of earth!
Lo! now, blest Home, thy circle made complete!
Thy pleasures full!   Now, in each throbbing breast,
All sweetest chords, unstruck before, are touched;
Vibrations exquisite, that slept, awake,
And the whole compass of the soul pours forth
Harmonious pæans; as some organ full —
Drawn every stop — its perfect volume swells,
And with its faultless chorus charms the ear.
Yet o'er the world, to each fond parent's eye,

A nameless change has passed.   A graver hue
Now tinges earth and sky, that laughed before
In flashing light and beauty ever gay.
Not less the light and beauty, nor the bliss
Of those beholding ; but all things seem charged
With meanings deeper far, that needs must lend
An aspect chastened and a tone subdued
To nature's face, softer yet richer too.
Emotions now first waked, and loftier aims
Than e'er before had stirred the conscious soul
Write on each brow new dignity of thought.

   As when is read some drama, rarely wrought
By genius' magic pen, the first act past,
That with strange power the attentive mind hath
   seized,
All note of time is lost, or heeded not,
While act on act succeeds till comes the last,
That disenchants the reader spell-bound long ;
So when thy scenes, dear Home, divinely planned,
Have opened as if bathed in silver light,
Have cheerily swept on beyond the days
Of love's first raptures and the blissful hour
When felt the first-born's brow a mother's kiss,
The plot fast thickens, and intenser grow
The sympathies that fill and hold the heart,
Ever yet more content, while through quick years
The changeful action hasteth swiftly on.
One charming prattler scarce hath learned to lisp

The names most musical to infant tongues,
Ere yet another cherub-face appears
In the pleased household, and in time's full round
Yet others still.   Come added cares with each,
And duties new ; but with such gushing love,
Such influx of deep joy, that all forgot
Or drowned in ecstasies, or tranquil bliss,
The weightier burdens seem.   Life richer grows,
As, with the years, fair sons and daughters rise
In beauty fresh, like olive-plants, to stand.

  Father and Mother !   How their hearts expand,
As large, and larger yet, becomes the sphere
Where sweet affections reign ; where brother blends
His rougher vigor with a sister's grace ;
Somewhat each borrows and each somewhat lends,
And all, as one, true filial honor pay.
Home, thou art richer so than piled with gold
And rarest gems, yet wanting loving hearts ;
Fairer than with all garniture bedecked
Of princely halls, with splendors cold, and pride.
If matched with thine, all other jewels pale ;
E'en God himself with pleasure thine beholds.
Brothers and Sisters ! what blest concord binds
Congenial souls that breathe in virtue's air !
How are they knit by inborn instincts kind,
By common blood and birth, by childhood's sports
Together shared in many a shining hour,
By transient griefs, and alternations quick

Of hope and fear, that each has felt with all,
All felt with each. Concord more perfect made
By such slight discords as in all have wrought
More watchful tenderness of patient love.
More of thy strength, divine self-sacrifice!

 Dwells then, O Earth, e'en in thy fairest spot,
A perfect bliss? Giv'st thou enduring joys,
Where nothing fixed abides? The circling years,
That swiftly chase each other in their flight,
Bring ceaseless change. Lo! Morning with her dews,
And song and bloom; still Evening with her shades;
Sabbaths with holy calm, that yield too soon
To seasons given to rounds of wearying toil;
Months marked by waxing and by waning moons;
Spring with its waking life, Summer arrayed
In robes that fade so soon; Autumn that strips
The teeming fields, and leaves them brown and sere;
Winter that with his storms deep buries all
Kind Nature's smiles beneath his chilling snows!
Each comes but to depart, nor long abides.
See how like withering grass all beauty fades,
And strength to weakness turns; how the firm rock
Slowly, but surely, crumbleth back to dust;
How life's uncounted forms dissolve, O Death,
At thy cold touch that blighteth all alike!
Hath earth one spot so sheltered, so secure,
That there no change, no pang, no sense of loss,
No fear of ill, no sorrow, e'er can come?

No : even within thy precincts, sacred Home,
Must it at last be known that 'neath the sun
No mortal heart can beat and feel no wound.

Edward, what aileth thee, that anguish sits
Where smiles, like glancing lights, were wont to play?
Mary, thy cheek is blanched ; thy restless eye
Turns frequent here and there, as if it sought
To rest on one with whom might come relief!.
Ah, yes! a tender lamb of that fair flock
O'er which to watch hath been by day, by night,
Thy life's chief joy, now by the wayside droops ;
Droops on from hour to hour ; no skill avails
To cool the fevered brow, or light again
The languid eyes that kindle now no more.
In vain, O mother, have thy faithful arms
Enfolded him and pressed him to thy heart.
No care, nor yearning of maternal love,
Nor father's wrestling hope, can stay the step
Of Sorrow — awful form ! — too clearly seen
Advancing ; in her hands the cup of woe,
Of which 'tis given all mortal lips to taste.

'Tis o'er.   Hark !   Hark ! soft on the startled ear
Music unearthly steals ! celestial notes
And melodies, as from the airy lips
Of spirits all unseen, with mingled lyres
Touched as by angel-fingers, seem to fill
The tranquil air.   Ye cannot catch the strain,

But well ye deem that lovingly it greets
The gentle spirit of its clay disrobed.
Bear — bear the cherub, angels, to His arms
Who in His mortal years such lambs did fold
Close on His heart with heavenly grace and smiles,
And blessed and called them His, and said, " Of such
Heaven's holy kingdom shall for ever be."
He hath its name already on His hands
Engraven, and hath watched it as His own ;
And with a tenderness surpassing thine,
O mother, He thine innocent will meet,
Will soothe its fears, and win its love with smiles
Of sweetness so divine that it shall need
No more e'en thy dear ministries, to fill
The measure of its bliss to full content.
What thou hadst thought to teach it, He will teach,
Of wisdom, goodness, beauty, truth, and love ;
His care will guard and train it till the hour
When thou shalt come, the blessed day arrived,
With thine own eyes, long waiting, to behold
The vision of the Lamb.   Back to thine arms
Then He, the faithful Shepherd, shall restore
Thy child, — still thine, — the same o'er which did fall
Thy bitter tears when lost to thee he seemed.
The same, yet not the same ! more beautiful
Beyond compare, e'en as the hyacinth
That perfect stands, unfolded every grace,
Is lovelier than the bulb that held it once,
And hid its purple hues.   Ah ! then thy joy

The memory of thy grief at last shall drown;
And with all ecstasies of thankful love
And praise admiring, shall thy soul o'erflow.

He lies upon the bier, pale, silent, cold,
Yet beauteous still.   Disease hath stolen away
But little from the face that late did seem
Almost a seraph's.   On the marble brow,
Chiselled so daintily, so calm, so pure,
Lies, as in carelessness, the flaxen hair.
In tranquil slumber one might deem he rests,
But that the leaden eye a sleep bespeaks
Too deep for waking.   Folded on the breast,
Now motionless, repose the snowy hands
With flowers o'er-strown; strange contrast! e'en as
        when
Thick clustering violets are seen to spring,
Or lilies of the valley, where the drifts
Of winter part, touched by the vernal sun.
Mary, they saw thee come and stand and gaze,
As if thy soul, with anguish wrestling long,
At last had mastered its fierce inward strife;
As if a self-command that awful seemed
Had changed thee to a statue; — saw thee take
Thy last, last look, and heard thy lips pronounce,
" My boy — thou'rt mine no more!   I give thee back
To God who gave thee!   O farewell! farewell!"
So triumphed faith when anguish wrung the heart;
And, as the rainbow spans the cloud o'erpast,

Emblem of peace that waits beyond the storm,
Thou saw'st with tranquil eye dark sorrow's gloom
Irradiate with the glow of heaven's own light, —
The pledge of days serene beyond these tears,
The harbinger of healing, rest, and peace.

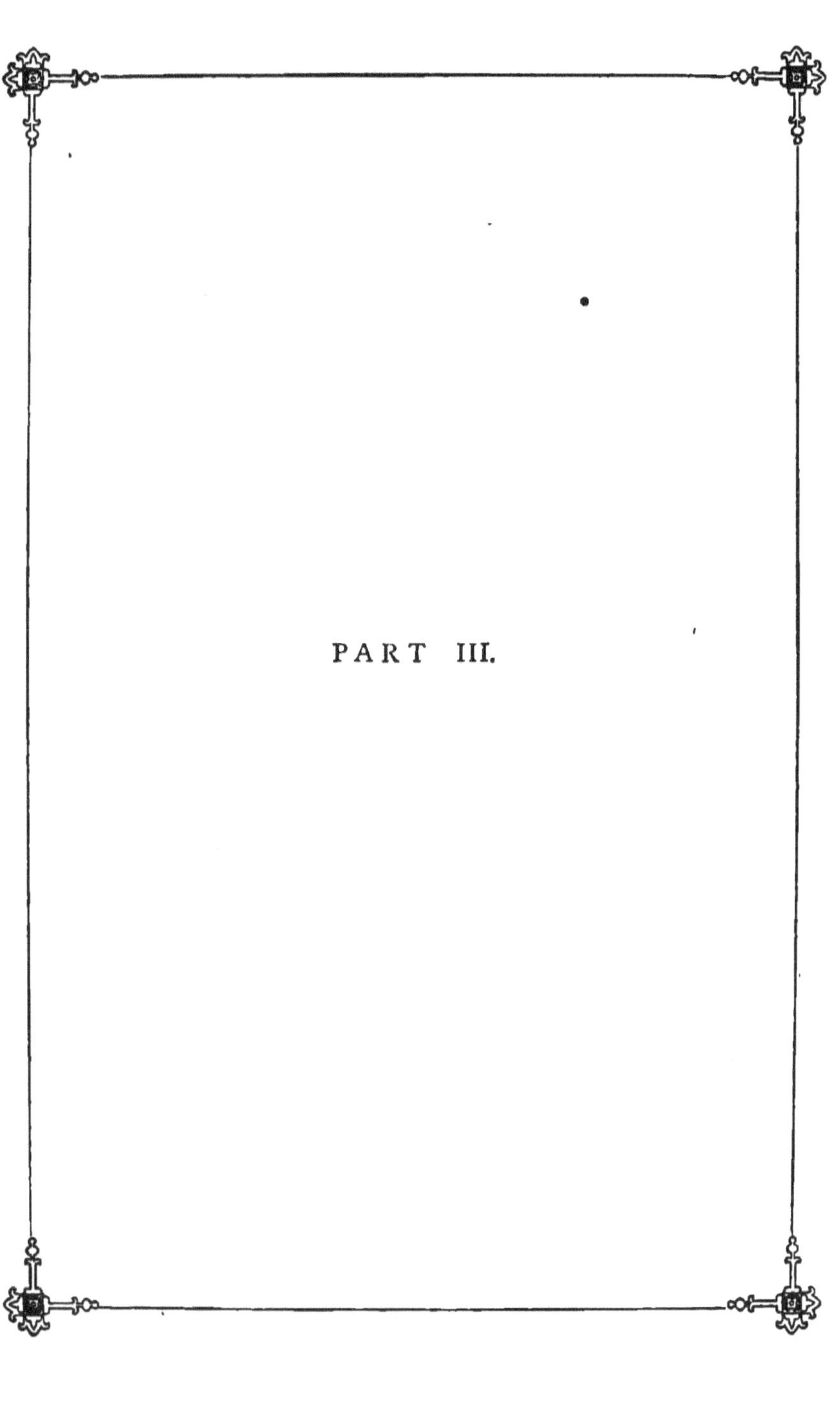

PART III.

WOULDST thou from sorrow find a sweet relief?
Or is thy heart oppressed with woes untold?
Balm wouldst thou gather for corroding grief?
Pour blessings round thee like a shower of gold!
'Tis when the rose is wrapped in many a fold
Close to its heart, the worm is wasting there
Its life and beauty ; not when all unrolled,
Leaf after leaf, its bosom rich and fair
Breathes freely its perfumes throughout the ambient air.

CARLOS WILCOX.

THERE blend the ties that strengthen
    Our hearts in hours of grief,
The silver links that lengthen
    Joy's visits when most brief!
Then dost thou sigh for pleasure?
    Oh, do not widely roam !
But seek that hidden treasure
    At Home, dear Home !

BERNARD BARTON.

PART III.

O SACRED spot of earth, where gentle hands
    Have laid the fragile form, so late suffused
With life's first glow, beneath the friendly mould ;
To slumber undisturbed where daisies spring
Unbidden, and the turf, with every dawn,
Seems wet afresh with tears ! There by fond hands
Ivy and myrtle have been taught to twine ;
The snow-drop spotless and forget-me-not
To bloom in simple beauty, — emblems meet
Of purity and of immortal love.
The friendly trees their drooping boughs o'erhang
As if in sympathy. The summer birds
Chant tender carols through the shining hours ;
And mingled lights and shades so softly blend,
That neither garish day nor gloom doth reign,
But grateful twilight lingers ever there.
Dear, oft-frequented scene ! 'Tis not that here
The sorrowing heart deems its lost treasure hid.
The living spirit that once blithely wore
The mortal robe that wasteth here to dust,

Dwells far, far hence, it knows, 'neath kinder skies.
But memories all undying centre where
This dust reposes, quick to stir anew ;
Oft as with lingering steps this scene is trod,
The past is lived again ; its bliss renewed ;
And grief becomes but tenderness and hope,
Till o'er the heart there steals a holy calm,
And balm from heaven hath healed its bleeding wounds.

Toil is no curse to mortals ; nor the cares
That make the price for life's best comforts paid.
Both have a charm — when on the saddened heart
Despondency and griefs, like clouds, have hung
Till into starless night day seems transformed —
The tide of ever busy thought to turn ;
That winding ever farther, farther on,
Behind it leaves the dreariness and wastes ;
And as, by slow degrees, new visions rise,
New scenes and aspects woo and win the soul,
Rekindle drooping hope and wake new joy ;
Till — how one knows not — all along life's way
Sweet landscapes smile again and days are glad ;
Welcome is duty's call, and future years
Invite to high endeavor, as they spread
Bright vistas opening far ; and every pulse
With healthful beating tells the heart is strong.
Thou that hast suffered, brood not o'er thy woes,
But to thy tasks !   Thy losses and thy pangs
Forget in cheerful toil ; thyself forget.

There be who love thee yet ; whom thou dost love ;
For God and these still be it thine to live ;
And, all unwearied, in love's ministries,
Go labor on and in thy works rejoice.

Edward and Mary! for you gather yet
Around the household board a ruddy band,
Like cluster roses that upon one stalk
Hang in their sweet luxuriance ; some in bud,
Some just revealing a first crimson line ;
Some half unfolded, some in their full bloom ;
One charming whole, of diverse charms combined.
'Tis yours o'er infancy kind watch to keep ;
To listen to the words half-formed that fall
From ruby lips just stammering to pronounce ;
And childhood's shout and laugh, perchance its cries,
Since showers and sunshine fill its changeful day.
'Tis yours to note youth's impulses, that swell
With passion's rising flood the heaving breast
That resteth not, but yearns with vague desire ;
That needs kind sympathy and wisest skill
To cool the fever of fresh life that throbs
With pulses too intense, and shape aright
The forming purpose and aspiring aim.
To these high tasks returned, your faces wear
A smile of peace again, and hope's bright glow.
The missing, not forgot, hath been transformed
Into a precious jewel of the soul,
That, in the dear fidelity of love,

With many a pensive, many a pleasing thought,
Is kept with memory's holiest trusts enshrined.
Sometimes, perchance, when on the vacant chair,
Some childish plaything needed now no more,
Or garment laid aside, the eye may rest,
A sudden tear, a shaded brow, may tell
How in the constant heart still lives the lost.
Yet steadily again life's current glides
Along the wonted channels, where the banks
Wave, as of old, with woods and summer flowers,
And bees hum softly, and the west wind plays,
And earth and skies once more are robed in light.

Childhood! thy bliss who hath not sung that e'er
The harp to tender melodies hath touched?
What is thy secret?   What thy hidden joys,
So pure, so full, that left far, far behind,
In memory still they live; yea, dearer seem,
As hoary age through gliding years steals on?
E'en thy glad morning is not without clouds
That cast their gloomy shades.   Not all unwet
With tears thy glowing cheeks; thy heart not free
From transient disappointments that corrode;
From chafing impulse and oft-crossed desire.
Yet art thou happy as the bounding fawn
That all day long, beside the lonely lake
And 'neath the arches of the forest deep,
Gambols at will, nor knows or want or fear.
Thy griefs abide not; soon the shadows flee

That cross thy path, and sunbeams gild again
Whate'er thine eye beholds, till all the world
For thee in gladness laughs and sings for joy!
As yet thou canst not know the fretting cares,
The toils and weariness and bodeful fears,
The buffetings with dark misfortune's tide,
O'erwhelming when too late for all retrieve.
These wait on ripened years.   'Tis meet that thou,
Dear child, to whom thy ignorance is bliss,
Shouldst drink the cup of innocent delight
Placed at thy lips, nor on the future draw
For aught to check thy heart's exulting play.

As in yon garden tastefully inhedged
And consecrate to beauty, rarest flowers
Of many a name thick clustering fill the place
That seems a realm, a kingdom, all their own,
Blending in rich variety their charms;
E'en so, O genial Home — secluded, made
By Heaven's kind law the nursery of joys
Only within thy loved enclosure known —
In thee all healthful pleasures, ever fresh,
Should spring abundant, and luxuriant grow
Filling all days and hours and months and years
With influences that wake and warm and cheer;
That send exhilaration through the soul,
And with refreshment bring a calm content.
Father and mother! yours the task to plan,
With tireless constancy and thoughtful skill,

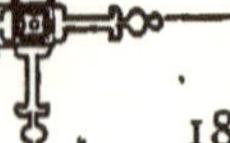

That boy nor girl, for lack of joy at home,
Shall from the hearthstone turn and wander far
To quench at poisoned streams the thirst they feel.
Brothers and sisters — let each have their sports
By instinct chosen oft, if choice be given ;
Sports such as best befit each sex and age
By nature's steady laws and inborn taste ;
With others that together shared shall best
Give fresh, young hearts delight, and make them bound
All joyously with sympathetic bliss.

Nor, O ye parents, let your hearts grow old ;
As oft your breasts have throbbed with childish glee
And youthful ardors, yet remembered well ;
Have felt the restlessness of keen desire
That seemed a quenchless thirst ; still let them hold
Kind fellowship with new-born life and joy.
Be ye with childhood, children ; youth, with youth ;
Nor deem that aught of dignity or grace
Is lost by nursery raptures, heard afar
In echoing laughs and shouts from lisping tongues ;
Scorn not to tell or hear the thrice-told tales
Of fairies, giants, and all monsters dire,
And chant quaint melodies, tradition's trust,
Safe handed down through generations dead !
Fail not, when merry girlhood courts thy smile
With lips carnationed and her locks of gold,
To greet the baby-house and black-eyed dolls,
Dressed and undressed, and nursed through blissful
    hours.

Frown not when roisterous boys or toss or strike
The bounding ball, or leap or run, or ride
The mastered steed, that, as the rider, loves
The rushing course ; or when with ringing steel
The polished ice they sweep in winter's reign.
All pleasing pastimes, innocent delights,
That gladden hearts yet simple and sincere,
Let love parental gather round the Home,
And consecrate by sharing ; let it watch
With kind, approving smiles each merry game
That quickens youthful blood, and, in the joy
That beams from crimson cheeks and sparkling eyes,
Its own renew, and live its childhood o'er.
So shall the scenes where life's fleet-footed years
Glide by with noiseless speed at last become
Memory's rich treasure-field, be all o'erspread
As with a radiant flood of golden sheen ;
Such as, on cloudless days in eastern climes,
With the still, hazy air seems interfused,
Enrobing with a dreamy loveliness
All visible things, transfigured in its glow.
'Tis so that tottering age, with fading eye,
Still sees thee, childhood, glorious as of old,
And of all earth's delights thine last forgets.

But childhood's glory fades ; its visions change:
For sweet simplicity and guileless trust,
Come youth's unrest, and thoughts that wider sweep,
With keener search and wishes reaching far ;

And yearnings vague that crave they know not what ;
Imaginations of all shapes and hues
That make earth seem a dreamland, and bright hopes
That in all gorgeous tints life's future limn.
Deep in the breast the sense of powers divine
Yet slumbering, stirs the eager soul with thirst
For wisdom's living streams, impels to curb
The impulses by pleasure's luring call
Awakened oft, and give to high pursuit
And silent solitude where knowledge dwells,
Long years whose disciplines may manhood yield.
Yes, Learning, 'tis of Home that thou art born !
Its needs demand thee and its tastes create.
Thy schools, thy classic halls and tranquil shades,
Haunted with memories of the nobly great,
Whose storied deeds and names that cannot die,
The pride of ages dead, enchantment lend
That seems like perfume breathed on all the air ;
Where linger still the echoes ever sweet
Of lays renowned that Time's great bards have sung ;
Where yet resound the words of fire pronounced
By orators who spake when balanced hung
On the swift moment destinies sublime ;
Where, in fit gallery and alcove ranged,
Stand art's grand triumphs, wisdom's treasured lore,
All wonders most divine by genius wrought,
Of centuries the lesson and the light ; —
These — these of household culture are the fruit ;
Culture that early, as with heaven's own fire,

Inflames the generous heart ; refines, exalts,
And with ambition's purest glow inspires
The youthful soul, not yet by sense enchained.[1]

O spectacle divine, where, heart to heart,
Father and mother, sons and daughters, blend
Their inborn sympathies in concert blest !
One body well compact by love's great law ;
Each member fit, in its own native grace,
To fill the measure of the perfect whole.
Envies and jealousies, ye grow not here
Indigenous, as hated nettles spring
'Mid rows of marjory and beds of thyme ;
Or, if ye start, — since e'en earth's fairest spot
Yields still some noxious weeds, — are quick subdued,
As all unmeet to root and flourish thus.
Oft by attrition in its torrent-bed
The precious gem may wear its roughness down,
Till from its polished surface back the beam
That brightly falls is thrown as bright again ;
So generous souls in daily contact lose
The excrescences of nature and the faults
That, left unheeded, must ere long become
Deformities, of God and man abhorred.

As year on year fulfils its circling round,
Thou, Edward, notest with a father's pride
Thine Edith's maiden charms that ripen fast

[1] Appendix, note D.

Toward fairest womanhood.   Oft o'er thy heart
Steals there a tranquil joy, a deep delight,
As 'neath thy watchful eye, that wearieth not,
New dignity and grace her form invest ;
New beauty tints her cheek, new thoughtfulness
Sits on her brow and lends her beaming eye
A deeper meaning and a milder fire.
Thou, Mary, on thine Alfred lov'st to fix
With tenderness profound thy earnest gaze.
God-given was he in place of thy first-born,
That Christ desired and angels bore away !
So doubly dear ; and now that in his face
Thou readest thoughtfulness, and seest revealed
Reason's calm light, and wakened intellect,
Imagination, hope, and purpose high ;
Now that with quickened heart-throbs thou dost mark
His manly form and mien ; whene'er thou wilt,
Dost find in him companionship, his arm
Thy strong support ; his words a daily joy ;
Thy mother's heart exults, nor would exchange
Its deep, deep bliss for Ophir's glittering heaps,
Or widest fame 'mid noisy contests won.
Thy woman's nature rests with full content
In these thy household treasures — asks no more.

How beautiful art thou, O Youth !   Not lost
As yet in thee the sweetness and the grace
Of childhood left behind ; but, richer far,
Thou wearest graces that are all thine own.

More full the sympathies that warm thy breast;
Thy thought more searching; keener far thy ken —
The vision of the soul athirst to know
Where hides true wisdom; larger thy desires
Far wandering, like the wanton summer-winds
That rove o'er regions wide and dalliance hold
With all sweet odors, ever restless still;
Loftier thy purpose, more sublime thy thought
Than childhood ever knew, or e'er could know.
A youthful band — their souls all closely knit
In the pure love that of one blood and birth
By nature's law doth ever richly spring,
As from full fountains, in the cloistered Home,
A scene present on which e'en Heaven must smile.

Nor moves the round of household pleasures on
In dull monotony that needs must cloy.
Home hath its festal days — its holy times —
When fresh delights exhilarate; when Mirth
Seizes the sceptre and asserts her reign,
And Laughter, her prime minister, she bids
Wake rapturous echoes all her realm around!
When on affection's altar, with one will,
The gathered household their fresh offerings lay;
Intent that there, like holy altar-fire,
Love's quenchless flame may ever brightly burn.

Dear old Thanksgiving! How the hallowed word
Restores, as in a moment, vanished years!

How back to life the honored dead it calls,
Whose hoary heads and venerable forms
The bounteous board of old were wont to grace!
They seem to come and sit and smile again,
And with their children's children share the joy.
How brothers, sisters, all companions dear
Of life's unclouded morn, together flow
From regions wide remote, and young again,
At least in heart, renew the scenes of yore!
This from the crowded city; that from where
The Prairie's naked bosom tempts the plough;
Perchance another, from beyond the flood
Where Mississippi pours his torrent down;
Or from fair Florida, beneath whose skies
Magnolias spotless open all their charms,
And orange-blossoms scent the tranquil air.
But, come they whencesoc'er, they come to prove
Unlost, unweakened, the old love of Home.
Joy! joy! Thanksgiving that, o'er all the land,
To-day a Nation's benison thou art.

And thou, too, ancient festival, whose name
A word of joy through centuries hath lived —
Christmas! thou com'st with carols as of old
When angels chanted, 'neath the midnight sky,
"Glory to God on high, good will to men!"
Methinks angelic choirs beyond the stars
Still warble round Messiah's throne the strain.
Earth well may lift her voice in jubilant praise,

And all true hearts exulting greet the day
That tells the world anew the Christ is born !
Let holly, box, and fir tree lend their boughs,
Symbols of life immortal, to adorn
Each Christian temple.   Ring, ring out, ye bells,
Sweet chimes that shall afar glad echoes start !
Then while the very air with love and peace
Seems all surcharged, within thee, happy Home,
Childhood and youth and hoary age may tell,
With many a gift and many a token kind,
With chastened merriment and generous cheer,
How beat in holy unison all hearts.
O Babe of Bethlehem ! to Thee we owe
Home's dearest ministries and purest bliss,
Not less with mortal pleasures innocent,
Than mortal pains and tears, thy loving heart
Hath sympathy, for Thou art Goodness' self !

Next for the household comes the opening year
With greetings fervent, wishes true and kind,
From each to each, of countless happy days !
With the old year deep buried all neglects,
Now friendship's record, as on a fresh page
Unsullied, the New Year once more begins.
As with a chastened tenderness, farewell
Is said to the departed months, whose round,
On Time's great calendar, has been fulfilled.
Age, ripe in piety, with faith confirmed,
All thankfully recalls the past, yet still

Looks onward to the Father's House on high,
Well pleased the golden gates more near to see.
Childhood and youth, exultant, note how fast
Years bear them forward to the longed-for scenes,
So gorgeous to their thought, of life's broad stage,
On which parts all heroic, as they dream,
Wait for their entrance, pre-ordained for them!
Nowhere, as where abides domestic love,
So richly " Happy" dawneth the New Year.

But best and dearest to the household comes
The day of holy rest, — God's sabbath day;
From the world's early morning consecrate
To piety and peace, to prayer and praise,
And all the sanctities of worship paid;
To pleasures such as days of toil know not;
To love, the grace that the whole law fulfils, —
Mother of virtues, — of all thoughts and deeds
That to the pure in heart divinest seem,
And e'en to earth some semblance lend to heaven.
With the fresh morn, while grateful stillness reigns, —
Stopped the great treadmill of the world awhile, —
Parents and children meet with greetings kind
Around the wonted altar.   The calm hour
No haste demands; and first to heaven ascends
In one sweet harmony, from joyful lips,
The hymn that to the ear of Love divine
Tells of each heart's deep, fervent thankfulness,
More welcome than frankincense.   Then the sire,

Priest of the family by God ordained,
From prophet old, or Psalmist, words of life
Reads reverently, as if afresh they came
From God's own lips to gladden trusting hearts ;
Or lessons from His mouth who, Light of men,
Spake as no mortal tongue e'er spake besides ;
Or from the story of His mighty deeds,
His lowliness, and grace that reached to all,
His shameful cross and wondrous sacrifice !
Then at the mercy-seat together bowed,
One tender voice, the worship of all hearts
Pours forth in utterance simple and sincere ;
Forgiveness asks for common faults confessed,
And praise heartfelt, for blessings shared, presents
To Him without whom not a sparrow falls ;
Life, health, and comfort, all most dear, commits,
For coming days, to His o'erwatching care ;
And 'neath the shadow of His wings to dwell
Entreats, one brief request including all.
So pass the peaceful hours.   From morn till eve
Pleasures succeeding pleasures fill the day.
When the glad bells up to God's temple call,
With one consent the household join the throng
That tread the hallowed aisles, their hearts the while
Drawn to each other closer, while they rise
God-ward in prayer and song, and hear the word
That life eternal tells.   Then home returned,
With books, and cheerful talk, and songs that stir
All pure affections, the loved day they close.

Of sabbaths such as this the memories kept
Among the heart's best riches, shall remain
Till earth's last week shall end and brightly dawns
The endless sabbath, the sweet rest of heaven.

A time for all things, — thus the wise man spake, —
And beautiful in its own time is each.
Not always, Edward, round thy bounteous board
Will greet thee youthful faces wreathed in smiles ;
Not always, Mary, will thy quick ear hear
Mother ! — earth's dearest word, — from morn till eve
Fall lovingly from many a coral lip.
Ye have been sowing long.   With line on line,
Lessons of wisdom and of heavenly truth,
No season lost, it hath been yours to pour
Into fresh opening souls, that to receive
What from your lips distilled were ever fain.
Have ye not sought to form for virtue's tasks,
To shape to some true life-work, these the sons
And daughters given from God, your highest trust ?
Draws nigh the reaping-time.   What most your hearts
For many a year have wished, your eyes shall see, —
Your children, girded for life's contests high,
By Providence led forth.   For this ye prayed.
Arrows not always in the quiver rest ;
Fledged birds not in the nest for ever stay ;
Arrow or bird, each at its hour must fly.
Onward, still onward, is the call divine
That all of mortal birth must hear and heed.

'Tis so that pleasures ever new are born
Out of new issues and oft-shifting scenes;
E'en things that most delight, unchanged should sate
From sheer monotony.   Thy pleasures, Home,
Can only live through never-ceasing flow;
As brooks that hasten leaping, babbling on,
Are pure as crystal ever; but, pent up,
Forbid their course to run, do stagnate soon,
And with green ooze breed noisomeness and death.
Ay, parents, send them forth, as God shall call, —
Your best and dearest, — not with fainting heart
And tears regretful at what Home must lose;
But thankfully, since unto you 'tis given
To God and man offerings so rich to bring.

The gentle Edith, ripe in maiden charms,
Yet more and more the magic power reveals
Of cultured womanhood.   Not wholly lost
The witching artlessness of childish years,
The airy freedom, the instinctive grace,
So winsome, till by fashion's hateful code
To chilling stiffness changed.   Radiant she moves
Amid Home's cheerful band, in beauty's light,
As floats a planet in the evening sky,
Bright and still brightening as it higher climbs.
No bird of Paradise, of plumage gay,
In thought or wish she seems; no trifler weak,
With vain conceit inflate, self-conscious, quick
With fluttering pulse to note each watchful glance

Of kindling admiration.   Such as these,
Ye who would find may seek in Fashion's halls,
Where dwell not Home's simplicity and truth.
Yet on her brow she wears, all clearly writ,
Intelligence ; and in her beaming eyes,
The joyousness that tells a guileless breast
And yet unsounded depths of hidden love.
Parental hearts grow warm at sight of her,
And brothers look and worship.   O, there's naught
Can touch so tenderly the restive soul,
Of youthful impulses o'erflowing full,
And urged by uncurbed will and passion's power
The tempter's voice to heed and choose the wrong,
As a fond sister's love, that wooes and wins,
Attempers what is wayward unto good,
And by its own pure effluence maketh pure.
Thou, Edith, art e'en as the warm south wind,
That, from the lips of Spring breathed o'er the fields
Whate'er is loveliest, waketh into life
With silent power, till all are robed in bloom.
While Home thou blessest, thou thyself art blest.

Goodness, to beauty joined, is like the flame
That from the light-house on some towering cliff
O'er the wild waters throws its beams afar
At nightfall, welcome to the wanderer's eye.
Its glory streams abroad, nor can be hid ;
But many an eye beholds it and admires.
Ah ! maiden, thou that in thy freshness wear'st

With modesty and gentleness and grace
The charms that nature gave and goodness lends,
With power these charms invest thee, — power per-
    chance
Beyond thy utmost thought, — to scatter wide
Influence that light and guidance both shall be
To many a heart sincere, that so inspired
Shall be by thee to nobler virtue won.
The power to bless by charming, — wondrous gift!
How rich who hath it! how made like to God!
Woman, this most exalts thee and adorns;
Gives thee a sovereign sway, if so thou wilt;
And makes thee as a spirit of the skies.

To all, such Edith seemed.   But most to one,
Young Arthur, from her childhood playmate, friend,
Sharer of frolic hours, and o'er the fields
And thro' the shadowy woods, when summer glowed,
Leader of many a ramble.   Always kind,
Homeward from school her satchel oft he bore,
And through the winter snow her pathway trod;
Or cross the swollen brook, with friendly hand,
By the rude stepping-stones, he safely led.
With changing years advanced to manhood now,
Transformed he seems, yet not another made.
In manners courteous, almost distant grown,
Yet is he near her oft, with calm content
On his fair face clear written, and an eye
That back reflects her glance, as she for him

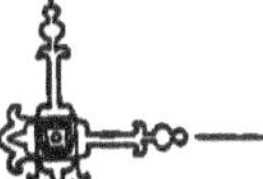

And he for her some secret fain would guard ;
As if by some keen instinct each did read
The other's thought, to words not trusted yet, —
Not uttered in full phrase, — yet half expressed,
Perchance not seldom, by some act or look,
Some pressure of the hand, some opening bud
Given to adorn the hair and meekly worn ;
Some book together read, or some soft strain
In the still twilight by two voices sung !

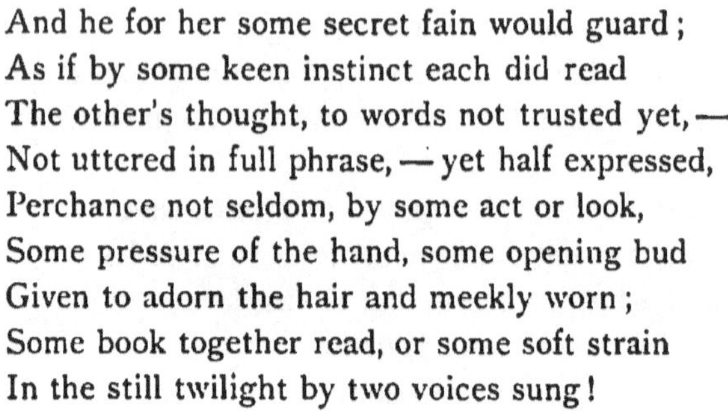

There is a time to love ! — a holy time
When from deep well-springs in the throbbing breast
Gush forth affection's purest, richest streams;
And flow unchecked, bearing through all the soul
Mysterious happiness ; when fleet-winged thought,
As finished occupation sets it free,
To the loved being flies and lingers long, —
As the wild bee, tasted the nectared cup,
Delays, and yet delays, its homeward flight, —
Or, all impatient, in the busy hour,
Full oft it plays the truant and escapes ;
Forgets all time and distance, and afar
Seeks the secluded walk or well-known bower.
O blissful season, when the unfolding soul
Puts forth all sweet affections ! when bright shapes
And visions, of imagination born,
And yearnings vague, and hopes and wishes, blend
With a deep restlessness that is not pain,
But rather seems a rapture ; and all things,

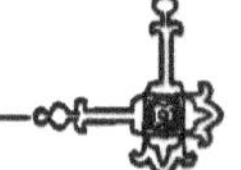

The heavens, the earth, life's many shaded scene,
Past, present, future, — future most, — appear
Glorious, enchanting, in love's aureate light.
So in some grand cathedral, when the sun,
Through the stained windows, his full lustre flings
On priest and altar, and the reverent throng
Of worshippers that crowd the solemn aisles,
'Tis as a new Shekinah filled the place,
And heaven's own splendors threw o'er all the scene.

   She is betrothed!   The changeless word is said!
Two souls are each to each for ever bound!
Is freedom then abjured, — for bonds exchanged?
Arthur and Edith, each once free as air
In thought, word, feeling, purpose, aim, and end,
Sold each a royal birthright when they sware
Henceforth to have one name, one life, one lot?
Or hideth seeming loss some priceless gain?
By somewhat yielded is it, Heaven's great law
That the young heart, with conscious need disturbed,
Must find its fulness, what it restless craved?
Bound! Bound! Ah! thou that doubting askest, know
That unto thee love's mystery as yet
Is all unopened; thou art but a child!
Thou hast not learned how, in the blissful sphere
Where love triumphant reigns, a soul gains most
When most it loses; that when giving all
It takes all and is blest.   Two hearts made one
In mystic unity of trustful love,

Constraint know not, nor liberty e'er lack ;
With full consenting wills as one they choose ;
Or, differing aught, for this alone contend,
How each to other first and most may yield !
No bonds like thine do bind, O heaven-born Love,
Yet as the angels free are loving souls !

Edith and Arthur, be the vernal days
Of your betrothal arched with azure skies
And glad with melodies of warbling birds !
Enchanting be the twilights, and the sheen
Of silvery moonlight on your evening paths !
Taste the dear joys of early love, and wait
In ecstasy delicious for the hour
When at the bridal altar blest ye stand.

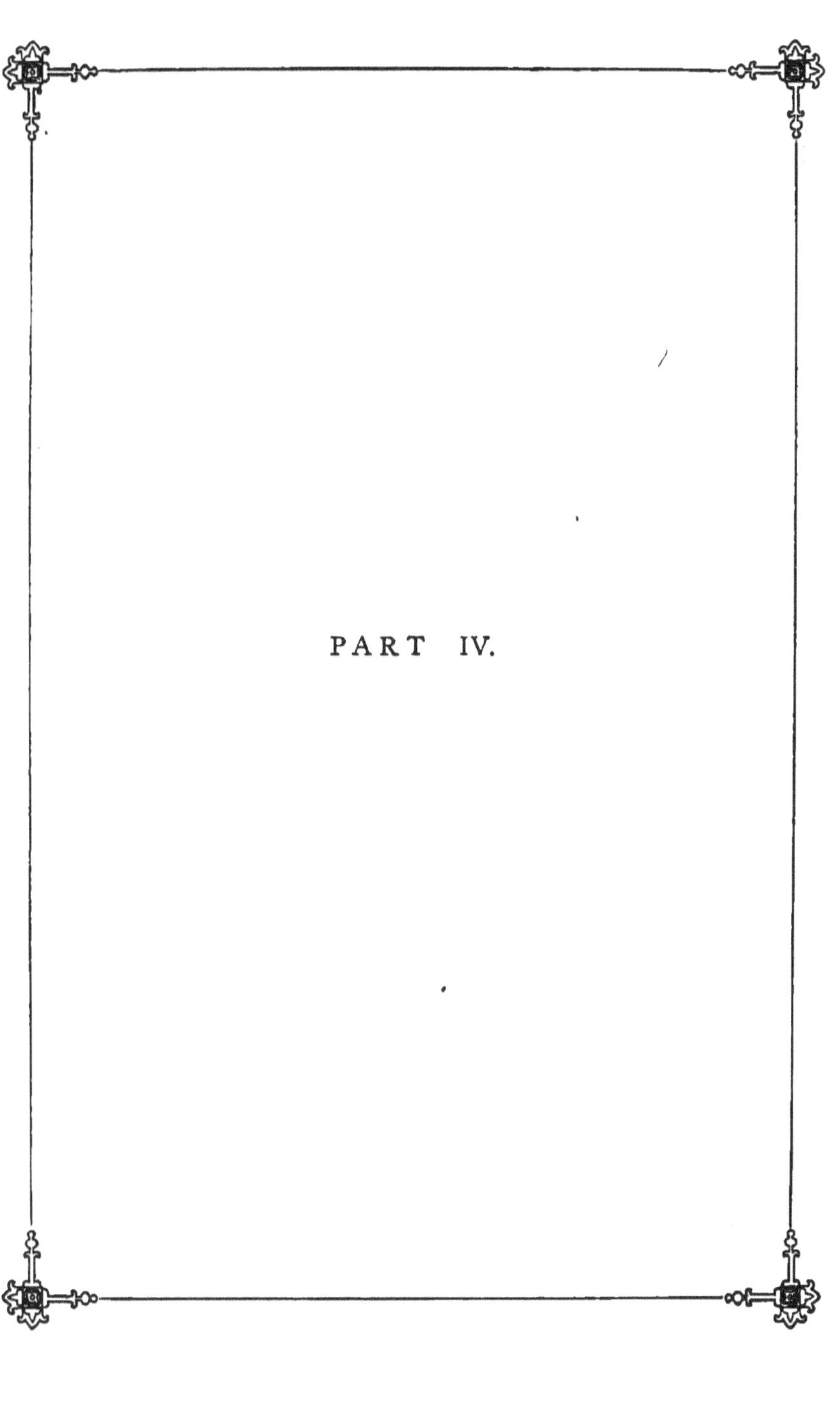

PART IV.

Oh, hush the song, and let her tears
Flow to the dream of her early years !
Holy and pure are the drops that fall
When the young bride goes from her father's hall ;
She goes unto love yet untried and new,
She parts from love that hath still been true.

MRS. HEMANS.

How happy he who crowns, in shades like these,
A youth of labor with an age of ease !
Onward he moves to meet his latter end,
Angels around befriending virtue's friend ;
Sinks to the grave with unperceived decay,
While resignation gently slopes the way ;
And, all his prospects brightening to the last,
His heaven commences ere the world be past.

GOLDSMITH.

PART IV.

THE bridal came.   The holy vows were said,
        As on some April morn the changeful sky
Lets fa1l, e'en through the sunshine, fitful showers,
As each contending which the hour should rule ;
So on that day alternate smiles and tears
On each face came and went.   O Edward, thou
Thy struggling heart in vain dost strive to still ;
Nor canst thou, Mary, when the sudden flood
Of gushing tenderness o'erflows thy breast,
Repress its heaving, or the quivering lip
At once compose, or dry the moistened cheek.
To-day a priceless jewel ye resign,
That has adorned your casket, flashed for you !
A heart that made sweet music in its beat
Of harmony with yours ; an eye whose glance,
To you, like light from heaven, bore only joy !
Brothers and sisters, from your blissful bower
The full-blown rose ye loved is borne away,
Elsewhere to shed its fragrance.   Yet grieve not,
As those who miss some treasure gone for aye.

Love chooseth ever what the loved shall bless,
And e'en in sacrifice finds sacred peace.
Edith but goeth, at the will of Heaven,
To kindle for herself a household flame,
Whose light afar shall shine.   Herself on all
Who in her bliss are blest, not less henceforth,
With Arthur at her side, shall gladness shed,
And to the Home she leaves shall not be lost.

As some prolific tree whose boughs with fruit
Bend earthward, yet through months of glowing suns
Keeps all its treasure till the harvest-hour
Hath come at last; and, ripening once begun,
The process hastens till there naught remains
Save a bare gleaning on the plundered boughs,
That look all lonely; so the Home where long
Young hearts have lingered, clinging each to each
And to the hearthstone where they first drew breath,
Must see them parted at the appointed bound.
When comes the day of ripeness and the spell
That held them one is broken, soon — ah! soon
The bands seem loosened all, and, one by one,
Mature for life's high calling, goeth forth
With many a backward look and secret pang;
Till where but now there stirred a cheerful throng
Reigns the hushed quietness of emptied halls!
'Tis so, O Time, that thy resistless hand
With scene on scene the mortal drama fills.[1]

[1] Appendix, note E.

Alfred and brothers twain too soon are missed
When meet the household band.   One burning heart
Hath kindled into generous, passionate love
At Learning's shrine, by names illustrious fired,
That, shining as bright orbs through ages gone,
Lit up the darkness, and, for coming time
Together blended, form a milky way
Glorious as that which spans night's ebon vault.
In cloistered halls he hides for toilsome years,
Youth's passion curbs, its restlessness subdues,
And, e'en as if to Learning's self betrothed,
Life's busy throng forsakes with her to dwell.
Another to the marts of hurrying trade
His steps hath turned; eager to tread where sweeps,
Now this way and now that, the surging tide
Of rivalries that chafe and ventures high ;
Where men for gain in life-long wrestlings strive,
Now win, now lose, and oft, ere manhood's prime,
Its sturdy strength wear out and die too soon.
Thrice happy they whose hearts die not, nor lose
All sweet humanities, though years be long
And crowned with rich successes all unstained !
Turns fondly to his mother-earth a third,
By some deep impulse urged ; and far away
Toward sunset-regions he hath wandered forth,
To fix his dwelling where beyond the flood
Broad Iowa her billowy bosom spreads.
There, 'neath his hand, the virgin soil shall soon
Grow genial, opened to the mellowing sun ;

Quicken the scattered seed, and in its time
Reward the sower with the reaper's joy.
Around the new-made Home his tasteful hand
New beauties shall create. Well pleased his ear
Shall note the voices, echoing far, of flocks
And herds that 'mid abundance graze content;
Nor need he envy here the city's din,
As glide, in healthful toil, the peaceful years.

Ah! Time, at once giver and robber thou!
Ere life hath reached its noon, each year beholds
Some gift possessed made richer, or some grace,
Some power or pleasure, all anew bestowed.
But high noon passed, each year shall filch away
Somewhat of beauty's charm, of manhood's strength,
Of lustre from the eye, and from the ear
Of quickness to perceive the subtile thrill.
Thou stealest from the agile limb and step,
Elastic beyond art, the lithesome spring;
From golden locks, or raven, their bright hues
Thou plunderest silently, till all are gone;
And keen desire, and love of high pursuit,
And buoyancy of hope, and courage firm,
And aspiration restless evermore, —
Whatever life's great tasks made seem but play, —
So stealthily thou takest that the robbed
Scarce note their loss, or, noting, half believe.
Yes, Edward, thou and Mary, yet thine own,
Still dear, far dearer than when thy young heart

Felt love's first pulses beat, are not the same
In thought, wish, purpose, taste, or mien and air,
As when around you glowed the bridal morn.
The brows, then fresh and fair, with deeper lines
Are furrowed by that skilled engraver, Time;
Then life lay all before you, like some scene
Of rarest beauty to the eye made clear
And magnified by telescopic glass ;
Now, through the glass inverted, ye behold
Reduced to littleness what once seemed great,
And dimmed, by half, the glory that did charm.
Grown calmer and more wise, ye, well content,
Resign your old ambitions ; pleased to dwell
Amid Home's peacefulness, and with such tasks
As here the tranquil days may best beguile,
To wait till evening shadows gently fall.
Home hath not lost its sweetness, its content,
Though missed the cheerful voices, heard of old
Echoing through hall and chamber; though the night
Descend in solemn silence, where so oft
At close of day, for many a year, did float
On the still air enchanting harmonies.
No lonely hearts here dwell, that do but live
In sad, submissive patience, and earth's joys
For them all vanished deem, to come no more.

No, no ! Not such the transformation wrought
By Time and Change, though wondrous be their power.
While creepeth stilly on life's closing scene,

And with the hoary head and trembling hand
Come signs of weariness, and for itself
Toil seems no more a pleasure; yet 'tis left
On the fled past to muse; and still to find
Companionship in books, or friends, around
The evening table where the loved were wont
Nightly to gather; or at will to sit
Beneath the old familiar trees that hang
O'er-arching by the door, as long ago,
And seem of all things least to have changed with
        years.
Ay, more: 'tis given to greet the oft return
Of children who, to filial duty true
And childhood's fresh remembrances, come back
To tread again the haunts for ever dear;
To hear grand-children's prattle, and to watch
Their childish raptures as on grandsire's knee
They drink in, all attent, the well-told tale.
These are the tranquil pleasures left to age
When towards the sunset verges life's long day.
With these, deep in the trustful, loving soul
That 'mid life's turmoil walked by faith with God,
And, far above earth's ever-shifting sands,
Builded on solid rock immortal hopes,
There come, as night draws nearer, glimpses oft,
And blest anticipations, of the realm
For ever fair, beyond the rolling spheres,
Where years no more shall ravish youth away,
Nor love be parted from its loved again.

Edward, thy Mary's voice for thee hàs lost
Naught of its sweetness ; it delights thee still,
Like old familiar music.   On that brow,
Mary, that in its manliness did charm
Thy girlhood's eye, not less thou lovest still
To gaze, though o'er it Age hath spread his snows.
Ah ! richer now, in either breast, the flow
Of love's pure current, than when ye did speak
With trembling ecstasy the marriage vow
Before God's altar.   Then that current welled
From confidence and hope ; from knowledge now,
And mutual virtues tested, till, like gold
Fresh from the crucible and proved by fires,
They shine with lustre that no doubt can dim ;
Blest in each other, ye are doubly blest.

Nor are ye lonely left.   One daughter still,
Fair Ella, youngest of the household band,
Like some bright minister of heavenly love,
Each morning greets you, fresh herself as morn,
And watches, all the day, if she may read,
In look or motion, even your rising wish !
Or with some sweet surprise may light a smile
On your calm, reverend brows, perchance provoke
To merry laughter, never hard the task.
A kind good-night she says when silent hours
Call you to tranquil sleep.   Good-morrow sweet
She bids you with each dawn.   For you she lives ;
Herself forgets ; forgets the brilliant halls

Where Fashion holds her court, ever best pleased
With acts of filial duty done, she seems.
Nor till her eyes shall see you pass the gates
Of life eternal, shall aught else divide
Her constant heart, whose every beating pulse
Tells that for you her very life-blood flows!
O faithful love! that, self-devoted, deems
All toil and care for you a mighty debt,
And to the utmost the full score would pay!

   Yes, Woman!   Though ofttimes to thee 'tis given
Thy heart-kept hopes, at duty's call, to yield
All cheerfully; for God and those that else
Were left forlorn and loveless, thine to make
The lot of those who nobly much resign;
Though thy life's course be like a modest stream
That through the vale in grateful coolness winds,
And hidden half, with tree and bush o'erhung,
Freshness exhales e'en when itself unseen;
Though Providence, or thine own choice, deny
The household throne and dear connubial bliss,
Yet beautiful and blest thy life may be;
Rich in self-culture, and each grace and charm
Of mind or manners, loveliest in all eyes;
And filled with deeds that the recording pen
Shall chronicle in heaven.   The world yet teems
With griefs and groans; with pierced and bleeding
      hearts,
To stanch whose wounds there needs the hand of love;

With sin, and souls debased, and dark despair ;
With ignorance perverse and error blind ;
With mercy's tasks untold, that well befit
Thy delicate fingers and thy facile skill ;
On thee it calls, and wide before thee spreads
Such fields where love's best triumphs may be won,
As make it grand to live and toil and bear.
If thou wilt be a trifler, deep the shame !
If frivolous and vain, with all the gifts
Of God conferred to make thee seem divine,
Demons must clap their hands in fiendish glee,
And pitying Goodness turn in tears away !
Be a true woman, whatsoe'er thy place,
In solitude or crowd or youth or age,
And life shall be to thee no joyless waste,
But rich in pleasures that sate not the soul.
Thyself revere ; nor suffer without need
Thy robes to draggle in the common dust !
Be as God would, — in thine own sphere a sun,
And round thee glorious planets shall revolve,
Glow in thy light, and life and comfort find.
So shalt thou bless thy kind, and all shall gaze
Admiring, and like Parsees worship thee !

   As in late autumn, when the frosty earth
With withered leaves is strown, the forests bare,
And many a signal tells drear winter nigh,
Comes Indian Summer with her gentle reign,
And charms which, tempered by the golden haze,

Half veil and half transfigure Nature's face,
That with pale, pensive beauty still delights,
As peacefully go by the tranquil days;
So, while age ripens, and when whitened locks
And the dimmed eye and faltering step forewarn
That not now distant lies the vale of shades,
Earth's darkness parting from eternal day,
Full oft there comes a season all serene,
Whose sunshine mellowed falls, whose airs are mild
As softest breath of May, whose tempests sleep,
Whose peace is like the Sabbath stillness, when
A hushed world waits and worships.   'Tis as if
O'er the calm spirit silently there steals
Some effluence celestial, that inbreathed,
As from the throne of God, a baptism seems
Of love divine, before the mortal strife,
The waiting soul from ties of earth to free,
And heavenward lure her towards her coming bliss.

'Tis in this hallowed time that Edward now
And Mary, side by side, like ripened sheaves
With yellow grain rich laden, bide the hour
When the great Husbandman, with faithful care
Shall bring them to his garner.   Ella's hand,
With love's instinctive gentleness, delights
To bear for them each burden, and each day
Some pleasure new to bring.   The furrowed brow,
Soothed by her touch, seems ever half to lose
Its look of weariness; and at her voice,

Whose tones are cheering as the morning lark's,
The languid eye grows brighter; and the ear
Tires not that listens to her pleasing talk,
Or readings, that beguile the loitering hours;
The genius of the place, she lives and moves
Like some kind, ministering spirit of the skies,
Sent forth the aged pilgrims Home to lead.

But mortal years must end.   Mary, thy cheek
So touched with crimson once, now paleness wears;
Falter thy footsteps on the lengthened path
Where thou of old didst tread like the gazelle
That scaleth with fleet limb the mountain side;
Faintness invades thy heart, so wont to beat
With ardor healthful and with purpose brave.
Beside thee bends thy Edward's reverend head;
Grieved not for thee, so soon to see His face
Whose beauty to behold ye both have pined;
But for himself, that he may not as yet
Enter within the veil, but without thee,
Still in the outer court must linger lone.
Thy children too, Edith and Arthur soon,
Then those who dwell afar, in hurried haste,
With Ella, gather in the chamber hushed,
And watch the failing pulses.   O dread hour,
When hearts long loving and in love made one
Are each from other rudely rent away!
Yet Faith can triumph here, and calmly say,
"Thy will be done!" can hear the symphonies

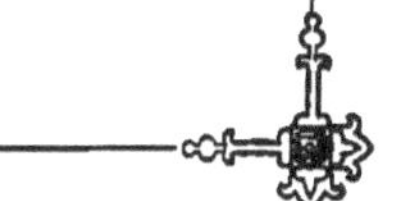

Soft floating on the air, from unseen harps,
That welcome to the invisible host of God
Another sister spirit, pure and free!
She is translated, and with Christ abides!

    Edward, not long shall Earth detain thee now!
Her lights grow dim, and like a vision fade
Her transient glories; heavenward look thine eyes.
Thou wouldst not linger, and the hour is nigh
When thou shalt hear kind voices bid thee come!
And see, beyond the flood, thy Mary stand
With arms outstretched to beckon thee away!
Then, Ella, thy dear, loving hand shall close
Thy father's dying eyes; that placid brow
With thy last filial tears thou shalt bedew,
Thy filial tasks all done.   Then farewell Home!
Thy Home from infancy, through long, long years,
Whose histories upon thy soul are writ,
As if, with iron pen and diamond point,
Graved on the eternal rock.   Go, thou true heart,
Well trained by duty for all holiest deeds!
Go forth where sin lays waste and sorrows spring,
And round thee scatter gladness, light, and joy!
In thee let it be seen that woman, true
To love's best impulses, must needs command
All honor from the world, by all revered.
So shall thy name, enshrined in grateful hearts,
Be as a jewel kept; and thou at length
Shalt hear the Ever-blessed say — Well done!

And pass the threshold of thy Father's House,
The HOME OF HOMES where changeless love abides!

O haste the happy day when o'er the world, —
The wide, wide world, — bright altar fires shall burn
On household shrines all countless as the sands!
When homeless thousands shall no more be found
Far scattered without shepherd, wandering sheep
Unpitied, left of savage beasts the prey!
Ye who with ruthless hand would madly tear
From the chaste maiden's brow the marriage wreath,
The sanctities destroy that God ordained
To guard domestic joys; the springs would taint
Of pure affection and foul lust unchain
To work its will till Homes are known no more;
Could the base wish succeed, the race undone,
And conscious of its wrong, on you would pour
Its curses without measure, — well deserved!
Religion's ministers! lift up the voice
On your high watch-towers, and assert His law
Who to unbind what God hath joined forbade.
Statesmen! loose not with sacrilegious hand
The holy tie without which perish Homes.
Know that when Homes shall perish states shall fall,
And earth, e'en as the nether world, be hell!
The citadel of hope for earth is Home;
Home the best type that earth affords of Heaven.

Yes! though like all beneath these changing skies,
The joys of Home abide not; though itself

By its own law dissolve, when circling years
Have finished, one by one, its shifting scenes,
And sundered far the hearts once closely knit;
All ends not here.   Hath not the Master said
That, in His Father's House, for loving souls
Are many mansions, whither safely led,
And made one family, they shall with Him
Their Elder Brother dwell, for ever one?
There the great anti-typal palace waits,
Thronged with the sons and daughters of our God
Made like unto the angels; and the feet
Of all the pure in heart shall thither come.

O mortal! whatsoe'er thy lot hath been,
If, half bewildered, thou hast seemed to stray
A homeless wanderer o'er a barren waste,
If one that much hath loved and much hath lost,
Or one that loveth much, and much doth fear
What most he loves to lose; let thy stilled soul
Repose itself in peace.   Though on thy head
Fierce tempests frequent beat, and all too oft
Clouds, dark o'ershadowing, veil the cheerful skies,
And gloom brood o'er thy path; though round thy
        steps
Perils thick-clustering wait; though cares oppress,
And each day hath its strifes, and Sorrow pours
From her exhaustless flagon for thy lips
Full cups of bitterness; though life's best joys
Seem half to lose their sweetness, and no more

Enkindle keen desire, nor yield delight
To the tired sense, worn with the round of years;
Still be thou calm!   Be strong and falter not!
Teach thy chafed spirit, that, in weariness,
Pants for her rest and longs for wings to soar
To kinder skies beyond this land of storms,
Her restless thoughts to stay; and in the strength
Of Hope, that, like the needle, trembling oft,
Is steadfast still, to wait the coming hour
When she well pleased the mystery shall read
Of earth's stern disciplines.   Then on thine eyes,
Beaming with life immortal, full shall break
The wonders hidden long.   Then Love Divine
Wide open the effulgent gates shall fling,
And bid thee enter; there, beside the throne
Where sits the Lamb, shall show thee the bright Home,
For Him and His for ever dear redeemed
Builded of God ere yet the worlds were made.
Lift, lift thy glance, O mortal, troubled, sad,
And lose thy griefs and fears in thoughts of Heaven!

There wait thee solid joys.   What most thy heart
Hath yearned to find, yet ever sought in vain
Through perished hopes and crosses ever new, —
Sweet rest, with full content, — thou there shalt know.
Thy cup of blessing filled, thou shalt behold
Divinest splendors, all things bright and fair;
With which compared, earth's purest loveliness
Remembered shall all unsubstantial seem,

A shadow and a type.   Thy treasures lost,
By stern Death wrested from thy warm embrace,
Now clothed in spiritual beauty and complete
In all celestial graces, still thine own,
There thou again shalt find.   Theirs the old love,
Changed only as made richer in its flow
And deeper far; as if, checked for a time
By separation, it the while had swelled,
Till ready, like a flood, to force its way.
These shall such greeting give thee as shall thrill
Thy raptured spirit, ne'er again to know
Unquenched affection's thirst ; while high above
Thou seest writ in words of flashing light :
" No pang, no death, no partings, evermore ! "

   Heaven ! 'Tis no misty dream. What mortal eye,—
Unlifted yet the veil, — hath never seen,
Nor can, with keenest glance ; what mortal ear,
Though listening all attent, hath never heard,
Even in faint echoes, God himself hath shown
To loving hearts and true.   By visions clear
And words celestial, whispered soft and sweet
In the rapt spirit's depths, revealed have been
Mysteries of life and beauty, love and joy,
That from of old await the sons of God,
Their heritage, reserved till their glad feet
Shall pass thy gates, Jerusalem the New !
In thee, O Holy City, crowned with grace,
Builded of gems imperishable, with walls

Of adamant that sin and woe debar,
O'erarched by skies serene without a sun,
And watered with pure, living streams, that flow
For ever from beneath the Mount of God, —
In thee fulfilled, and more, each promise stands.

Nor this alone.   For, lo! the Lamb Himself
From the eternal throne, — where, " in the midst
As one that hath been slain " He yet appears,
Wielding all princely power o'er earth and Heaven,
With " many crowns " on that once bleeding Head, —
Full oft descends, with gentlest mien, to walk
All lovingly, a Bridegroom with his Bride,
Rejoicing o'er her in her bridal robes,
White as the light and lustrous as the sun.[1]
In dear companionship amid the throng
By His own pangs redeemed, now tenderly
He talks of Golgotha, the tomb, the morn
When the rent sepulchre resigned its trust,
And He, triumphant, first-born from the dead,
Death's sceptre broken, trod the earth again ;
When His own saw Him, heard Him, and believed
That He, whom on the tree they saw expire
In agony and shame, was LORD OF ALL!

Ah! how their blessed spirits now respond
In rapturous praise, and thanks, and burning love, —
Love that not blindly burns, like theirs of old

[1] Appendix, note F.

Who to Emmaus walked, — while heavenly words
Fall like soft music from those lips divine !
His glory they behold, that glory share,
Even as on earth He said.   All human grace
With the full Godhead's dignity combined,
And lowly gentleness, enrobed He seems
With beauty infinite !   They, all intent,
And ravished, gazing on His unveiled face, —
O vision long desired ! — themselves transformed
And in His likeness made, exultant see ;
To know as they are known supremely blest.
He feeds them, — He whom seraphim adore !
He leads them where eternal fountains rise,
That they may thirst no more ; and from the eyes
That wept on earth so oft, His loving hand
All tears hath wiped for evermore away.

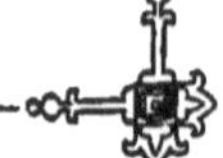

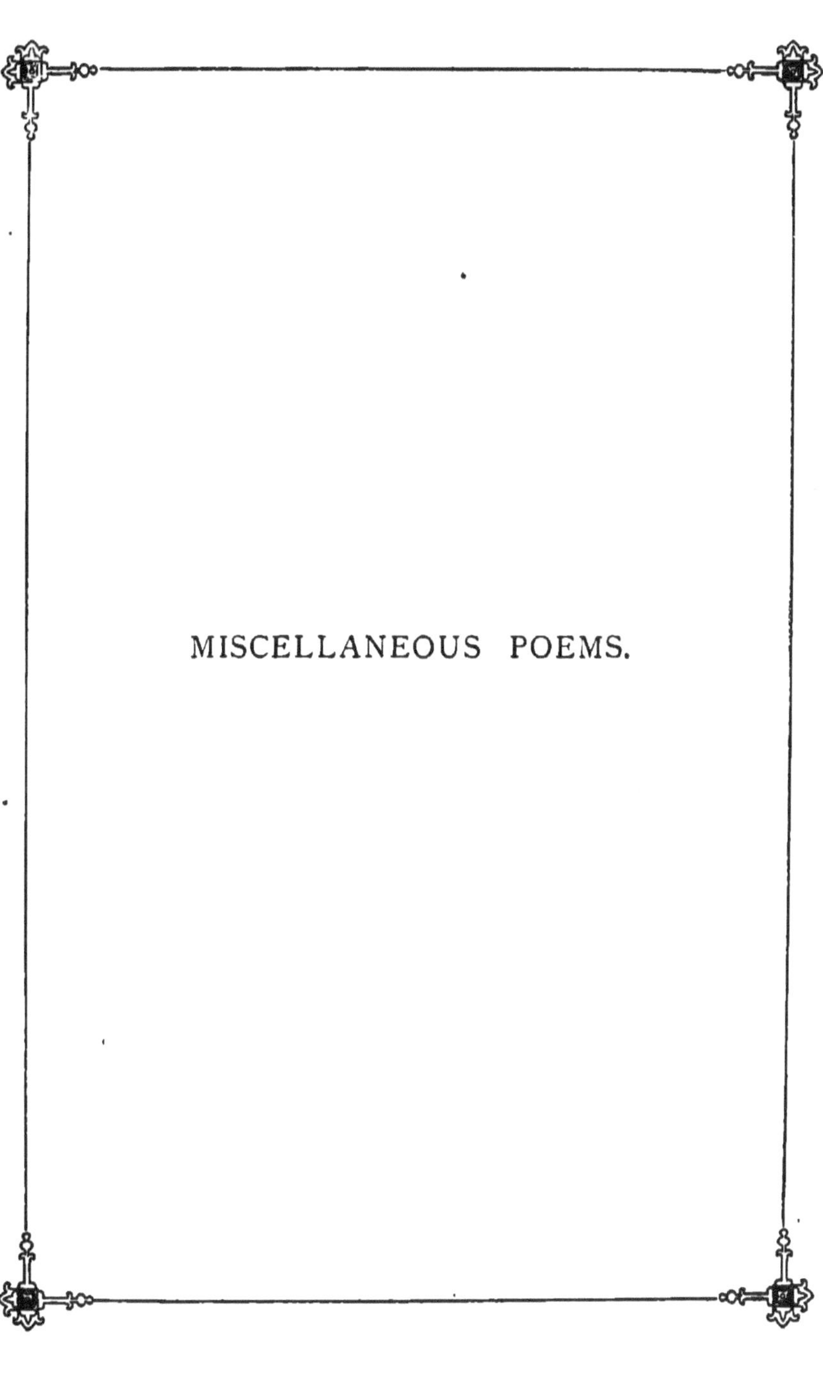

MISCELLANEOUS POEMS.

MISCELLANEOUS POEMS.

THE SEASIDE.

I SIT beside thee, murmuring sea,
  And watch thy ever-changeful motion;
Note where soft clouds float over thee,
  And where commingle sky and ocean;
White sails are scattered here and there,
  Of swift ships o'er thy bosom gliding,
That in the hazy, shimmering air,
  Move dream-like on the wave dividing.

I mark where on yon pebbly shore,
  Along the crescent bay far-sweeping,
White waves are breaking evermore,
  E'en when the winds are calmly sleeping;
I gaze when storms are on the deep,
  Like unchained demons wildly roaming,
When billows huge their tumult keep,
  In frantic fury madly foaming.

Thy deep and still abysses, where
  Dwell life and beauty all-abounding,
Where pearls are born and mosses rare,
  And sea-flowers bloom, the rock surrounding;

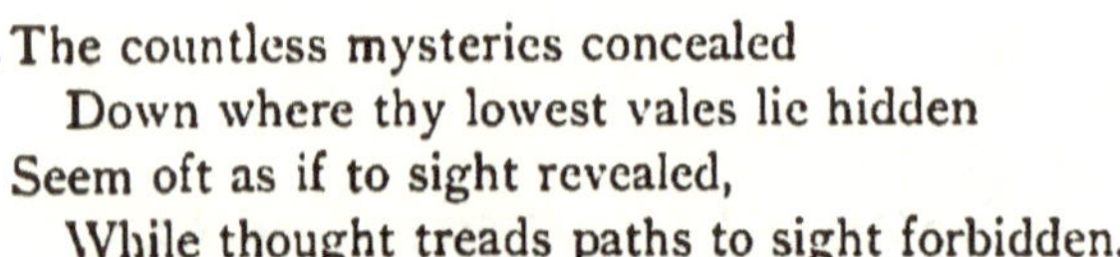

.The countless mysteries concealed
   Down where thy lowest vales lie hidden
Seem oft as if to sight revealed,
   While thought treads paths to sight forbidden.

Yet, mighty Sea! 'tis not the glow
   Of thy broad face when calm and smiling;
'Tis not thy wrath when heavenward go
   Thy surges into mountains piling;
'Tis not the secrets of thy breast,
   Thy countless marvels all unspoken,
That make me with thee ever blest,
   Held long as by a spell unbroken!

'Tis that thou stirrest in my soul
   Thoughts all too deep and vast for telling;
Thoughts free as thine own waves that roll
   On and yet on with ceaseless swelling;
'Tis that emotions, memories, loves,
   And buried joys, thou dost awaken;
Flown hopes dost call, like nestling doves,
   Back to the heart too soon forsaken.

'Tis that far o'er thy wide expanse
   I know that sunny lands are lying;
And at thy side, full oft, perchance,
   To those fair climes my thought is flying;
I scent the orange groves afar,
   I see the tufted palm-tree spreading,
I rove where Orient gardens are
   In endless bloom their perfumes shedding.

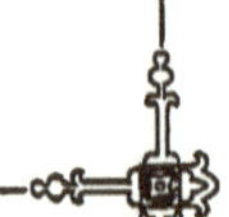

'Tis that in years far, far away,
  When youthful pulses high were beating,
I joyed by thee at eve to stray,
  True hearts in high communion meeting ;
And now thou givest back once more
  The faces whose bright smiles have perished;
I see them, greet them, as of yore,
  Though lost, in faithful memory cherished.

'Tis that, when on thy strand, I feel
  A reverent tenderness come o'er me,
Am moved by thy gray rocks to kneel,
  With all thy grandeur spread before me,
And breathe my worship in His ear
  Who, in His greatness thought out-reaching,
Is ever to the lowly near,
  The glory of His goodness teaching.

'Tis that by thee I feel the love
  That, like thy floods, no measure knowing,
From the Eternal Fount above
  To mortal man is ever flowing ;
And hear His footsteps who of old
  Sublimely trod the troubled billow,
Who with a word the storm controlled,
  Rising majestic from his pillow.

'Tis that, at sight of thee, inspired
  With conscious power, my soul, ascending,
Shoots high her flight with wing untired,
  Her heavenward yearning impulse lending ;

Till fairer visions greet her sight
   Than charm where tropic suns are gleaming,
Realms bathed in uncreated light
   From God's high throne for ever streaming.

Long as my mortal years shall roll,
   Grand Sea! thy sights and sounds shall cheer me,
Bring calm sweet musings to my soul,
   And God and kindred spirits near me;
Then, when these eyes behold no more
   Thy noble face, its charm still keeping,
O let thy long-loved, solemn roar
   Be as a requiem o'er me sleeping!

THE CHORUS OF ALL SAINTS.

Suggested while hearing Haydn's Imperial Mass.

THE choral song of a mighty throng
   Comes sounding down the ages;
'Tis a pealing anthem borne along,
   Like the roar of the sea that rages;
Like the shout of winds when the storm awakes,
   Or the echoing, distant thunder,
Sublime on the listening ear it breaks,
   And enchains the soul in wonder.

And in that song, as it onward rolls,
   There are countless voices blended,
Voices of myriads of holy souls
   Since Abel from earth ascended:

Of patriarchs old in the world's dim morn ;
  Of seers from the centuries hoary ;
Of angels who chimed when the Lord was born,
  " To God in the highest, glory ! "

Of the wise that, led by the mystic star,
  Found the babe in Bethlehem's manger,
And gifts, from the Orient lands afar,
  Bestowed on the new-born stranger ;
Of Mary, the blessed of God Most High ;
  Of the Marys that watch were keeping
At the Cross where He hung for the world to die,
  And stood by the sepulchre weeping.

The voices of holy Apostles rise,
  The symphony grandly swelling,
And land to land with the strain replies,
  As they go of Messiah telling ;
And with them the martyr host conspire,
  A host as the stars for number ;
They sing from the rack and from out the fire,
  From the dust in which they slumber.

From the saints obscure, that in every age
  Have fought the good fight unheeded,
Whose names ne'er graced the historic page,
  Who thought not of fame, nor needed,
Come tones that tell of a tender love,
  Of a spirit calm and holy :
O, sweet to the ear of the Lord above
  Is the praise of the meek and lowly !

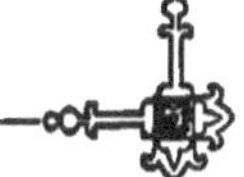

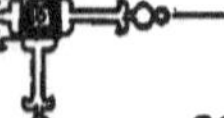

He hath heard, well pleased, when the psalm awoke
   Dark caves and the dismal prison;
When the stillness of lonely glens it broke,
   Or on damp night-winds has risen;
When up from the cot of the poor it came,
   Or from meanest cabins stealing,
'Twas an offering dearer than altar's flame,
   The love of true hearts revealing.

And hark! from the joyous infant choir
   Which the Lord to His arms hath taken,
Notes sweet as breathe from the trembling lyre
   That the softest touch doth waken!
And from childhood's band who, when life's fresh glow
   On their early bloom was lying,
Felt the shaft of death to their young hearts go,
   And His love enfold them dying!

So onward, long as the queenly moon
   Shall float through the azure nightly,
Or the sun ascend to his throne at noon,
   Or the evening star burn brightly,
Shall the choral hymn of the saints resound
   That chants of the Cross the story;
It shall rise and blend with the trumpet's sound
   When the Lord shall come in glory!

MIDSUMMER NIGHT.

O'ER the dim, empurpled mountains,
   Fades the ruby light away;
Shadows sleep where late the fountains
   Sparkled 'neath the glance of day.

Tranquil streams that, smoothly gliding,
   Mirrored tree and cliff and cloud,
All their placid beauty hiding,
   Gathering night-shades now enshroud.

Flowers that in the jocund morning
   Drank with blushing lips the dew,
Folded wait another dawning,
   And their wasted sweets renew.

Hurrying life's last murmur dying,
   Stillness broods o'er vale and hill,
Startled only by the crying
   Of the wakeful whip-poor-will.

Spirit of the peaceful hour,
   Now while nature sinks to rest,
Let thy sweet, subduing power
   Still each passion in my breast!

Give calm thoughts of tasted sorrows,
   Tender memories wake again,
Bring me dreams of bright to-morrows,
   Hopes that shall not all be vain.

While, with darkness vigils keeping,
 Here I linger silent, lone,
Come there, like the soft wind sweeping,
 Breathings from the realm unknown.

As yon watching stars above me
 Greet me, though afar they roll,
May not those in heaven that love me
 Speak in whispers to my soul?

As if some new sense possessing,
 May I not those whispers hear?
Catch from airy lips a blessing?
 Know that holy ones are near?

Night's deep shade the world concealing,
 Makes the soul's quick glance more keen;
In serener light revealing
 To her eye the things unseen.

Sights of unthought glory hidden,
 Sounds unheard by mortal ear,
Are not to her sense forbidden
 When she wakes to see and hear.

Beauty greets her, ever vernal,
 Melodies for earth too sweet;
Glows for her the Throne Eternal,
 Of Incarnate Love the seat!

On my spirit, heavenward turning,
  Falls celestial grace like dew ;
Waking all afresh her yearning,
  Angels, to ascend to you !

O, while hushed is each commotion,
  While, my soul, thy thought is free,
Fervent breathe thy pure devotion :
  God and heaven are nigh to thee!

ETERNITY.

A MEDITATION.

ETERNITY ! What art thou, — when and where?
  With awe and bated breath men speak thy name,
And think of thee as of a dread unknown,
A gloomy mystery from mortals hid ;
To be unveiled then only when shall fall
These vestments that for earth enrobe our souls.
They who now tread the globe, and darkly walk
Their toilsome round of years, are prisoners held
Of Time's close realm ; encircled and pent in,
As if beneath o'erarching, massive walls,
Fixed by heaven's law, impassable, and all
Impervious to the flooding light beyond ;
Barriers that, till arrives the destined hour,
Must shut them from the infinite, and make
Thee, grand Eternity, a shadowy dream
Of the sealed future, waiting till at last
Unfold the ponderous gates, and breaks the glow
Of thy full day on each enfranchised soul.

Nay, dote not thus.   Eternity is HERE!
In thee, Eternity, I live this hour;
Not more than now shall I inherit thee
When the last fires have lapped the flowing seas
And wasted the firm earth.   Thou wast before
Time and its shifting scenes; thou art while lasts
To-day, with its bright sun and laughing hours;
Thou shalt be while unreckoned ages roll,
That shall make up the record not yet writ
Of man's long disciplines.   Whatever is, —
Being and forces finite, systems, orbs,
That, by God's fiat once divinely set
In harmony, thenceforth chime tuneful on, —
Change may know ever, but no end can know.
What seem the many do but make the one,
The mighty whole, throughout with Law instinct,
Where Love and Wisdom reign; where evermore
In grand progression silent sweepeth on
The march of all-embracing Providence.
God's secret counsels in thy bosom sleep;
Counsels that wait their hour, and thoughts divine,
Whence shall be born new worlds and wonders new;
New mysteries of life; new nameless forms
Of beauty, wisdom, strength; new truths sublime;
New purposes, whose ripening shall reveal
New marvels of his goodness; splendors new
Of all perfection, glories infinite;
And thou, Eternity, enfoldest all!
Within thee stands insphered the universe,
Substance and being; all save God himself.
He filleth thee.   He claims thee as his own;
And thine infinitude, in which is lost
Man's loftiest thought, can fathom in Himself.

Eternity!   Time is in thee ; — a part
Of that which hath no whole.   Its centuries
Are as the strokes of a vast pendulum,
That, measuring ever, leaves thee ever still
Immeasurable.   Time's histories to thine
Are nothing.   E'en the events that sounded far,
That shook the world, kindled prophetic fire,
Woke rapturous lyres, made lips grow eloquent ;
That planted empires, thrones, and dynasties,
Or these o'erthrew with vast convulsive strifes ;
The miracles of art by genius wrought ;
The massive temples, pyramids, and towers,
O'er which the suns of ages dead have watched ;
Whate'er of mortal works divinest seem,
In presence of the mighty thought of thee
To trifles sink, yet in thee are not lost.   .
Thou losest nothing.   All that earth hath seen,
Or men achieved, or shall to Time's last hour,
Thou in thy hidden depths dost ever keep,
As keeps the soul its memories and thoughts ;
The long-forgotten oft again to be
Unveiled, lived over, seen and felt anew,
With tears or smiles such as they stirred of yore.

Remember, man !   Remember, O my soul !
Thou shalt not wait till passed yon silent gates
To know the grandeur and to feel the power,
The impress, of Eternity.   E'en now,
Unconscious though thou art, o'er thee it broods,
And on thee falls its effluence every hour.   .
Say, hast thou dreamed that when the lifted veil
Should on thine eyes the eternal full unfold,

The vision would endow thee all anew;
Exalt thy thought, thine aim, enkindle flames
Of heaven's own love, and make all good thy choice,
Wisdom thy treasure, virtue thy delight?
Then let thy quickened heart now firmer beat;
Fresh in thy breast all pure affections bloom,
Like vernal flowers waked by the coming sun.
To all best deeds, deeds that shall bless mankind,
That shall most honor Him who most deserves
Thy loyal duty, give thy noblest powers.
Time's boundary thou shalt pass; this earth shalt leave;
And, seen no more, shalt thence hold on thy way,
Climbing the heights of being yet untried.
But know that now, not less than then, — to-day,
Thou dwellest in Eternity at home;
To-day its grandeurs compass thee around!

THE MOUNTAIN MAID.

WHILE riding among the Alps, you continually encounter flocks of sheep and herds of cattle, wherever there are grassy spots, under the care of young women, who stand or sit all day beside them, occupying themselves, generally, with braiding straw. There is something highly picturesque in the appearance of these herds with their fair attendants, as you find them in these mountain solitudes.

SHE sits upon the mountain side,
    The herd is grazing by;
At hand soft murmuring waters glide,
    Around cool shadows lie.

Beside her on the grass are laid
    The well-adjusted straws,
With which to weave the tasteful braid
    That o'er her knee she draws.

Upon her nut-brown cheek there glows
  Of health the blushing hue ;
Her eyes, like dew-drops on the rose,
  Are pearly, soft, and blue.

All blithe and happy is her air
  Throughout the livelong day ;
As to her breast corroding care
  Hath never found its way.

And yet she bears, full well I know,
  A tender human heart ;
Where deep and warm affections glow,
  And wishes fondly start.

Perhaps, adown in yonder glen,
  A mother's grateful smile,
As with each eve she comes again,
  Awaits her all the while.

And well the thought of such delight
  May cheer the lonely child,
As pass the hours their lingering flight,
  'Mid solitude and wild.

Perchance, as thus alone she sits,
  Intent her task to ply,
A dream of some fond lover flits
  Before her inward eye ;

And fancy paints her happy lot,
  In days when she shall be
The matron of a mountain cot,
  With children round her knee.

Perchance she hath a lofty soul,
  The gifts of genius rare,
Reads on each crag a written scroll,
  Hears voices in the air.

But what she hath of hopes or fears,
  It is not mine to know;
Yet will I wish, fair maid, thy years
  All peacefully may flow.

That time may thy best hopes fulfil,
  And all thy visions bright
Be changed to truth; yet upward still,
  Still upward be thy flight!

MORNING WATCHES.

SEASIDE, LITTLE COMPTON, R. I.

'TIS not yet dawn; from troubled sleep
    And strange bewildering dreams I rise;
Here at the casement will I keep
  Still vigils with the sea and skies:
I know not why, a tender sadness
  Broods o'er my spirit at this hour;
Perchance the dawn may bring me gladness,
  And give my soul fresh hope and power.

Yon ocean, stretching far away,
  Blends in the darkness with the sky,
Hither its low, dull murmurs stray ;
  Now hoarsely swell, now sink and die:
That restless sea is heaving ever,
  Kissed by the breeze or tempest tossed,
Type of the soul that resteth never,
  By pleasure stirred, by sorrow crossed.

But see ! o'er yonder deep afar,
  Wreathed in soft mist, yet purely bright,
Ascends the glorious morning star,
  And sheds serene her placid light:
Sweet pledge of day ! thy radiance glowing
  'Cross the dim ocean's heaving breast,
Like some kind influence o'er me flowing,
  Brings to my spirit peace and rest.

O, ever when 'mid trouble's night,
  With drooping hope and saddened heart,
I wait and watch for cheering light,
  And falls the tear unwont to start ;
May some fair messenger of heaven,
  All bright and beautiful as thou,
Be to my anxious vision given,
  And all my griefs be healed as now !

BURIAL HILL.

THE most interesting moment in the session of the National Council of the Congregational Churches, 1865, in Boston, was that when, standing on Burial Hill at Plymouth over the graves of the Pilgrim Fathers, its members solemnly reaffirmed, with prayer and singing, their fidelity to the system of Christian faith from which those noble men drew their highest inspiration.

O N Plymouth's Burial Hill we trod,
   And high each heart was beating ;
It seemed indeed " the field of God,"
   Each stone his praise repeating.

'Twas not mid chill December's blast
   O'er sea and land wild sweeping :
June's longest day, — too soon 'twas past, —
   Its carnival was keeping.

Soft skies were o'er us as we stood,
   With summer zephyrs breathing ;
We saw God's smile on field and wood,
   And flowers the earth enwreathing.

Beneath our feet the Pilgrims slept,
   The brave, the true, all lowly,
Their humble graves by angels kept ;
   The ground to us was holy.

Ah ! then all tenderly we thought,
   We thought with pride and wonder,
How, — Freedom's price divinely taught, —
   They stood unflinching yonder ;

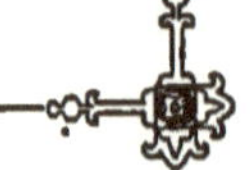

Though wintry chillness reigned around,
  And wintry winds were howling,
Though only savage man was found,
  And savage beasts were prowling.

Anew we felt their hopes and fears,
  When want and sickness wasted;
As through the lingering, weary years,
  Of sorrow's cup they tasted.

Grand souls! that with heroic will
  The waves of trouble breasted;
Not e'en did woman falter, till
  Beneath that turf they rested!

For God, for truth, for man, they bore
  Loss, exile, grief, and danger;
As Christ, the Lord they loved, of yore
  Accepted earth's low manger.

And there above their sacred dust
  Whose names shall never perish,
We vowed THEIR FAITH, a holy trust
  For all mankind, to cherish.

O God, who heard'st our prayer and song
  'Neath heaven's high dome ascending,
Bid us in thine own might be strong,
  For that pure Faith contending.

From regions wide where Plenty fills
  Her lap to overflowing;
From rugged realms where rocks and hills
  With gold and gems are glowing;

From northern lakes that, cool and bright,
　　Their sparkling waves are spreading,
To where fresh orange groves delight,
　　Perpetual fragrance shedding;

From all the wide, wide land, the cry
　　For God's good Word is speeding;
And Freedom lifts her hands on high,
　　No more enchained and bleeding!

O wake, ye sons of Pilgrim sires!
　　Go, live in power and beauty
The life sublime their Faith inspires;
　　Its watchword — GOD AND DUTY!

MOUNT WASHINGTON.

HERE let me gaze in silence.   Awed, entranced,
　　And stilled as if to worship reverently;
Moved to all thoughts most noble, pure, and calm,
To the strange heart-thrills which the vast awakes,
I seem o'ermastered by a mighty spell:
Exalted, yet subdued, my heart I yield,
In this rude solitude, to eye and ear.
Beauty and grandeur and a sense of God,
Commingled all, enchant my willing soul,
Stir it to longings vague and infinite,
Fill its profoundest depths, and hold it charmed
In tranquil wonder and sublime delight.

Ye massive domes, ye towering cliffs and crags,
Ye purple summits that lift up your brows
Bathed in pure azure, or enwreathed with clouds,
Far, far ye rise above our mortal paths, —
Paths resonant with groans and wet with tears;
And, in soft sunshine glowing, now ye smile,
As if exulting in a living joy;
As if, in ever-peaceful, grand repose,
Ye feel not the rude shocks that shake the world,
Heedless though battles rage and kingdoms fall.
Yet know I well that ye not ever thus
Serenely stand; that oft around your heads
Fierce tempests rave and cleaving lightnings gleam,
And thunders peal that from each rifted gorge
To gloomy skies are echoed awful back.
Changeless ye seem, as if in giant might,
Defying elements and hoary time,
'Twere yours the flow of ages to abide,
While man and his proud works are turned to dust.
And yet I mark that ye bear countless scars;
That down your rugged steeps torrents have swept
Gashing your sides, and avalanches plunged,
Baring your rocky breasts to sun and storm.
Exult not proudly o'er frail, mortal man,
That naught for him endures; ye too at last,
By earth's fixed, unrelenting law, shall waste.
Yet shall your term be long.   Man oft shall mourn
His perished hopes and joys; shall weep full oft
His heart's best treasures ravished all too soon;
Shall see his laurels fade, his honors die,
His empires pass, his palaces decay,
His canvas mould, his marbles crumble down,

His noblest words of eloquence and song
Lost in forgetfulness, and known no more ;
While yet unchanged your majesty remains.
O, ye are worthy, venerable forms,
That on the long-gone centuries have looked,
And wait to look on ages yet to come,
Of the deep reverence that my spirit feels.
Helpful ye are to lift my heart to Him
Whose hand of old your strong foundations laid,
And piled, with power almighty, your huge towers.
Therefore I love to climb your rocky steeps,
To note each outline, drink the spirit in
That breathes through all your glens and forests wild ;
To feel the influence of your changeful moods,
And gain from each some joy or impulse new.
I love, as now, to watch with you alone,
When morning greets you early with her smile ;
When evening bids you late a kind good-night !
When ye are holding converse with the stars,
At midnight clustering thick around your heads,
Like jewels in some august monarch's crown.
I love among the pines, far down your slopes,
When winds breathe softly in the cool, still eve,
To linger for the latest notes of birds, —
Notes sweetly tender as befits the hour ;
While rills and distant waterfalls respond,
And with their chimes the diapason fill.
Ah ! then I seem with God, and almost hear
Voices celestial speaking words of love.
And lingering still, well pleased, I dare to dream
That the soft cadences that swell and die
In your thick shades, are harmonies divine

Wafted to earth from holy choirs of heaven ;
Or greetings kind of saintly souls from whom
Long since I parted at the gate of death ;
Who, loving and well loved, were wont to speak
Words that were ever music to mine ears.

Long it were joy to stay.   But now again,
To duty's call attentive, I return,
As if from holy ground, to meet the shock
Of life's rude jars, and wrestle with its ills.
But from your base, O mountains ! I shall go
Stronger, with loftier purposes inspired,
With fresher thoughts and calmer life within,
And firmer rest in God.   His changeless pledge
Of love, and love's best gifts to faithful souls,
Shall stand when even ye, crumbled by time,
And lost by slow decay, shall be no more,
And earth itself hath vanished as a dream.

THE SONG OF THE SEVEN.

Auld Lang Syne.

THESE stanzas owe their origin to a delightful tour to the White Mountain region,
several years since, by "the seven" in their own carriages.   After wandering for several days together among the glorious scenery, they ended with an Oration by one of
the company, and the Song of the Seven by another, at the hotel of the pretty village
of Ossipee.

WE SEVEN kind souls, by friendly chance,
  Together hold our way :
All with one impulse we advance,
  Or with one will we stay.

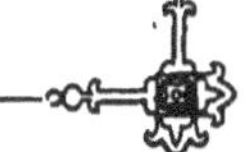

Far, far away each well-loved home,
    Our absence may regret ;
But, since awhile we needs must roam,
    We joy that we are met.

These gliding days have seen us climb
    The mountain's lofty side,
And from the top, all gray with time,
    Gain prospects rich and wide.

The valley sweet, the wandering stream,
    Green woods and arching skies,
Have seemed like some bright, lovely dream
    To our enraptured eyes.

The winding ride o'er plain and hill,
    With everchanging scene,
The headlong brook, the gentle rill,
    Calm lakes green slopes between :

The basin in the solid rock,
    Where crystal waters lie ;
The dell 'neath cliffs by some rude shock
    Left frowning dark and high :

Where, when o'er all the moon-beams sleep,
    And silence reigns profound,
Fairies may bathe, and vigils keep,
    And lightly trip it round :

Oft coming the rough way to smooth,
    The cup of balmy TEA ; [1]
And oft, our weariness to soothe,
    The merry laugh and glee :

The morning when, each day, begin
    Fresh joys and fresh desire ;
The social evening at the inn,
    Where climbs some village spire :

The peaceful hour of prayer ; the day
    Of holy sabbath rest,
When, bidding earth's best joys away,
    We worshipped and were blest :

All these our memories shall keep
    While years shall wing their flight,
As gems in fountains clear and deep
    Lie sparkling pure and bright.

All lovely forms, and shapes sublime,
    Shall float before us long ;
Shall tempt aspiring thought to climb,
    Or wake the breathing song.

When scattered far, and toil and care
    Shall cloud the troubled brow,
Fresh smiles the thought shall kindle there
    Of pleasures tasted now.

[1] A beverage of which one of "the seven" was particularly fond, and which at every hotel he gave particular directions to have made *strong !*

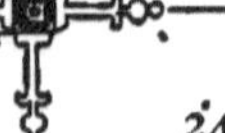

When wanderings cease with us, — THE SEVEN,
   Life's weary way all trod, —
May friendship's chain grow bright in heaven
   Around the throne of God!

THE UNKNOWN KNOWN.

O FATHER Infinite, the hidden One,
   Before all worlds Thou art.   Nor space nor time
Hath measured Thee, nor can.   Nor line nor bound
Hath limit set Thee, nor Thy power defined.
From everlasting is Thy going forth ;
Unchanging, ever-blest, all-perfect, Thou
Hast lived, hast wrought, and in Thy works rejoiced.
All substance and all being, forces all,
Of Thee are born, their primal fount and ground.
'Tis but the fool, howe'er accounted wise
By others weak as he, whose heart hath said,
No God, no God! who, in the names revered
Of science and of law, would Thee dethrone,
Thy sceptre wrest away, Thy name forget,
Forth from whose bosom law and science spring,
And of whose thought the boundless universe
Is but the grand unfolding and the sign.
Thy sovereign will is power, — the power supreme
That through the mighty whole of Nature rules
And moulds and moves and permeates evermore.
The cause of causes, Thou, the force of force,
Motion of motion, and of life the life.
Of Thee are all things, of Thee, not Thyself ;
Before all, over all, above all, Thou!

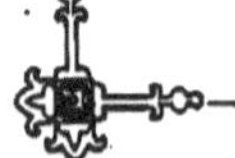

Such thoughts o'erwhelm me.   How may I unawed
Before Thy mystery unfathomed stand !
When to ascend the height, to sound the depth,
The length and breadth to scan, my kindling soul
With daring wing the venturous flight would try,
Hopeless and weary, back at length she sinks,
And veils herself before Thee and adores !

In vain with suns and stars that fill the abyss
Of space illimitable I talk of Thee,
And ask them how my feeble thought may reach
The secret awful, how may find Thee out.
From their still spheres no answer give they back,
Articulate and full, my soul to teach.
In vain, with Time communing, I demand
What, in the circuit of the ages dead,
His sleepless eye hath seen, his wisdom learned,
That my deep questionings at last may end.
He answereth not, — he hath not found Thee out.
Not e'en the first archangel near the throne,
Where light insufferable to mortal gaze,
Unveiled and cloudless, falleth evermore,
Hath all Thy grandeur and Thy fulness known,
Nor can, though ever learning, Thee reveal.

And yet I know Thee ! Know Thee, though in part ;
E'en as I know the ocean, when, reclined
On some tall cliff beside its broad expanse,
I take the circle of clear vision in ;
Feel all the vastness, note the power sublime
Of the huge tumbling billows as they foam,
And lift in deafening roar their mighty voice ;

While yet my searching eye attempts in vain
The bound to pass where sky and sea embrace,
And reaches not the hidden vast beyond!
I know Thee as I know the sun, that pours
A flood of light around me, o'er me sheds
His vital warmth, in which I live and move,
Arrays in glory all the visible world,
And gladdens my whole being; while unknown,
Unreached by thought, his thousand wonders lie.

O yes! since love ineffable Thou art,
To souls that love, Thyself Thou dost unveil
In ways ineffable.　By light divine,
Flooding their inmost being, Thou dost give
The knowledge, incomplete, but sure and true,
Of Thy great fatherhood, Thy wondrous grace,
And all Thy power and will to make them blest.
What though my spirit finite cannot take
The riches of Thine infinite being in,
Thy glory cannot bear?　Enough that Thou,
In mortal form arrayed, the Word made flesh,
To me, to all, a brother's name dost own,
Immanuel! God with men! Image express
Of the Eternal Father, known in Thee;
Thee I behold and love!　Through all my soul
I feel the throbbing pulses of Thy life
For ever flowing, and Thy brooding love
Warming my chilled affections, till to Thine
My love makes glad response; and life and joy,
And worship reverent, and pure desire,
And hope immortal fill my glowing breast.
Thou walkest with me; and Thy hand doth guide

My erring feet through each bewildering maze,
My head doth shield when life's fierce tempests beat,
And evermore my cup with good doth fill.
Thee I behold in all things ; earth and heaven,
As with one voice, declare Thee to my soul.

Ay! go, ye doubters, tell the countless tribes
That in free, gladsome life do ever rove
Through all the abysses of the mighty deep
There is no water!   Tell the joyous group
That in the genial spring-time, on the bank
Soft with fresh clover, sit and bask themselves
Beneath the noontide beam, there is no sun !
Tell ye the friend that with his friend beloved
Is wont to walk, and high communings hold,
In many a tranquil, many a twilight hour,
He knows but his own shadow, hath no friend !
When so ye are believed, then tell my soul,
That in a present God doth live and move,
That in His smile doth bask, and in the glow
Of His sweet sympathy is deeply blest,
She worships but a dream, a fond conceit,
Or, granted most, a being all unknown.
Till then be sure herself she will account
No orphaned waif, by unrelenting fate
Helpless and hopeless left, of chance the sport ;
But ever with deep joy, with holy rest,
In God her Father's love will she abide,
A trusting child, till up through parting clouds
Her way she wings and comes to his embrace!

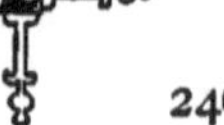

THE VOICE OF FREEDOM.

THE NEBRASKA BILL. 1854.

'TIS Freedom's voice, the joyous tone
  Swells loud and far o'er sea and main;
The tyrant, on his tottering throne,
  Shall strive to hush that shout in vain:
Man, long oppressed, awakes, and stands
With soul erect and stalwart hands.

Breaks the bright morn, in days of yore
  By holy seers so fondly sung,
When, crushed by wrong to earth no more,
  The chains shall from his arms be flung;
When all that feel oppression's rod
Shall tread the earth, — the freed of God.

Once waked and fired, the god-like soul
  Sleeps not again; no force can stay
The glancing thought that spurns control;
  Truths on it flash, as lightnings play,
While clouds and darkness thick surround,
And thunders shake the solid ground.

From Tiber's banks, from Arno fair,
  From many an Alpine cliff and glen;
From Rhone and Rhine; from Danube, where
  The Magyar waits to strike again:
Come murmurs which the day foretell,
When sounds the last oppressor's knell!

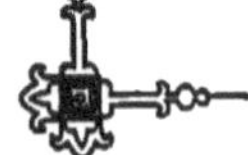

E'en the stern Turk has caught the word,
   And Mejid swears in Freedom's name ;
For Freedom flashes Omar's sword,
   And Schamyll burns with Freedom's flame ;
O'er Asia's plains her echoes sweep,
And China breaks her ancient sleep.

My native land ! my native land !
   Art thou not Freedom's chosen home ?
Her place of rest, where many a band
   Of sorrowing exiles cease to roam ?
Joy, joy to see the nations wake
To lofty deeds for Freedom's sake !

Ah ! joy thou shouldst ; but burning shame
   Mounts to the cheek, to think that thou,
Mother of heroes who o'ercame
   In Freedom's holy cause, shouldst now
Permit the bondman's groans to rise
And cry against thee to the skies !

Shade of Virginia's mighty son !
   Disturbed it not thy peaceful sleep, —
That deed of wrong, ignobly done,
   A faultless woman doomed to weep ?
Woman, — the generous, noble, kind,
Virginia, thou hast stooped *to bind !* [1]

To bind for tender pity shown
   To captives who thy bondage bear ;

---

[1] A respectable lady was just before imprisoned in Virginia for teaching some colored children to read.

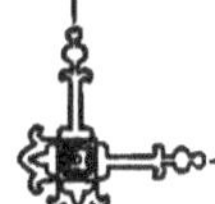

For Christ-like love, that should have sown
  The seeds of truth bedewed by prayer,
In saddened hearts by thee consigned
To shades that dim the immortal mind!

Land of my birth! shall virtue be
  In thee a prisoner sent to dwell,
Oppression's martyr, — while I see
  False, recreant statesmen Freedom *sell?*
THE WORLD'S DEEP SCORN the man must brave
Who gives Nebraska to the slave!

TO MY WIFE.

JAN. 1, 1864.

I'VE sought the city o'er to find,
  Dearest! a fitting gift for thee;
In vain! There's nothing to my mind,
  Of all the tasteful things I see.

'Tis not that works of taste and art,
  Books, pictures, jewels, I despise;
These have their uses, and impart
  Some pleasure, even to the wise.

But these are trifles to my thought,
  When this full heart would fondly prove
What price by years it hath been taught
  To set on thy pure, faithful love.

Each gift most beautiful and rare
  Seems all unequal to express
The fervent gratitude I bear
  For all thy life-long tenderness!

To every year that speeds its flight
  Each must, 'tis said, some grace resign ;
But flying years, to my pleased sight,
  Add grace to every charm of thine.

Thy riper judgment, richer mind,
  Enlarged experience, firmer will,
Leave no regrets for days behind,
  But bless and satisfy me still.

Time, the arch-robber, hath no power
  To steal thy solid worth away ;
He cannot touch thy peerless dower
  Of virtues that know not decay.

My heart's best offering, dearest, take ;
  Its changeless love, its steady trust ;
'Tis thine till earth's last tie shall break,
  And I shall sleep in silent dust.

Ay, where immortal life shall glow,
  Where endless years serenely glide,
Firm is my faith that I shall know
  THEE as my fair, IMMORTAL BRIDE !

THE LORD GOD IS A SUN.

I SEE the rose-bud, wet with night's cold dew,
   Smile through her tears, as if some joy new-born
Stirred at her heart.   To some deep instinct true,
   Her eyelids part, kissed by the waking morn.
Softly her wondrous beauty she reveals;
   Opens her crimson bosom full and fair,
To drink thy beams, O Sun! and, drinking, feels
   Warmed with fresh life and filled with pleasure rare.
On thee I see her waiting all the day,
   As by thine influence filled with sweet content,
And anxious only not to lose one ray,
   While thy pure glory to her gaze is lent.

So my own spirit, what time sad and chilled
   By earth's dark shadows that do close me o'er,
Looks up through streaming eyes, and smiles as filled
   With kindling joy, when Thy kind beams once more,
O God, my Sun, do chase the shades away:
   And when full-orbed Thou breakest on her sight,
My soul expands herself to catch the day;
   Athirst, her inmost being drinks Thy light,
Thy cheering warmth, all influences benign;
   Till her immortal essence, 'neath Thy glow,
Blossoms with graces, throbs with joy divine,
   And back to Thee her loftiest ardors flow!

NELLY.

I KNEW a gentle maiden,
  Her cheek was pale, but fair;
Her eye was blue, of the softest hue,
  And a golden brown her hair.

She used to cross the meadow,
  Skip nimbly o'er the stile;
Her motion light as the swallow's flight,
  Like a sunbeam's play her smile.

As o'er the grassy common
  To school she blithely went,
In grace she seemed like a fairy dreamed,
  Like an angel in content.

With every Sabbath's dawning,
  Up to the house of prayer
The maiden came, — for she loved the name
  Of the Saviour worshipped there.

She went and came so often,
  That each returning morn
My eye would stray down the winding way,
  Till she had come and gone.

One day, — the sun shone brightly, —
  I watched, but watched in vain;
With a weary eye saw the day go by,
  For she came not o'er the plain.

No more I saw her coming
  With light, elastic bound ;
The frost of death, it had chilled her breath,
  And she slept beneath the ground.

O, there was bitter anguish,
  And there were floods of grief ;
A home made sad, that before was glad,
  · In that life so bright and brief.

But goodness liveth ever,
  It cannot, cannot die ;
When lost to earth by a holy birth,
  It is born to a life on high.

And still sweet Nelly liveth
  Beyond the stars of night ;
Where all are fair, she is shining there,
  Herself a star of light !

FOREST WILDS.

'TWAS morn, — a beautiful morn of May ;
  I sought to refresh an exhausted mind ;
And I led from the stable my faithful bay,
And toward the deep forest I took my way,
  Leaving men and their haunts behind.

My path was lonely and rude ; it wound
  A devious way over hill and through glen ;

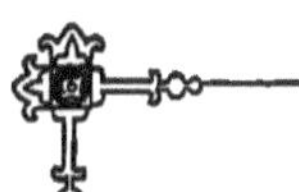

Of the tree-felling axe there was heard no sound,
But the grandeur of nature unmarred I found,
  As if Eden had bloomed again.

I pause and listen ! and hark the sigh
  Of the soft wind stealing among the trees ;
And see ! the pine waves 'mid the clear blue sky,
And the fir, as it lifts its proud head on high,
  Just nods to the passing breeze.

There a mountain stream, down a deep ravine,
  Leaps babbling by like a child at play, —
O'erbending the old moss oak is seen,
Like Age óver Youth, as the rocks between
  It rushes with foam and spray.

From the wanton school-boy's eye remote,
  The birds here nurture their unfledged young ;
And the robin, the thrasher, the blue jay's note
Like a chorus of angels seems to float
  The wild forest boughs among.

The squirrel peeps from his snug retreat,
  In the hollow trunk of an aged tree,
And along the bough trips with his fairy feet,
And frisks his tail as he takes his seat,
  As if to contemplate me !

Where yonder cliff lifts its bald, blue head,
  On a leafless branch sits an eagle proud ;
Scared at the sound of the horse's tread,
His broad, brown pinions are slowly spread,
  And he soars to the floating cloud.

O Nature! how pure, how majestic thou!
  I joy to behold thee thus lonely and wild;
And whene'er I gaze on thy beauty as now,
To the Infinite Beauty my soul would bow,
  And love like a dutiful child.[1]

THE WATCH OF LOVE.

COME, thou loved one of my heart,
  Wander with me here alone;
While day's latest beams depart,
  Be this trysting-time our own.
Here beside the tranquil sea, —
  Tranquil while the tempests sleep, —
Far the restless world shall be,
  While our watch of love we keep.

Look how on the arch of night
  Kindling stars serenely glow;
See their pure, celestial light
  Gleaming from the deep below;
Fires of heaven! ye seem to shed
  O'er our souls some influence kind,
While the lonely strand we tread,
  Closer yet our hearts to bind.

Deeper, deeper grows the shade;
  Closer, closer draw our souls;

[1] This piece was written earlier than the "Spirit's Life," and three
or four lines were transferred from it to that.

'Tis an hour for friendship made,
  That each selfish thought controls.
While o'er Nature's face around'
  Silence falls as from above,
Wake affections deep, profound ;
  O sweet mystery of love !

While the drowsy ocean heaves,
  Lulling with his murmurs low,
Tears, not as of one that grieves,
  But of those o'erhappy, flow !
As when one who fain would pray
  Deems that words the half conceal,
The few gentle things we say
  Are but signs of all we feel.

Many a hope and many a dream
  In our quickened souls arise ;
Bright enchanting vistas seem
  Opening on our eager eyes ;
Busy thought within each breast
  Strives to paint the coming scene
A fair landscape, gayly dressed
  In rich hues, with skies serene.

Yet we may not all forget
  That fierce tempests oft deform
Yonder deep, till billows fret,
  Lashed to fury by the storm ;
So swift years perchance may fling
  Storm and gloom athwart our sky ;
Cares and strifes and contests bring
  Ills from which we cannot fly.

Fear we not; to-night we know,
  While these hallowed moments glide,
While our hearts more fervent grow,
  As we wander side by side,
That where'er our steps shall tend,
  And whate'er the pains we bear,
Heart with heart shall ever blend,
  Hand to hand our lot we share.

'Twere not life to live untried,
  No stern battles fought or won;
No fond wishes e'er denied,
  No high deeds of duty done;
Nobler shall our purpose be;
  Father! witness from above
That these hearts are true to Thee,
  While we keep this watch of love!

THE RIDE.

WILLIAMSTOWN, MASS.

I.

WE rode, in genial mood, a friendly band,
  Where climbed a winding path o'er many a
    steep,
And caught from height to height, on either hand,
  Visions of beauty in the valleys deep;
There gentle Hoosic holds his peaceful way,
  With meadow banks of green, and trees o'erhung;
  There are sweet pastures where the blithe lambs play
And sober herds repose; fields where is sung

The reaper's troll, as o'er his arm is flung
   The ripened grain that for the sheaf he binds;
   There gleams the village spire; and, deep among
Thick elms and maples hid, the eye yet finds
   The classic halls whence, with each year, are sent
   Men of high soul on noble ends intent.

II.

There lift the mountains their majestic forms,
   Wearing their forest robes, a rich attire,
   Unharmed by wasting time or raging storms,
   Serene when thunders on their brows expire.
So blend the lovely and the grand around,
   Fix the pleased eye and charm the admiring soul;
   Joy warms each heart, pure, tranquil, and profound;
   O'er each, blest impulses·delicious roll;
We snatched each view, drank in each rural sound;
   The brook's dull murmur and the wind's soft sigh;
   And while, 'mid scenes of beauty on we wound,
Each troubled thought seemed in the heart to die;
   Peace filled each breast, and hope that friendship's
      chain
   Might firmly bind till perfect love should reign.

17

THRICE BORN.

I.

AGE! On my brow now falls thy frost;
    But o'er far years I wander back,
Till, as in golden mist, is lost
    All note or memory of the track
      These pilgrim feet have trod,
      Since forth they came from God:
Remote the day doth seem a thousand years,
When woke for me this life of smiles and tears.

    Unknowing, not unknown, I came,
      A gasping babe, a helpless thing,
    Unrobed as yet, not e'en a name,
      Or word, or thought, 'twas mine to bring;
        Yet was I fondly prest
        Close to a gentle breast,
In which there woke the sweet maternal love,
Of all on earth most like to God's above.

    About me, with no heed of mine,
      Earth's tenderest ministries were found,
    As if the angels all divine,
      Heaven-sent, did compass me around;
        Each feeblest cry was heard,
        And, like a callow bird
In safety nestling 'neath the covering wing,
I soft reposed till time full life should bring.

And so I knew myself, at last,
  A prattling child upon the lawn,
'Mid flowers, and swallows shooting past;
  And then like a swift-bounding fawn,
    That sports the long day through,
    Youth's strength and pride I knew;
Then on, until beneath life's climbing sun
A man I stood, its strifes sublime begun.

II.

But, Childhood, ere thy laughing eye
  Youth's graver shade began to wear,
Rose deep within my soul a cry,
  And troubled thoughts were wrestling there;
    Thy shafts, O Truth, had sped,
    Pierced was my heart, and bled,
Till Love Divine the inward storm had quelled,
Had healed the wound and every fear dispelled.

Ah! then myself I found once more
  A child, a babe, life fresh begun,—
True life in God for evermore;
  Above me shone the Eternal Sun,
    And on my opening way
    Let fall a flood of day,
As when, in the clear noon, the winds at rest,
Falls the full beam on ocean's trembling breast.

And fairer visions charmed my sight
  Than erst had gladdened childhood's morn,
Serener was the pure delight
  That kindled in my soul new-born:

Like some ascending star,
Heaven's lustrous gate afar
Gleamed clear and bright, and fixed my ravished
eye;
E'en earth in fresher beauty seemed to lie.

Then, O my Father, owned a child,
From strength to strength I learned to tread
The way, with many a song beguiled,
That heavenward, though through crosses, led.
Intent to do Thy will,
Till I may drink my fill
Of love and joy, and see, my Lord, Thy face,
Onward I press with ever-hastening pace.

III.

There waits another birth.   Not yet
This being's measure is attained;
Not yet the final seal is set,
Nor God's lost image all regained;
'Tis mine to know above
The life of faultless love;
And death, in Thee, O Christ, a birth shall be,
The last grand birth, to immortality.

Why should I tremble to be born
All-glorious, peer of angels bright?
What terror hath the effulgent dawn
Whose day God and the Lamb shall light?
Oh! when with dying throes
These eyes on earth shall close,

Forth shall I pass all vital, free, and strong,
See God's high seat and Heaven's innumerous
      throng.

Nor shall thy glories, unveiled Throne,
  O'erwhelm my soul, unused to gaze ;
Nor shall I, timorous and alone,
  See flashing splendors round me blaze ;
    The love that o'er me bent,
    And by my cradle lent
Sweet offices, at my first birth below,
Will then not less to keep and cheer me know.

O birth divine ! O bliss complete !
  In purity enrobed, to stand
Where all earth's best and noblest meet,
  Christ and His own, the spotless band.
    E'en now I catch some notes,
    As through the concave floats
The harmony of their eternal strain, —
" WORTHY THE LAMB THAT DIED, TO LIVE AND
      REIGN ! "

THE HON. WILLIAM A. BUCKINGHAM.

There are names that cannot die. That of Governor Buckingham is one of these. Without the highest advantages of education, without professional training, without ambition or desire for political distinctions, by his sound wisdom and spotless Christian integrity he attained to an eminent degree the confidence of his countrymen, and by his distinguished public services well deserved the veneration in which his name and memory are held.

I.

WHAT is true glory? . Not the loud acclaim
    Of heedless throngs that shout, they know
        not why,
Clamorous hosannas, when some favored name
For the brief hour is echoed to the sky;
Not eminence of place that sets on high,
    And gives to wield the power that rules the state;
    Nor royal splendors that enchant the eye
    In gorgeous palaces where courtiers wait;
Ambition hath not reached it when the prize
    Long coveted by strifes or guile is won;
    When, like the eagle soaring to the skies
And bathed in light beneath the unclouded sun,
    It proudly triumphs in its daring flight,
    And on a world looks down in conscious might.

II.

True glory is the lustre pure and fair
    In which exalted virtue stands-arrayed;
    No changeful, transient blaze, no meteor-glare
    That e'en while yet beheld doth straightway fade;

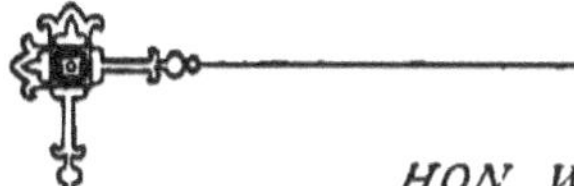

'Tis as a robe, of sunbeams deftly made,
  That glows undimmed through the long flight of
      years ;
  That whoso wears, unreached by envious shade,
  As dressed in Heaven's own livery appears :
'Tis won by patient service, loving deeds
  Wrought for mankind in firm self-sacrifice ;
  By treading the rough path where duty leads ;
By trust that e'er on God and truth relies ;
  By courage that knows not to yield, or fly,
  But, battling for the right, can calmly die !

III.

'Tis thine, O Christian statesman, thus to shine
  In vestments of true goodness undefiled,
  Wearing the virtues that are most divine ;
  By bribe unbought, by flattery unbeguiled,
Without or word or deed that, justly weighed,
  Touched with dishonor.   Goodness made thee
      great,
  When in thy country's peril, undismayed,
  All firm and steady at the helm of state,
Thy wisdom through the surging billows steered ;
  When our great Martyr proved thee prompt and
      true,
  And on thee leaned as trusted and endeared.
Henceforth, enrolled among the faithful few
  Who for mankind have lived, thy name, sublime
  In glory's light, shall glow to latest time !

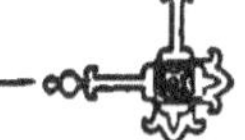

SUMMER SHADES.

FROM the scorching noontide heat
　Welcome is this cool retreat;
This dark grove, where all o'erhead
Thick, inwoven boughs are spread,
Yielding grateful, solemn shade,
E'en as for a temple made.

Silence keepeth here her reign,
Hushed is e'en the cuckoo's strain,
Save at intervals a note
That, half-audible, doth float
On the breeze that, whispering low,
Lingers as if loath to go.

Peace hath here her chosen bower,
All o'ergrown with vine and flower,
That, in close embrace entwined,
Types of friendship seem designed;
Here she bids calm thought to stay,
Wooes from aught that chafes away.

Eva, 'neath this ancient tree,
Lo! a mossy seat for thee;
Velvet ottoman it seems,
Where to lounge in waking dreams!
All the scene our stay invites,
Welcomes us to pure delights.

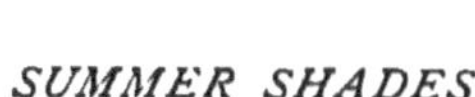

Nature, thou in hearts that love
All sweet sympathies canst move ;
Voiceless to the listening ear,
Thou hast words the soul can hear ;
Many a secret rare they tell
In lone wood and cloistered dell.

Secrets to the schools unknown,
Learned by childlike souls alone ;
Truths, that make the spirit pure ;
Balm, of power its wounds to cure ;
Spells, that work it deepest joy ;
Sweetness, that hath no alloy.

Dearest ! into souls like thine,
Quick to feel each force divine,
Scenes like this do evermore
Fresh life-currents richly pour,
Make thy softly beaming eye
Glow and flash with ecstasy !

While we drink the stillness here,
No intruding footsteps near,
All our kind affections seem
Mingled into one full stream ;
And there stealeth o'er each breast
The sweet joy of hearts at rest.

Who, O who would share the race
Of yon throng, that blindly chase
Pleasure false through glittering halls,

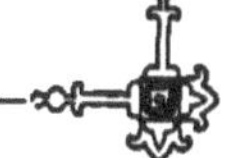

Whither with feigned voice she calls,
Oft to fix her poisoned dart
Quivering in the bleeding heart!

When on us to weariness
Life's thick-coming cares shall press,
When the noon-tide sun doth burn,
Oft our feet shall hither turn,
And where these thick shades o'erclose
Find in Nature's lap repose.

Gladder, sweeter, so shall be
Summer hours for you and me;
Pleasures true our hearts shall taste,
Purer grow as years shall waste,
Till, where noontide scorcheth never,
Joy's full cup we drink for ever!

TO MY MOTHER.

I.

MY angel mother! Long, long years have gone,
　　Since thou, yet young and fair, passed from
　　　　my sight,
　Translated to the world where all is light,
　From earth's dim shadows evermore withdrawn;
O, bright on thy awaking broke the morn
　Of life immortal; for thy soul even here
　Angelic seemed, lent to this mortal sphere,
　And waiting till the eternal day should dawn:

Yet thou did'st not forsake me when they bore
   Thee sadly forth, and fresh turf o'er thee laid ;
   E'er since, I see thy gentle face each day,
And in the silent night, and still there play
   In those soft eyes the self-same smiles that made
   Thy presence a deep joy, in days of yore.

II.

Dark mystery of death !   I may not break
   The grave's dread silence, but, O mother dear,
   Is it a dream that thou art ever near,
   And smilest on me when I sleep or wake ?
Is it not granted thee e'en yet to take,
   With that same overflowing tenderness
   That gave me at thy knee the fond caress,   .
   Kind note of all my steps ?   Let me not wake,
If dream it be, that thou my angel art ;
   That 'tis thy presence with me, though unseen,
   Which sometimes makes the tender tear to start,
And sometimes fills my soul with peace serene ;
   As when in childhood folded to thy breast,
   Thy calm, sweet look still charms my griefs to rest.

THE MAIDEN.

'TWAS on a summer evening, when the sun was
    set in flame,
And the golden hues were fading, and the twilight
    shadows came,
That I walked with one I loved, — one who felt with
    me the power
Which o'er the heart comes tenderly in nature's peace-
    ful hour.

By a river-side we walked, — 'twas a softly flowing
    stream ;
Its murmur like sweet music stealing o'er the sleeper's
    dream :
Green and mossy were the banks, clustering shrubs
    and arching trees
Here and there, beside the waters, whispered ever to
    the breeze.

If there are aerial spirits, as 'tis often said in song,
That love 'mid scenes of beauty to keep revel all
    night long,
Surely there they oft had gathered, on the moonlit
    grassy bed,
And danced their mystic dance till the morn was
    blushing red.

As arm in arm we wandered with a quiet step and
    slow,
And communed in such discourse as kindred spirits
    only know,
And, in thought, from earthly beauty mounted up to
    worlds of light
Where beauty is immortal, — ever fadeless, ever bright;

There came a plaintive voice through the stillness on
    the ear ;
Hark ! how soft and sweet its murmur, it is melody
    to hear !
We stay our steps and listen: clear on the tranquil
    air
Breaks from a leafy covert the holy words of prayer !

'Twas a gentle maiden's voice : from the busy world
    away,
To this lovely, lone retreat, at the hour of dying day,
She hath stolen out unseen, and on faith's bright wing
    she soars,
Breathing out her soul in worship to the God whom
    she adores.

We would have bowed in silence, for the place was
    holy ground;
God's awe was on the spirit, and 'twas heaven all
    around !
But profane it seemed to hear as that guileless heart
    aspired,
And we turned our footsteps silently, and from the
    spot retired.

Perhaps she came there nightly by the kindling stars
　　　of even,
To kneel upon that fragrant turf, and pray and think
　　　of heaven ;
She was, doubt not, a sweet sister, bore a faithful
　　　daughter's part,
Was in all things like an angel, — " Blessed are the
　　　pure in heart."

LEILA.

I SAW thee, Leila, when the light
　　Of youth's fresh dawn was on thy brow ;
When joy and hope and visions bright
　　Beamed in thine eyes, thou knew'st not how.

Thou wast all sweetness, and thy smile
　　Was born of thy pure, loving heart, —
A heart that knew nor art nor guile,
　　But seemed of truth itself a part.

Fair was thy neck, and round it hung
　　With careless grace thy unbound hair ;
Thy words were music, from thy tongue
　　Breathed forth as if without thy care.

In manners, motion, air and mien,
　　Thou wast as simple as a child ;
Yet to perceive wast quick and keen,
　　Not soon by idle words beguiled.

Was it strange chance that oft we met
  To while a careless hour away,
Just when the summer sun had set,
  And witching twilight round us lay?

Ah, why it was we could not tell,
  But when we met it ever seemed
As if some sweet delirium fell
  On both our spirits, and we dreamed!

We read, — but reading always found,
  Whate'er the tale or song might be,
Some influence all unknown that bound
  Our souls in closer sympathy.

We chatted, chatted hour by hour;
  Those hours, — too soon they hasted by!
We heeded not; but sure some power
  Taught them on swifter wings to fly.

I said not, — Leila, lov'st thou me?
  I read thy secret in thine eyes;
I said not, — Leila, I love thee;
  Thou wouldst have heard without surprise.

And so our souls together grew,
  Each formed to each with passing years;
We asked not how or why, nor knew, —
  Our life one joy undamped by tears.

O transient joy! O'er thy fair cheek,
  As if by stealth, strange paleness spread;
I saw what yet I dared not speak,
  What fear and hope alternate fed.

Thy face a holier sweetness wore;
 A deeper tenderness thine eye;
I heard thy ringing laugh no more,
 Nor wonted song as days went by.

I saw thy glance its lustre lose,
 Yet brighten when it turned on me;
And oft it seemed, might I but choose,
 'Twere joy to part from earth with thee!

But, no! an angel thou, and meet
 For heaven's pure bliss and nobler life;
On me earth's storms must longer beat,
 For me remained yet many a strife.

At last I stood beside the bier
 On which thy precious form was laid,
So stunned with grief I shed no tear,
 Nor heeded when the prayer·was said.

O day without a sun to cheer!
 Without a star to glow, the night!
All on before looked dark and drear,
 No cheering ray my path to light.

But, Love divine, Thy healing word
 Recalled my soul to peace and Thee;
And oft Thy gentle voice is heard
 That brings fresh hope and strength to me.

And now the hour I calmly wait,
 When Christ shall bid my steps ascend;
When, where He sits in kingly state,
 We two before His feet shall bend!

DYING WORDS OF NEANDER.

" I'm weary, — I'm weary, — let me go home !"

I'M weary, weary, — let me go !
    For now the pulse of life declineth ;
My spirit chides its lingering flow,
    For her immortal life she pineth.

I feel the chill night-shadows fall ;
    The sleep steals on that knows no waking ;
Yet well I hear blest voices call,
    And bright above the day is breaking.

Not now the purple and the gold
    Of trailing clouds at sunset glowing,
These dim and fading eyes behold ;
    But splendors from the Godhead flowing.

'Tis not the crimson orient beam,
    O'er mountain tops in beauty glancing ;
Light from the throne ! a flooding stream ;
    'Tis the eternal Sun advancing !

As oft, when waked the summer morn,
    Sweet breath of flowers the breezes bore me ;
In this serener, fairer dawn,
    Perfumes from Paradise float o'er me.

As when by sultry heats oppressed,
  I've sought still shades cool waters keeping,
So long I for that holier rest,
  Where heaven's own living streams are sweeping.

The joy of life hath been to stand
  With spirits noble, true, confiding:
O, joy unthought, — to reach the band
  Of spotless souls with God abiding!

Ye loved of earth! this fond farewell,
  That now divides us, cannot sever:
Swift flying years their round shall tell,
  And our glad souls be one for ever.

On the far off celestial hills,
  I see the tranquil sunshine lying;
And God Himself my spirit fills
  With perfect peace, — and this is dying!

Methinks I hear the rustling wings
  Of unseen messengers descending,
And notes from softly trembling strings
  With myriad voices sweetly blending.

O Thou, my Lord adored! this soul
  Oft, oft its warm desires hath told Thee:
Now wearily the moments roll,
  Until these waiting eyes behold Thee.

Ah! stay my spirit here no more,
  That for her home so fondly yearneth:
There joy's bright cup is brimming o'er;
  There love's pure flame for ever burneth!

THANKSGIVING.

NOVEMBER! draped in sullen gray,
   And veiled with withered leaves,
One ever-welcome, smiling day,
   Thy leaden gloom relieves.

Day of bright hours, that all too fast
   With noiseless feet go by,
O, give me back the buried past
   Ere thou thyself shalt die!

Let me tread o'er the misty track
   Of long, long vanished years;
Let childhood's dreamy days come back
   With all their smiles and tears.

On memory's canvas, fair and bright,
   The dear old home is drawn,
And o'er it falls the golden light,
   As of a cloudless morn.

I see the trees that hemmed it round,
   On which, each year anew,
The robin built her nest, and found
   A greeting warm and true.

I see the crib with ripened corn
   And yellow grain o'erflow,
The well-filled barn, the close-grazed lawn,
   The orchard's tempting glow.

I pass again the threshold where,
   A bounding child, I played;
When parents, brothers, sisters, there
   For me an Eden made.

I see again my father's smile;
   I hear my mother's song;
Sweet dream! so sweet, that still awhile
   I would the bliss prolong.

But onward hastes my restless thought,
   As onward trod my feet,
When, home and childhood left, I sought
   The strifes for manhood meet.

E'er since a man, with busy men,
   I've trod life's flinty path,
With crimsoned footsteps now, and then
   Amid the tempest's wrath;

Thou, loving God, my feet hast kept,
   That else afar had strayed;
Hast dried the tear when sorrow wept,
   And lit the gloomy shade!

Thy hand, o'er all the desert waste,
   My cup hath daily filled;
The Bread of Heaven hath made me taste,
   And every wish hath stilled.

Though childhood's lights and joys can greet
   No more my fond return,
Homeward, each year, shall turn my feet,
   Long as life's flame shall burn.

' Round the old hearth-stone met again,
    The old deep love shall glow,
And youthful mirth shall wake and reign,
    And hearts together flow.

O, ever-welcome, ever dear,
    Thou ancient festal day,
When home calls back to social cheer
    Its wanderers long away.

DAUGHTERS.

HAST thou a tone, O Harp, so rich, so sweet,
    That the deep, changeless love it can express,
That warms a father's heart and bids it beat
    Responsive to a daughter's tenderness?

Then would I wake with skilful touch thy strain,
    Till the full melody flow all abroad;
And, while my hand sweeps o'er thee not in vain,
    My heart shall vibrate to the quivering chord.

Dear daughters mine! whom Heaven in kindness left
    When others, dear as ye, away were borne,
To you this heart has turned as, though bereft,
    Forbidden all too much for them to mourn.

Kind ministers! Ye oft, with magic power,
    Have life's disturbing elements composed;
Have Home transformed, as to a fairy bower
    By ivy, rose, and jasmine thick enclosed;

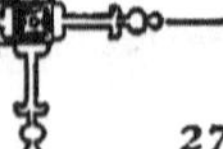

Where pure affection, from rude jars withdrawn,
    May kindle all unchecked and calmly rest ;
And fairest virtues, fresh as flowers at dawn,
    May bud and blossom in each gentle breast.

Oft when this head and heart have weary grown,
    'Mid cares and toils that crowd the passing day,
Your skill to cheer and charm full well I've known,
    Your sunny smiles have chased each shade away.

When glide those fingers o'er the tuneful keys,
    The tones wake echoes in my listening soul ;
And vocal harmonies, that soothe and please,
    In waves of music o'er me seem to roll.

Ah ! would ye knew how ever in my heart
    Live thoughts of you to me as treasures rare !
And love, that would to you all bliss impart,
    That would for you life's tears and anguish bear !

Thanks that kind Heaven hath granted me so long
    To shield you from the storms that fiercest beat ;
Thanks that ye both have learned, with courage strong,
    Where God would lead to tread with willing feet.

O Love Eternal ! through earth's fleeting years,
    Go Thou before, and guide them at Thy will !
Then, when they pass beyond the starry spheres,
    Let them abide with Thee, and serve Thee still !

PRESIDENT LINCOLN'S PROCLAMATION.

" Let my people go ! "

'TIS done ! 'tis done ! the word is spoken ;
   Oppression's final hour is nigh ;
The spell dissolves ; the charm is broken ;
   Freedom's glad shout shall rend the sky !

On the great dial-plate of ages,
   The light, advanced, no more recedes ;
On and yet on, the historic pages
   Reveal God's march to him that reads !

His word of ancient promise keeping,
   That wrong at last shall yield to right,
He comes, — no more His justice sleeping, —
   For judgment comes, and clothed with might !

His ear hath heard the bondman's groaning :
   His hand, of wrongs the score hath kept ;
His eye hath marked when mothers moaning
   Like Rachel, for their children wept.

As through the Land of Nile resounding,
   His voice rang out, — *Let Israel go !*
So rings it now, clear, loud, confounding,
   To ears that well the mandate know.

Like some swift, cleaving blow, 'tis falling
   On proud rebellion's vaunting crest;
The loyal and the brave 'tis calling
   To stand for freedom, breast to breast.

O ye who long in hopeless sorrow
   Have toiled, and wept, and seen no dawn,
There breaks, at length, a glad to-morrow;
   Wake! wake! and hail the joyous morn.

'Tis freedom's day!   Its splendor glancing
   From hill to vale shall flood the land;
'Tis freedom's sun to noon advancing:
   Chains burst, — they drop from every hand!

O, not in vain that blood is flowing
   That stains yon fields of gory strife;
With loftier hopes and wishes glowing,
   Millions are born to nobler life.

With freedom's flame glad hearts are burning;
   They throb with joy before unknown;
To visions bright glad eyes are turning,
   Gleams of a future all their own.

God haste it!   Holy souls are praying,
   Come freedom's hour with swiftest speed!
God haste it! long, ah! long delaying,
   Now, now our hosts to victory lead!

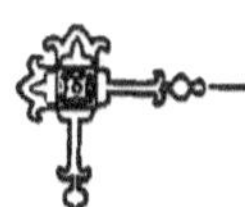

RESTLESSNESS AND REST.

I.

O TELL me where the skies are fair,
  Where mist and gloom brood never;
Where rise no fears and fall no tears,
  But gladness reigneth ever.

O tell me, pray, where no decay
  All loveliness must wither;
Show me some spot where death reigns not,
  And guide my footsteps thither.

Long tempest-tossed, oft well-nigh lost,
  With raging seas contending,
Some haven kind I fain would find,
  These toils and perils ending.

Give me a home, no more to roam
  Thenceforth, a lonely stranger;
A home secure, with joys all pure,
  That knows nor dread nor danger.

Some region blest, where peace and rest
  Abide, I would discover;
Where heart from heart no fate must part,
  No force wrench loved from lover.

Where zephyrs sweet with perfume greet,
  Nor fade for aye the flowers;
Where soft light gleams on tranquil streams,
  And sleeps on summer bowers.

All idly still its depths to fill,
  This restless soul is pining ;
Yet pines in vain, — with ceaseless pain
  Sees hope's bright star declining.

For life I long, where fresh and strong,
  Her vigor never waning,
My soul may climb to heights sublime,
  New visions ever gaining.

Where noble deeds win noble meeds,
  And glory is no bubble ;
Where joy's glad sun his race shall run,
  Undimmed by shade of trouble.

Where spirits blest profoundly rest,
  Their fruitless searchings ended ;
Yet vital still, achieve at will,
  No weariness attending.

II.

O mortal, hear !   A Friend is near,
  Whose heart to thee o'erfloweth ;
Thy love He seeks, to thee He speaks,
  Thy deep unrest He knoweth.

About thy path his way He hath,
  Though ne'er His tread thou hearest ;
Thy steps with power He keeps each hour,
  And in thy strait is nearest.

If tempter charm, or work thee harm,
  Thy heart's strongholds assailing,
To break the spell He knoweth well,
  Each deadly art unveiling.

All thou wouldst gain, hast sought in vain,
  And yearned for in thy sorrow,
Hast missed each day with feet astray,
  And sought again each morrow ;

With love's sweet care He doth prepare,
  And giveth without measure ;
Beyond thy thought and all unbought,
  Gives He the soul's best treasure.

From earth afar, beyond night's star,
  There is a sky unshaded ;
A clime all bright with God's own light,
  By no heart-pang invaded.

Lift up thine eye ! That home on high, —
  How like the sun it gloweth !
Within those gates a glory waits,
  Such as no mortal knoweth.

There, there at length, is life in strength,
  And being full of blessing,
And honor fair thy brow shall wear,
  Thy feet that pavement pressing.

O, there no more shall love deplore
  Its richest treasures wasted ;
For joy soon fled and beauty dead,
  No bitter cup be tasted.

Deep there shall glide the placid tide
 Of peace serene, eternal,
And high pursuit shall reap its fruit,
 Through seasons ever vernal.

Once reached that goal, thy longing soul
 Shall ache with longings never;
Thy spirit filled, its wishes stilled,
 In God shall REST FOR EVER!

TO TILLIE ON HER BIRTHDAY.

METHINKS that on this joyous natal morn,
 Backward, dear girl, thy gentle thought hath
  strayed,
And 'mid the golden blushes of the dawn
Of early childhood thou again hast played.
Ah! beautiful in the dim past appears
 That early twilight when all things were fair;
 When blithe birds carolled to the morning air,
 And thou as yet didst feel no boding fears:
Sweet memories! As they rise, thine eye doth wear
 A tender look, half sorrow and half joy!
 For childhood's dreams are vanished, and now care,
And sober thoughts, and noble aims employ
 Thy earnest woman's soul; the future calls;
 On! on! God give thee strength till evening falls!

VAUCLUSE.

Passing the bridge, you stand in front of a grand cliff rising perpendicularly nearly eight hundred feet. You ascend by a winding path along the rapid stream to the base of the mountain, and there, under the shelving rock, you find a natural reservoir, some fifty feet across, and said to be on one side more than a hundred feet in depth. The sun never shines into it. The water lies perfectly tranquil, is of the deepest blue, and, on the shallower side, you can see the pebbles go shelving down as far as the eye can follow them.

I.

STERN, solemn, grand, far up the dark blue heaven,
   Thou old gray cliff, thou heav'st thine awful form !
  On the wide waste of years a beacon given,
   Lonely and bare, and scarred by time and storm ;
·Hard at thy base, where all day shadows sleep,
   Spreads the wide grotto, overarching high ;
   Adown its mossy sides the cold tears weep,
   And in its lap the crystal waters lie,
In sweet repose, as if there ventured nigh
   This still retreat no rude disturbing power ;
   No sound to pain the ear, no sight the eye ;
Peace was not more profound in Eden's bower ;
   Far down the depths the pebbly slope is seen,
   Then azure shades unpierced by vision keen.

II.

'Tis such a spot as poets oft have sung,
   Or fancy pictured in her wildest dream ;
   A spot the which, while yet the world was young,
   Had peopled been with Naiads, and the stream,

Along whose murmuring course sweet odors breathe
 From beds of fragrant thyme and roses wild,
 Had been the haunt of Fays, that came to wreathe
 Their flowery garlands when the moonbeams smiled;
Now gushing forth through portals all unseen,
 And bubbling upward to the light of day,
 It dashes onward the rough rocks between,
With sparkling foam,—then sweeps its winding way
 Down the long steep,—then its rash speed re-
  strains,
 And bears fresh beauty to the blooming plains.

III.

Petrarca's Fountain! Yes, thou bear'st his name;
 A name that distant ages shall rehearse;
 A name that soareth not alone to fame,
 Married to Laura's in immortal verse!
Oft came he musing to the cooling shade,
 When scorched the summer's sun with noontide ray;
 At twilight thither oft his footsteps strayed,
 To while with thee the pensive hour away:
Now, seated thoughtful by thy rocky side,
 A soft, kind influence steals through all his soul;
 Bright, airy visions now before him glide;
Now, mark the tears of tenderness that roll!
 Fixed is his gaze, but the winged soul is free;
 He *thinks* on LAURA, though he *looks* on THEE![1]

---

[1] These sonnets, more than any others, perhaps, should have been constructed on the Petrarchian model, considering the *genius loci*. But, written as they were immediately under the inspiration of the visits, the author thought of nothing, at the time, but of giving expression to what he felt. The older English writers, however, as Shakspeare, for example, commonly used this simple construction.

SUNSET.

" Sol occidit, nulla nox secuta est."

I SEE the sun of life descend ;
   The mountains gather deeper blue,
The shadows on the plain extend,
   The forests wear eve's saffron hue.

I know that sun, ere long, must set,
   And darkness shut the eye of day ;
That night's chill dews this brow must wet,
   Where thinly spread these locks of gray.

Ye silvery paths, that childhood's feet
   Through many a dreamy hour have prest !
Ye fairy scenes that, all too fleet,
   Swept by like visions of the blest !

Far, far away your morning, bright
   In cloudless beauty, seems to lie ;
Then earth and heaven were bathed in light,
   And rich in splendors, — soon to die !

Long gone the years of youthful prime,
   When life was strength and striving play ;
When duty's rugged steeps to climb
   My heart beat quick and asked the way.

Thou, manhood ripe, art left behind ;
   Thy many a battle lost or won,
Thy many a burning hope resigned,
   Thy many a patient labor done !

Not all in vain the toil and care,
  When on thy hard fought fields I stood,
Well pleased each contest high to share,
  For God and duty, with the good.

Yet might I vanished years bring back,
  I would not choose their round restore ;
Lest smaller joy should mark their track,
  Or pangs yet keener than before.

Why should I ask again to try
  Pleasures once chased with eager feet,
That in the tasting seemed to die ;
  To cheer a famished soul, unmeet ?

Why should I wish afresh to drink,
  At sorrow's hand, the cup of gall ?
Or press in tears the grave's dark brink,
  Wide yawning to engulf my all ?

No ; pains and perils of the past,
  Enough, — enough !   Return no more !
The sailor, near his port at last,
  Would not rewake the tempest's roar !

Though steals the deepening twilight on,
  And day's last beams must soon depart,
Yet deem I not that joys are gone,
  Nor onward tread with saddened heart.

Ah ! life is more than earth's brief years ;
  Beyond, there wait, — O gift divine ! —
Ages that know nor pangs nor fears,
  But life's perfection, — these are mine !

Then, sunset, bring the welcome shade ;
  Though o'er me deepest darkness lowers,
No terrors shall this breast invade,
  No vain regrets for vanished hours.

O Love! that all my steps hast led,
  To thy dear hand I trustful cling ;
O blessed night! that, swiftly sped,
  Heaven's sweet and holy dawn shalt bring.

TO MY SISTER.

ON HER WEDDING DAY.

THE hour is come, my Sister,
  When thou givest thy plighted hand,
And the nuptial throng are gathered,
  A youthful, brilliant band :
Each heart is filled with gladness,
  As the bridal wreath they twine,
And 'twere wrong that a shade of sadness
  Should cloud that brow of thine.

True thou leavest now, my sister,
  Youth's bright and careless ring,
And graver thoughts await thee,
  And cares in thy pathway spring ;
Yet let not a tear-drop falling
  O'ercast thy smiles to-day,
'Tis the voice of love that's calling
  From the old dear scenes away.

The heart thou hast loved, my sister,
  The heart thou hast loved is warm ;
Doubt not thou wilt find it faithful,
  True alike amid calm and storm :
In the calm it will tenderly cherish,
  In the storm it will firmly defend,
And, though other trusts may perish,
  This, this shall not fail till life end.

I have loved thee well, my sister,
  I have watched thee many a year ;
Can I see thee from me passing,
  And stay the uprising tear ?
Yes, go ! long nurtured flower,
  Yes, go ! and I'll not repine ;
Though plucked from my own dear bower,
  I yield thee, — thy joy is mine.

Heaven send thee its blessing, dear sister,
  The light of God's love be o'erthrown,
The angels be ever around thee,
  Thy heart be as blest as my own :
Then when death, which earth's ties must
     dissever,
  Shall bear thee o'er the dark tide,
Go wander and love for ever,
  The calm waters of heaven beside.

TO DEATH.

MEN wrong thee, Death !
    They fashion thee a monster grim,
  With lifted dart,
Intent to strike thy victim's heart ;
The light of day to quench for him,
To wrench him from his joys away,
And doom to moulder in decay,
  The turf beneath.

  Thou seem'st a foe ;
And mortals quail to see thee come
  With tread so still,
With sable robe and breath so chill,
And finger beckoning to the tomb,
Thy heralds hollow groans and sighs,
And breaking hearts and streaming eyes, —
  All signs of woe.

  To shun thy hour
The living deem the chief of cares ;
  With hurried flight,
As from some horrid spectral sight,
They speed till their hot haste prepares
The worn-out springs of life to break,
And thine an easy triumph make
  O'er mortal power.

The few who dare
To seek thee are the rash, the mad,
    In frenzy wild,
By some delirious dream beguiled ;
The wretch, the hopeless, blindly glad
From present misery's rack to fly,
And reckless, though they see on high
    Thy shaft made bare.

What hidden lies
Beyond thy bourne for souls unshriven,
    By guilt deep stained,
When at the eternal bar arraigned,
Where just award to each is given,
Thy victims, Death, may well appall,
Whom no celestial voice shall call
    Heavenward to rise.

To Faith's keen eye
Thou, Death, art life ; 'tis but to sense
    That thine are dead ; .
No cruel shaft by thee is sped ;
'Tis not thy will that hurries hence,
Sets life's brief limit and ordains
The gloom, the sorrows, and the pains
    That speak thee nigh.

Heaven's high behest
All these hath fixed for wayward man ;
    Offspring of sin,
The terrors round that gate have been
Through which, ere since thy reign began,

All mortal steps must tread to see
The dawn of immortality,
 Its visions blest.

 Kind Death! 'Tis thine
To cool the fever of the brain,
 At once to still
Of fretted nerves the torturing thrill,
To end the lingering days of pain,
To dry all tears for evermore,
To lift the veil that hid before
 The Home divine.

 When lifted high,
The Son of God in anguish hung,
 And on His head
The burdens of a world were laid,
Till groans from His parched lips were wrung;
'Twas thine to come with sweet relief,
To end the Sufferer's mighty grief
 In one last sigh!

 From yon blest shores,
When souls redeemed shall backward turn
 To look on thee,
All beautiful thy form shall be;
Thy ministries, once deemed so stern,
Shall seem sweet ministries of grace
For ever to unveil the face
 That Heaven adores!

     Death! Death! The word
No more shall be a name of fear,
     My joy to kill,
While years, or days, life's measure fill;
My soul, when she thy voice shall hear,
Aside her mortal robe shall cast,
Stretch her swift wing and mount at last
     To meet her Lord!

SONG: THE WIFE.

WHEN through dark wilds and doubtful
      mazes,
  O'er thorny paths perplexed I rove,
And many a luring meteor blazes,
  And patience many an hour hath strove;
When worn with care, my spirit sinking,
  No more elastic, strong, and free,
Despondency's sad draught is drinking,
  And hopes like fading shadows flee;
Oppressed, half-weary of my life,
Thou art my solace, faithful wife!

Like some lone spot of verdure springing,
  The desert's dreary waste to cheer,
Which, chance the weary wanderer bringing,
  Yields soft repose by fountains clear;
E'en thus, on earth's wide desert smiling,
  Appears my home, one fairer spot,

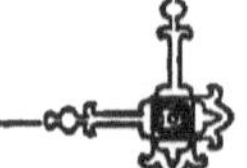

Where joy springs fresh, each care beguiling,
  And noise and discord enter not;
Of home, bright resting-place of life,
Thou art the soul, my noble wife!

When, duty's urgent call obeying,
  I wander from that home and thee,
My truant thought is ever straying
  Backward thy gentle face to see;
And when again my footsteps turning
  Bear me thy warm embrace to meet,
That thought with fond impatience burning
  Sweeps onward than the wind more fleet,
And stays not till, life of my life,
It rests with thee, my charming wife!

When comes at length the hour of meeting,
  I give and take the fervent kiss;
Oh, with the thrill of such a greeting
  Can earth compare another bliss?
The joy of that eternal union
  That ransomed spirits round God's throne
Unites in heaven's own blest communion,
  Excels it, but excels alone;
That be it mine, to endless life,
With thee to share, my angel-wife!

THE SPIRIT'S LIFE.

THE following poem was delivered before the Literary Fraternity, Waterville College, and the Porter Rhetorical Society, Theological Seminary, Andover, at their anniversaries, August and September, 1837.

WHEN from her course, o'er stormy billows driven,
　　Some gallant ship on fatal rocks is riven,
The hapless sailor, cast upon the shore,
To see his home and native land no more,
Deems all around him desolate ; and vain
The hope that he shall e'er be glad. again :
But when revolving years prolong his stay,
They steal, by slow degrees, his gloom away ;
Till used, — the heart is o'er the world the same, —
To call it Home, — he loves it for the name.

So is it with us all : since when exiled
From the dear spot where early Eden smiled,
Where perfect man 'mid perfect beauty trod,
And innocent, like angels, walked with God,
Strangers and friendless on the lone world thrown,
We sigh for blooming seats no more our own :
But doomed returnless, wisdom bids us prove
What ills we may but suffer, what remove :
By hard experience taught the priceless skill
From sorrow joy to draw, and good from ill,
Yet a few flowers we teach around to grow,
And though we reach not bliss, escape from woe.

We live a twofold life: the grosser sense,
Allied to earth, must draw its life from thence;
A life oft harassed by unfilled desire,
Whose joys are transient, and whose hopes expire:
Not by the noble mind too highly prized,
Nor yet, by God appointed, all despised.

The Spirit, of an essence half divine,
Hath its own proper life; nor may resign
The high prerogative, that bids transcend
Dull sense, and make the invisible its end,
Its home the universe.   It LIVES but where
It finds the PERFECT and the TRUE and FAIR.

Not they who eager throng the crowded mart
Where Fortune waits her favors to impart;
Nor they who sit where pleasure wreaths her bower;
Nor they who climb the giddy heights of power;
Nor they who curious rove from clime to clime;
Nor they whom learning tempts to plunder time, —
Attain what may the inward thirst supply,
And gild life's moments as they hasten by:
'Tis theirs whose youth, whose manhood, and whose
    age
The BEAUTIFUL, the TRUE, the GOOD, engage.

Say what is Beauty, and direct us where.
What hearts may feel, but never words declare.
'Tis nature's mystery, — a silent spell,
That chains the soul like music's gifted shell;
'Tis the pleased spirit's harmony; the thrill
Of chords by unseen fingers touched with skill;

Of power to calm, when stormy passions move,
And wake the soul to tenderness and love.

Where is it, askest thou : expand thy soul
To grasp of finite things the mighty whole :
Scan with attentive eye each part in turn ;
The stars that glitter, and the suns that burn,·
Far as the assisted orb can stretch its view :
The broad expanse, where God's own finger drew
The path of moving worlds, through which they urge
Eternally their flight, nor once diverge :
The azure air, where fleecy clouds repose,
And float majestic as it ebbs and flows ;
Or kindle in the sun's departing glow ;
Or, darkly frowning, arch the mystic bow :
The sea, that moaning heaves its foaming crest,
Or sleeps unruffled, when the tempests rest :
The earth, that once accursed when sin began,
Forgetful of the wrong still blooms for man :
Morn, when it purples all the eastern hill :
Eve, when the stars are mirrored in the rill :
All nature's noble· face is bright and fair,
The smile of beauty plays for ever there.

But nicer shades the searching eye may trace ;
Minuter study shows diviner grace :
Each single object, perfect in each part,
Each scene complete, with wonder fills the heart.

Exchange the busy city or the town
For the lone wilderness.   There sit thee down
Where waves the pine amid the clear blue sky,
And greets the breathing zephyr with a sigh :

The Gothic fir, that lifts its head in pride,
Nor bows, though tempests sweep the forest wide,
Stands in still majesty.   Encircling round,
A thousand names in wild disorder found
Blend all their thousand shades of varied green,
And open far retreating glades between.
Like a fair child at play, the mountain stream
Leaps babbling by, and sparkles in the beam
That falls where parted boughs a path disclose:
Athwart the old moss oak its long arms throws,
As age bends over youth; while o'er the brink
The rose and lily stoop, as if to drink.
The timid fawn is there to slake his thirst:
The thrasher and the blue jay safe have nursed
Their unfledged young, and pour their clear wild notes,
That one may deem an angel chorus floats:
And flowers by God's own care unnumbered spring,
And 'mid the maze of beauty fragrance fling.

Turn next where man essays, with patient toil,
To disembowel earth; and mark the spoil
Which forth he drags, his labor to repay.
See where the sunbeams on the crystal play,
Or fall, refracted by the brilliant gem,
Destined to grace a monarch's diadem;
Note the bright masses of the precious ore,
Henceforth to swell the rich man's coffered store:
On all the products of the teeming mine,
Beauty is writ in characters divine.

Or, leaving nature, fix thy roving thought
On the fair works that human skill hath wrought.

Eternal Rome's proud Vatican go tread ;
Rich mausoleum of the gifted dead :
Where sculpture bids the marble bosom heave,
The lip to utter, and the eye to grieve ;
Give to the wretch Laocoon a tear ;
Or gaze in silence on the Belvidere ;
Pause where, with pencil dipped in magic dye,
Painting transcends all hues of earth and sky ;
And while thy rapt soul feels the mighty spell
Of gorgeous Titian, or bold Raphael,
That fixed in wonder, thou couldst ever wait,
Learn what the beauty genius can create.

And there is beauty on the classic page ;
Immortal product of each perished age :
Where graphic Homer, master of the lyre,
Or melts to pity, or inflames to ire :
Where Plato, half divine, intensely soars,
And wide, unfathomed realms of thought explores :
Where breathes, chaste Virgil, thy sweet, tuneful lay ;
Or the thronged forum owns rich Tully's sway ;
Or where Petrarca sighs in later time ;
Or Dante's numbers roll, — dark, wild, sublime ;
Or our own Milton, with adventurous flight,
Sweeps heaven and hell, and " chaos and old night ; "
Where gentle Addison provokes a smile,
And to fair virtue wins the heart the while ;
Or splendid Burke pours his exhaustless stream ;
Or Johnson kindles on the moral theme.

But close the eye of sense, and thou shalt find
Yet fairer forms of beauty in the mind.

The inward eye hath vision more serene;
It sees a world no eye of sense hath seen;
Ideal all, transcendent, ever bright:
Imagination thither bends her flight,
Bids the charmed soul 'mid radiant forms to range,
And hues that fade not, yet for ever change;
And there where soft eternal sunlight gleams,
Find calm repose, and dream bright glorious dreams!

AND WHAT IS TRUTH? Thou Source of truth
     benign,
Light in whose light we see, to say is Thine!
'Tis the great sum of all Thy will hath wrought:
The antitype of THINE ETERNAL THOUGHT.

Go, grave inquirer, search the plan profound,
Of God ordained, or ever years rolled round;
Which firmly fixed what nature's laws we call,
That bid the planet roll, the pebble fall;
That atoms join, by close attraction held,
Or sever, by repulsive force impelled;
That send the Spring's sweet blush, the Summer's
     bloom,
The Autumn's riches, and the Winter's gloom;
That all the changes of all things control,
And bind in wondrous harmony the whole.

· Enter man's inmost soul; the search pursue:
A voice, than Delphic oracle more true,
Shall utter its response, nor once deceive
What ear may listen, or what heart believe;
Shall whisper truth by intuition taught,
Or drawn by reason from the wells of thought:

Shall bid thee to the Infinite ascend,
To God, Eternity, thy being's end;
Reveal thee subject to the changeless throne,
And speak unending ages all thine own.

The Book of God unfold.   There radiant shine,
By his own Spirit written, truths divine.
Lo! where thick clouds and flame his way attend,
On shuddering Sinai's top the Lord descend!
While the shrill trump affrights the startled ear,
And thrills the heart, rebellious Israel hear
Man's sum of duty down to latest time,
By God's own awful voice pronounced sublime.
The harp of Prophecy, in lofty lays,
Pours the rich notes of truth in after days:
Till He whose name is Truth, bright Morning Star,
Bursts on the world and spreads his beams afar!

O sacred Truth!   Say if thou may'st be found
Above, beneath, within us and around;
Why from the many liest thou all concealed?
Why to the favored few alone revealed?
Methinks I hear thy gentle voice reply,
'Tis these alone that search with single eye:
The many, or with pride or passion blind,
But seem to seek, and therefore may not find.
The schoolman, learned, mystical, acute;
The pedant, vain, conceited, and astute;
The skeptic, ever on suspicion bent,
To evidence too weak to yield assent;
The caviller, who each argument gainsays,
Of tact or wit ambitious of the praise;

The reckless, who, if Truth or stand or fall,
Alike unheeding, never think at all;
Such, self-deluded, I forsake to cheer
The childlike spirit, humble, yet sincere.

CELESTIAL GOODNESS! may we speak thy name,
Nor feel each cheek consume with burning shame?
We've banished thee!   Yet deign'st thou to return,
With them to linger who unheed or spurn?
Ah! how unlike this sombre world of crime,
Of violence and wrath, to that fair clime,
Thy native seat, where myriad harps are strung
To hymn thy praise, and dulcet strains are sung!
Earth's hapless region, grating discords fill;
Dark malice roams unchained, intent on ill,
And leering envy lurks in many a breast,
And reign insatiate lusts that know no rest:
Now calumny lets fly the envenomed shaft;
Now murder grimly pours the noxious draught;
Or strength gives weakness to rewardless toil;
Or lawless rapine revels in its spoil;
War fiercely waves the desolating brand,
And scatters ruin o'er a smiling land;
And peaceful where the towering city stood,
Leaves smouldering ruins reeking human blood.

Yet Goodness hath not bid the earth farewell.
Come with me to yon lowly cot, where dwell
Want's wretched children.   Pale disease is there:
The ghastly cheek and wasted limbs declare
Its mortal ravages: the fevered head
Throbs restless on the hard and cheerless bed:

It is a widow pines ; doomed to behold
Victims of hunger, nakedness, and cold,
Her lonely babes ; and many a bitter tear
Weeps for them fatherless, — no friend is near !
But stay.   Like some kind ministering angel sent,
A gentle stranger comes, to soothe intent
The sufferer's anguish, and to bring relief
To instant woes ; while for the soul's deep grief
She offers balm eternal love hath given,
And points the dying eye to God and heaven !

Come listen to the pining prisoner's moan :
'Mid the deep dungeon's gloom, desponding, lone,
He lies immured, remote from cheerful day,
To noxious air and foul disease a prey.
No mother's love, no tender sister's smile,
No wife's caress the dreary hours beguile ;
Too blest might end his anguish with his breath,
Impatient chides he the slow pace of Death.
Hark ! swings the massy door with grating sound !
'Tis but the warder treads his daily round :
No ! there are tones of kindness : how they roll
Like waves of blessedness o'er that crushed soul,
Long, long resigned to desolate despair !
Some Howard, breathing goodness, enters there.

Where Gunga wanders to the distant main,
Embanked by spicy grove and blooming plain,
Come sit thee down awhile.   The sultry day
Is o'er ; and gorgeous twilight fades away
In the far west ; cool down the rippling stream
The perfumed breezes sweep, while every beam

The moon lets fall from the transparent sky
To greet the wave, reflected meets the eye.
And all is silent, save the measured dash
Of yonder oars, that in the soft light flash.
How beautiful!   But hark! that piercing cry,
That tells some tortured heart's deep agony!
See! 'tis a mother! and her arm hath pressed
Her cherub infant closely to her breast!
Ah! 'tis her last embrace, or e'er she throws,
And o'er the innocent the waters close!
Stay, frantic mother! nor unclasp thine arm!
Lay not thine hand upon thy babe for harm!
A voice as if from heaven, ere yet too late,
Prevents the sacrifice, arrests the fate.
Yes! there is one shall bid that mother care,
With nature's yearning, for the babe she bare;
From home self-banished, and from kindred dear,
He came to light her soul, to calm her fear;
And so he may but lift her thoughts on high,
Consents 'neath burning suns to toil and die!

If finite Goodness move thee to admire,
Thy soul shall to the perfect next aspire:
Thirst for the Infinite, resigned no more
To dwell with sin and hate, and upwards soar:
Through purer regions, worlds serenely bright,
And ranks of spotless beings, urge its flight;
And past all things create, shall last ascend
To God Supreme, in Him the quest to end.

O, come the better day, when every gale
That sweeps from heaving hill or sunny vale

Shall sweetly breathe of purity and peace!
When passion's rage and party strife shall cease:
When Learning, from her venerated halls,
Shall send forth sons whom no fierce summons calls
To noisy conflict, that lays waste the mind,
Nor leaves one noble sympathy behind;
When like the surges spent upon the shore,
The waves of tumult shall forget to roar:
Society grow calm; and men begin,
Withdrawn from outward life, to live within.
That life earth's every joy shall twice endear;
Give nature language, and the soul an ear;
Make reason utter truth, the soul approve,
And pure affections the pure spirit move!

Ah! who would quench the nobler spirit's fire
In sensual life, — the life of low desire?
Who spurn the holy birthright nature gave,
To be ambition's fool, and pleasure's slave?
Let such, inglorious and perversely blind,
Grasp meaner things, and madly starve the mind;
Ignoble let them live, and nameless die,
And "Infamy" be written where they lie!

But ye, whom loftier purposes impel
To choose the richer meed of living well:
Who feel the spirit's heaven enkindled flame
Mount upward to the source from whence it came;
And nerve your fervent souls for worthier strife,
Instinct with inward energy and life:
Ye gaze, alternate filled with hopes and fears,
Adown the vista of approaching years,

As conscious many a storm shall fierce assail,
And trembling, lest or strength or courage fail;
That ye may calm abide, when billows roll,
Commune with God, with Nature, and the Soul:
Nurture the Spirit with a Spirit's food;
O, love the BEAUTIFUL, the TRUE, the GOOD!

CLOUDS.

WRITTEN during an extraordinarily protracted season of cloudy weather in November and December, in which, for five or six weeks, dull, leaden-looking clouds covered the sky, with very little rain, scarcely a few hours of sunshine breaking the oppressive monotony.

WE looked when wintry winds should sweep,
   For bright blue skies and clear keen air,
That should all life in motion keep,
Make glad the soul to its lowest deep;
   Should bid all faces a lustre wear,
Give nerve to climb the slippery steep,
   Or over the smooth ice firm and strong
   With glee and shouting to course along.

But dull gray clouds for days have spread
   O'er the wide arching heaven; and earth
Hath lost its smile, its glow hath fled,
As if no sun were high o'erhead;
   And hearts are heavy, and joy and mirth
Are half suppressed, or wholly dead:
   Life hath put on a sombre hue,
   And eyes look drooping and words are few.

So nicely are our spirits strung
   Responsive to each sound or sight;
The plaintive wail by the wild wind sung,
The leaden look of the sky o'erhung
   With vapors that darken the day's pure light,
Bring sadness, like cypress shadows flung
   Darkly athwart our path, till slow
   And solemn the tread, as we come and go.

Break forth, bright, ever-shining sun!
   These brooding, earth-born mists dispel;
In the blue serene thy circuit run,
Pouring thy splendor till day is done;
   Till with glad thoughts our bosoms swell,
And all life seems as if fresh begun:
   Full of vigor and hope and power,
   Crowding with deeds each joyous hour.

O for that fairer clime, where flow
   Eternal days of health and gladness!
Where never a howling wind shall blow,
Nor cloud the gloom of its shadows throw,
   To tinge the immortal life with sadness;
No dreary moments that life shall know,
   For while the unending cycles fill,
   The UNVEILED THRONE shall be cloudless still!

THE VIOLET'S COMPLAINT.

WHAT meaneth this? Methought the friendly
      Spring,
With glowing cheeks and smiles and perfumed breath,
Had come again, — grim Winter fled at last, —
To set up her glad reign. I heard her steps
Advancing, — so it seemed, — and, watching, saw
Her light robes waving in the sportive wind,
And knew her gladsome voice. Through every nerve
I felt the thrill of a new-waking life,
With vital warmth rekindling, after sleep, —
The long undreaming sleep 'neath wintry drifts, —
And trustingly unrolled the leaves that wrapped
And shielded me, baring my head, that now
Ached for the blessed sunshine. Ay, yet more,
All fearlessly I turned the drapery back,
And opened wide my bosom to drink in
Each vernal influence kind. O fickle maid,
Thou hast deceived me! Thou art a coquette,
Toying with Winter, who, beguiled by thee,
Lingers in dalliance long beyond his hour!
I feel his icy touch. Cold on my breast
Unveiled the chilling sleet and snow descend,
Freezing my life-blood, pressing me to earth,
And marring my fresh beauty. Cruel one!
How shall I trust henceforth thy promise fair
Or heed thy wooings and thy fond caress,
When thou wouldst call me forth? Thou shouldst be
      left

Without a flower wherewith to deck thy hair;
Without one pansy, violet, or rose
To sleep upon thy bosom, or to breathe
The odors that thou lovest round thy head.

All this and more thou hast deserved ; and yet
Full well I know that, should I but survive
This dreariness, and once more see thy face,
And hear thy train of songsters in the groves,
And all thy witching influences feel,
I shall forget this wrong, — shall straight relent,
And greet thee as of old, and to thy sense
Yield my best fragrance and my loveliest hues,
Thenceforth content to live and bloom for thee!
Such is thy power, — thy magic power, — to steal
The hearts of flowers ; and such the instinct deep
By Heaven implanted in the violet's breast.

THE BIRTHDAY.

MAY 2, 1834.

TO-DAY just eight-and-twenty years,
    A day of mingled hopes and fears,
Remembered well, though now afar,
Rose on the world an unknown star.
Unknown, yet not unlooked for, came
The trembling thing without a name!
Emerging from the eternal deep,
Where unthought mysteries ever sleep,

It rose in beauty on our sight,
A ray of the celestial light.
Tears greeted it, but not of sadness,
Tears warm with love and bright with gladness;
And grateful thanks to Heaven were sent
For this fair gift so kindly lent,
On life's dim shadowy way to smile,
And its oft weary hours beguile.

That glimmering star, as years have flown,
Has larger waxed and brighter grown;
And loving hearts have quicker beat,
And eyes have glowed its glance to meet.
Now clear, full-orbed, ascended high,
It fixes many a gazing eye;
And kindly influence lets fall
O'er a wide sphere to gladden all.
A guiding star, — it sheds its beams;
A star of comfort now it seems;
A star elect, set 'mid the band
The Highest holds in His right hand.
Purer and purer may it glow!
Wide and more wide its splendor throw!
When, — past its latest natal day, —
Its light for earth shall fade away,
More fair and glorious let it rise,
To blaze on the eternal skies!

THE MOUND.

THOU hast a charm, thou grassy mound,
   That draws my heart to thee;
And oft my footsteps linger round
   The spot so dear to me.

'Tis but of earth a simple pile,
   With mossy turf o'ergrown,
Where Spring's first-peeping violets smile
   When her soft winds have blown.

The summer birds around it sing
   Through all the glowing day,
And near it sit with folded wing
   When twilight melts away.

Pale Autumn, with her pensive mien,
   Strews o'er it withered leaves,
And seems as one that there unseen
   In silent sorrow grieves.

E'en wintry snows and storms seem kind
   When round that mould they sweep,
As they, with fleecy robes, would bind
   And shield what there may sleep.

The ever-wakeful stars, by night,
   Watch o'er it from above,
And cheer it as with glances bright
   Of eyes that beam with love.

The sun, when the sweet morn awakes,
  Each day through changeful years,
Makes glad the spot that man forsakes,
  And dries its dewy tears.

Full well, — O dearer thought! — I know
  That angels linger there,
And guard the slumbering dust below
  With sleepless, faithful care:

I know that e'en the Lord on high,
  Whose word all worlds obey,
O'er that dear dust, with loving eye,
  Watch keepeth day by day.

O moments blest! when, lowly mound,
  I sit alone by thee, ·
While genial Nature smiles around,
  And breathes her peace o'er me.

Then, floating on the tranquil air,
  I gentle whispers hear,
Feel deep affections waken there,
  And know that God is near.

Ah! then swift thought far onward flies
  To that bright, gladsome morn,
When this that mortal, mouldering lies,
  Immortal shall be born!

When He, of Life and Death the Lord,
  Who holds of both the keys,
Gives Death to death, and, with His word,
  The grave's last captive frees!

Then, then shall Love its harvests reap,
From tears of sorrow sown,
And its rich treasures safely keep
Through ages all unknown.

SONNETS ON CHRIST'S SACRIFICE.

I.

THE ANOINTING.

SHE came, — the sinful, — while He brake the bread,
Her broken heart now healed, and brimming ö'er
With holy, burning love; she came to pour
Sweet, precious odors on that reverend head;
And, — as by deep, prophetic impulse led, —
That sacred body, soon uplifted high
'Mid scorn and shame in agony to die,
Betimes to anoint for its sepulchral bed.
Ungrudgingly she did the loving deed;
For to that glowing heart no offering seemed
Too rich for Him, — no cost too dear she deemed,
If He with one kind look the gift might heed:
The selfish chid, pronounced her act a crime;
He praised, and bade it live to latest time!

II.

THE ALARM.

HE kept the Passover; it was His last;
For now drew near the great predestined day,
When of man's mighty guilt Himself should pay
With dying groans and blood the ransom vast:

The cross was in His eye, the hours flew fast;
  Yet calm He sat, and looked serenely round
  On all the twelve; while they with awe profound,
  And loving gaze on Him, revolved the past,
The future from them hid: then touched He said,—
  "Of you one shall betray me unto death!"
  At that dire word, BETRAY, they all did start,
As if a thunder peal had stilled each breath,
  Or sudden mortal pang shot through each heart:
  Lord! is it I? each cried with horrid dread.

III.

THE EXPULSION.

THE loved disciple lay upon His breast,
  Drinking sweet influence from that voice divine;
  He asked, the Master gave at once the sign
  That marked the traitor, justified the rest.
Then, with convicting glance, while yet dismay
  Sat on the faces of the innocent,
  He said,—and Judas knew the deep intent,—
  "What thou hast purposed DO without delay."
Heart-smitten, out into the murky night
  Went he, foul demons ruling all his soul,
  And floods of hate that surged without control.
Then Jesus cried,—His eye beamed heavenly light,—
  "Now shall the Son of Man, betrayed, denied,
  Before all men by God be glorified!"

IV.

THE INSTITUTION.

HE took the bread and blessed it.   Then He brake
  And gave to each, and said,—O words sub-
     lime!—
  This is my body broken! through all time,
  In memory of my death this emblem take.
Next for the cup gave thanks.   For His dear sake,
  He bade them taste the wine.   Drink, 'tis my blood,
  The seal and witness of all grace in God,
  Till when the judgment trump the dead shall wake.
O sacred mystery!   Communion sweet
  Of holy, loving souls! in which they flow
  All into one blest brotherhood, and meet
Ineffably their Lord ; and joy to know
  That at this simple board they feast with Him
  Whose face unveiled fires the rapt seraphim!

V.

THE HOLY BOND.

A LITTLE while,—He said,—and hence I go ;
  And ye shall seek me, but ye shall not find ;
  Ye may not follow now ; but left behind,
  My witnesses, the world by you shall know
The truth, that truth strike root and grow ;
  A holy kingdom rise and wide extend ;
  Till e'en earth's proudest shall submissive bend,
  And unto me all tribes and nations flow!

Behold ! a new command to you I give ;
   Love one another ; all who will be mine,
   Let love in one blest fellowship combine,
That each for all, and all for each may live.
   So, marked of men, shall ye 'mid earth's dim night
   Divinely glow with pure, celestial light.

VI.

GETHSEMANE.

SPREAD thick above, ye clouds, your dusky veil,
   Hide from yon stars the Saviour's bitter woe ;
   Breathe, ye night winds, in murmurs sad and low,
   Or lift, in fitful gusts, your mournful wail :
Listen, thou Olivet ! and Kedron's vale
   Catch the sad accents that are borne to thee
   From yonder shade, — thine own Gethsemane, —
   As when one pleadeth, and doth not prevail.
See, to the earth the Holy Sufferer sinks ;
   Weighs on His heart an anguish all unknown ;
   Bursts from His lips the thrice-repeated prayer,
Yet firm His will the utmost pang to bear ;
   Till for Him fainting while the cup He drinks,
   Angels bring succors from the eternal throne !

VII.

THE SACRIFICE.

WONDER of wonders !   On the cross He dies !
   Man of the ages, — David's mighty Son, —
   The Eternal Word, who spake and it was done,
   What time, of old, He formed the earth and skies.

Abashed be all the wisdom of the wise!
　　Let the wide earth through all her kingdoms know
　　The promised Lamb of God, whose blood should
　　　　flow,
　　For human guilt the grand, sole sacrifice:
No more need altar smoke, nor victim bleed;
　　'Tis finished! the great mystery of love ;
　　Ye sin-condemned, by this blood 'tis decreed
Ye stand absolved ; behold the curse remove!
　　O Christ! Thy deadly wounds, thy mortal strife
　　Crush death and hell, and give immortal life!

VIII.

MARY AT THE SEPULCHRE.

I.

WEEPING she stands.　Unmastered yet the
　　　　Word, —
　　"On the third day I will arise again."
　　She finds not in the open tomb her Lord,
　　Nor where to seek Him knows ; tears fall like rain,
Drowning her sight.　On the still air in vain
　　Falls the familiar voice.　It wakes her not
　　From the deep trance of grief's o'erpowering reign,
　　That seems all memory from her soul to blot.
But hark! Drawn nearer now, distinct and clear,
　　Breaks on her quickened sense the thrilling tone ;
　　"Mary!"　The word reached not alone the ear ;
Leaped the true heart with ecstasy unknown:
　　"Master!" she cried, all doubt for ever fled,
　　And ran to tell, — He liveth that was dead!

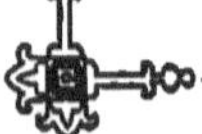

2.

E'en so full oft, methinks, the loving soul,
  Too much attent to its own griefs and fears;
  Bewildered, mazed, while quick emotions roll
  O'er it like floods, at first nor heeds, nor hears
That voice, which heard would scatter all its fears,
  Wake holy joy, and captive hope unbind:
  Though near He waits whom most it longs to find,
  And kindly speaks, with words of one who cheers
A friend 'neath sorrows bowed; though He would heal
  The bleeding heart, and with His own sweet skill
  Assuage its anguish keen, and bid it feel
The peace of happier days, remembered still;
  Yet, unperceived, unheard, the Master stands,
  And speaks, and stretches forth inviting hands.

3.

Look up, O sufferer, dash thy tears aside,
  Shake from thy soul the load of heavy grief;
  Behold thy best Belovéd at thy side!
  In His dear smile find a divine relief.
He bids thy sorrows fly, thy pangs be brief;
  To His own breast would fold thy fainting head:
  O joy of all divinest joys the chief, —
  To rest reposed upon the heart that bled!
To clasp the hand that erst the nail did mar!
  To hear the voice that from the cross did cry!
  To feel the arm that heaved death's mighty bar
Enfold thee when thy mortal hour is nigh!
  Hail Him who once earth's sharpest anguish bore,
  Thy Lord, thy Life, thy Friend for evermore!

4.

He liveth glorified, — set far above
  Angelic thrones and powers ; yet still He bears
  Within His human breast a brother's love ;
  His brow divine a brother's aspect wears ;
Still for the griefs of all His own He cares
  As when He dried the faithful Mary's tears ;
  The wounded spirit, that in meekness dares
  To call Him " Master ! " tenderly He cheers,
As her He cheered soon as His voice she knew :
  She wept, thenceforth, no more ; but rapturous joy
  O'erflowed her heart, — that heart so fond and true.
So when distrust would all thy hope destroy,
  O weeping one, such joy thy soul may thrill ;
  Sorrow's huge billows own His " *Peace! Be still!* "

※

THREESCORE YEARS.

The Sixtieth Birthday, Aug. 2, 1874.

WHEN first I saw thee, on thy youthful brow
  The light of dawning beauty softly shone
And drew the admiring glance, — thou knew'st not
    how, —
  Thy graces hidden from thyself alone.

Sweet gentleness was in thine eye and air,
  Yet thy whole being seemed with life aglow ;
And o'er thy face, in every feature fair,
  Played thought and feeling in their changeful flow.

Beneath all outward charms there beat a heart
  Rich in deep sympathies, and warm with love
That from itself did evermore impart;
  So blessing all, as angels bless above!

And so I loved thee; richer far to share
  Thy heart's affection than all gold to gain,
Than all ambition's laurel wreaths to wear,
  Or crowns that glory scatters in her train.

I sought and won thee; and thou gav'st thine hand,
  And with it heart and soul, and thou wast mine!
O 'twas a joy untold with thee to stand
  Before God's altar owned of thee as thine!

Then, glad, together we went forth to try
  Life's tasks and ventures, all as yet unknown,
To prove what in the future hid might lie,
  Each joyous as not sent to strive alone.

Perception keen and ever-restless thought
  Formed thee for action, waked to high desire;
E'en then thy eager soul with courage sought
  Some noble life-work worthy of its fire.

And thou art now threescore! I scarce believe
  The story of the swift-departed years!
Ah! crowding memories, ye may undeceive,
  Backward ye stretch till long their tale appears.

O faithful heart! true worshipper of good!
  In pure affections rich, in courage strong!
Through changes, changeless thou hast firmly stood,
  My best and dearest! constant, and so long!

Together we have trod the rugged way ;
   Together many a brimming joy have shared ;
Together borne the burdens of life's day,
   Together to its storms our bosoms bared !

Nor hast thou loved in vain : within this breast
   Hath lived and glowed unfathomed love to thee ;
In thee this heart hath rested, ever blest,
   And trusting e'en as thou hast trusted me.

Think not that face to-day for me less fair,
   Though changed perchance by care and grief it be,
Than when youth's brightest smiles were gleaming
      there,
   Like sunbeams dancing on a crystal sea.

With rapture ever new that face I greet !
   Dearest, I fold thee to my heart again,
As when I felt thy youthful pulses beat ;
   At threescore dearer art thou far than then !

Now on we tread, if other toilsome days
   Await us ere our mortal tasks are done ;
And, when fall o'er us life's last twilight rays,
   O may the hour of sleep for both be one !

EPITAPH,

FOR MISS J. H. A.'S MOCKING-BIRD.

ALAS, poor Bird ! How few there be
   That live, like thee, contented !
How many live to mock, like thee,
   And die far less lamented !

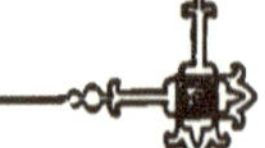

I SAW THEE.

"When thou wast under the fig-tree, I saw thee."

I SAW thee when, as twilight fell,
   And evening lit her fairest star,
Thy footsteps sought yon quiet dell,
   The world's confusion left afar.

I saw thee when thou stood'st alone,
   Where drooping branches thick o'erhung,
Thy still retreat to all unknown,
   Hid in deep shadows darkly flung.

I saw thee when, as died each sound
   Of bleating flock or woodland bird,
Kneeling, as if on holy ground,
   Thy voice the listening silence heard.

I saw thy calm uplifted eyes,
   And marked the heaving of thy breast,
When rose to heaven thy heartfelt sighs
   For purer life, for perfect rest.

I saw the light that o'er thy face
   Stole with a soft, suffusing glow,
As if, within, celestial grace
   Breathed the same bliss that angels know.

I saw, — what thou didst not, — above
  Thy lowly head an open heaven ;
And tokens of thy Father's love
  With smiles to thy rapt spirit given.

I saw thee from that sacred spot
  With firm and peaceful soul depart ;
I, Jesus, saw thee, — doubt it not, —
  And read the secrets of thy heart !

REST, SOLDIER, REST.

On depositing the body of Brigadier General JAMES C. RICE in the tomb.

REST, Soldier, rest ! thy weary task is done ;
  Thy God, thy country, — thou hast served them
    well :
Thine is true glory, — glory bravely won ;
  On lips of men unborn thy name shall dwell.

Rest, Patriot, Christian !   Thou hast early died,
  But days are measured best by noble deeds :
Brief though thy course, thy name thou hast allied
  To those of whom the WORLD admiring reads.

Rest, manly form !   Eternal love shall keep
  Thy still repose, till breaks the final dawn ;
Our Martyr stays not here, — *He knew no sleep !*
  On death's dark shadow burst a cloudless morn !

Live! live on fame's bright scroll, heroic friend!
  Thy memory, now, we to her record give,
To earth, thy dust: our thoughts to heaven ascend,
  Where, with the immortals, thou dost ever live!

THE CHRISTIAN SOLDIER'S SLEEP.

SERGEANT JOHN HANSON THOMPSON.

SMILE softly, skies, upon the grassy grave;
    Angels! about it holy vigils keep;
  Where calm reposes, in his dreamless sleep,
  The young and manly, generous and brave:
Deck it, ye flowers that tears of love shall lave;
  Let faithful hearts full oft beat quicker there;
  A glory not of earth the spot shall wear;
  For He, the Lord of Life, that died to save,
Of the still sleeper saith, " *He is not dead !*
  Whoso believeth, he shall *never die !* "
  The mortal resteth here; the immortal, — sped,
Swifter than wings or fleetest thought can fly,
  Above yon burning stars, — exults to climb
  Of heaven's own life the eternal heights sublime!

MRS. W. L. L.

I.

SHE hath but passed to heaven. As if from sleep,
    Sleep soft and peaceful, she awoke to find
  Earth with its pangs and tears all left behind;
  Rose her freed spirit up the airy steep;

On steady wing, beyond where pale stars keep
    Their watch o'er mortal griefs, she upward sped,
    Not lonely, but by sister spirits led
    To that dear home where eyes do never weep:
Strange rapture thrilled her there; and straight her note
    With sweet accord swelled the eternal hymn
    Of souls redeemed, led by the seraphim;
Whose echoes through the circling ages float:
    Now living, conscious, pure as angels bright,
    With God she dwells in everlasting light.

II.

Who would recall her to tread o'er again
    The mortal path, — from heaven's pure bliss recall?
    The wish were weakness, though full oft must fall
    Thick, blinding tears from eyes that once were fain
To catch her genial smile, ne'er sought in vain;
    Though many an hour fond hearts be sad and lone,
    And miss, and yearn once more to drink, the tone
    That lingers in the ear like some lost strain:
No; ye that loved her, now to Heaven resign,
    Nor wish her from that nobler life withdrawn;
    The night of grief shall pass; and with the morn
Shall come sweet memories; and a face divine.
    With all your worthiest thoughts shall seem to blend,
    And a fair form your wandering steps attend.

THE GATHERING HOME.

THEY gather there!   They gather there!
    The saintly souls of ages dead,
    The good that earth but late hath lost,
    O'er heaving seas and tempest tossed,
Have gained their port, — their fears are fled;
    Dies far away the surges' roar,
    The watch, the gloom, the dangers o'er,
All joyfully they press the strand,
Exulting to behold the longed-for land!

They gather there!   They gather there!
God's ransomed host, in long array;
    The burnished gates for them unfold,
    The wondrous city they behold
That shines in cloudless, changeless day!
    With glad, triumphal songs they come;
    Each hath his own, — no tongue is dumb;
Forgotten, in their joy, the tears,
The wasting toils and strifes of earth's sad years.

They gather there!   They gather there!
They tread the courts by seraphs trod,
    They wear the forms that angels wear,
    In faultless grace for ever fair,
Made in the likeness of their God!
    They feel of life the immortal thrill,
    Of life's prime fount they drink their fill;
And from the dazzling throne there fall
Sweet beams of love divine, suffusing all.

They gather there!   They gather there!
- This is the Father's house, the rest
        Prepared, O Christ, for Thee and Thine, —
        Household of God and Home divine;
They pass that threshold and are blest;
        Safe sheltered near Thy throne and heart,
        Reached nevermore by sorrow's dart,
Thou giv'st them, — the long waiting o'er, —
Thy blessed face to see for evermore!

They gather there!   They gather there!
No splendor of empurpled morn
        Such glory flings o'er hill and plain
        As pours o'er all the radiant train,
From that dear face for ever born!
        With Thee, the Lamb, they need no sun;
        From Thee, while ceaseless cycles run,
Light pure, serene, and full shall flow,
And all thine own bask in the genial glow.

They gather there!   They gather there!
They meet, the parted long!   Again
        Love finds its lost!   The husband grasps
        The wife's fond hand!   The mother clasps
Once more her babe, torn from her when
        Death snatched it in the long-gone years,
        Unmoved by all her prayers and tears!
And brother greets a sister's grace,
Raptured to fold her in the old embrace!

They gather there!   They gather there!
O Love, that yearned so oft in vain

Through mortal years, and baffled still,
    Still yearned, and sought with steadfast will
To find the lovely without stain,
    Unchecked pour forth thy fervors now;
    Not one of all the throng that bow,
The sons of God, about the throne,
But wears true beauty, save in Heaven unknown.

They gather there!   They gather there!
Not for ignoble ease; e'en song,
    Were there no tasks the strength to try,
    At last on wearied lips would die;
In that high world the spirit strong,
    And as the eagle bent to soar,
    Untired shall range creation o'er;
To work God's perfect will intent,
Forth by His Word on Love's great errands sent.

They gather there!   They gather there!
Ah! Life through death.   Life just begun
    When the full cup of joy they taste,
    Nor pleasures pall, nor treasures waste!
In Him they live, — the Holy One, —
    By whose dear cross each wears a crown,
    At whose dear feet each casts it down;
And, while all chant His matchless name,
Intenser burns in each love's quenchless flame!

They gather there!   They gather there!
Thou who, 'mid hopes and fears, art led
    As if through deserts wild, o'erborne
    With chafing cares or left to mourn

Lonely and sad o'er comforts fled ;
   Take heart !   Take heart !   The holy light
   Streams on thee from the eternal height ;
That home of love thy rest shall be, ·
There loving eyes expectant watch for thee!

THE STRAIN I LOVE.

AGAIN !   Those chords again !   As o'er the keys
   The fairy fingers glide, the strain swells forth
In harmonies that all entrance the soul !
It wakes pure thoughts, unlocks the fountains deep
Of tenderness, till thence the flowing tides
Of sweet emotion, — as each varying tone
Speaks to the heart of sorrow or of love, —
Well up and flood the breast.   Each nerve it thrills
With exquisite vibrations, till each yields
Pleasure ineffable ; as if some harp,
By angel fingers touched, were heard afar, —
The notes unearthly, such as charm in heaven !
It quickens my whole being ; fills, enchants,
And half bewilders, till I seem to float
A spirit all disrobed and light as air,
Borne upward on the melodies that rise
Like viewless exhalations ; or as one
Soaring in dreams, unfettered, free as thought,
Through realms of perfect beauty all unknown,
Losing himself in bliss !
               O, yet once more, —
Once more repeat the strain !   Break not the spell !

From out her opened casket Memory now
Brings forth her precious treasures, hidden long.
Ah! those dear, distant scenes!   I live them o'er.
Childhood comes back! its purple lights, its flowers
Unmatched by all the bloom of riper years;
Its fantasies, that ever came and went;
Its rich exuberance of joyous life.
And youth returns.   Its bounding pulses throb
With ardor for high contests now so near.
I see again its visions, share its hopes,
And taste anew the raptures that are born
Of youthful love, when first it fires the breast,
Stay! stay! ye blissful fancies.   Let me feel
Yet some brief moments the delights ye bring.

.   .   .   .   .

That change of key!   How soft and tender now
The plaintive tone.   It touches my rapt soul
With a subduing power.   I seem to sit
As in the twilight of a summer's eve,
When clamorous day has passed and all is still,
Or when the moonlight broodeth over all,
And the cool dews descend, that fall as tears
Wept silently by loving eyes in heaven
O'er mortal griefs.   And lo! the airy forms
Of childhood's playmates and of youth's bright band,
And of the numbers loved in bygone years,
But missed long since on earth, who one by one
Were counted with the blest beyond the stars,
Around me seem to gather; and intent
I hearken, if perchance some well-known voice
May fall, as oft of yore upon my ear,
And with the old affection fondly gaze
On faces dear, remembered, O how well!

Strange transport, wrought within my yielding soul,
So quick responsive to the trembling string!
Dies now the strain I love, and I must weep, —
Weep not of grief, but of ecstatic joy,
Which these delicious sounds do ever wake
While yet I listen, and which, dying, still
In lingering echoes round me seem to float.

TO CLARA.

LADY of gentle mien and eye,
   We every hour have missed thee,
Since when we gave the last good-by,
   And, at the parting, kissed thee!

The stars above grow dim at dawn,
   Are lost in day's full beaming;
But thou, our star, on that last morn,
   Didst shine with brighter gleaming.

Thy winning ways and witching smile
   Seemed all enhanced in losing,
And sweeter grew each tone the while;
   Ah! — 'twas not of our choosing, —

But thou wouldst leave us! Yet perchance
   Kind hearts for thee were pining,
Which saw their sun of joy advance,
   As we saw ours declining!

I saw thee last upon the deck,
  A manly hand warm grasping;
Who, who in thought or wish would check
  The fervor of that clasping!

Ah! happy all thy future years,
  Where'er thy steps are bending,
So thou may'st have, through toils and tears,
  That manly form attending!

Nay, do not blush; some smiling cot
  Awaits thy charms to grace it;
Heaven send thee earth's divinest lot,
  Till heaven itself replace it!

THE MONKS OF CHESTER.

I FELT, as I wound my way along the echoing passages, a solemn awe, and a vague and indescribable sympathy with the long-forgotten past. My imagination restored the old monks to life.

WHERE are they then? those hooded men,
  Whose footfalls now no more
Yon arches echo back again
  That echoed oft of yore?

Here, in the olden time, they strolled
  Along the well-worn aisle,
And swelled the solemn chant, that rolled
  Through all the massy pile!

The reverend abbot, trim and sleek,
  With well-feigned look demure,
The burly friar, whose aspect meek
  Expressed devotion pure, —

Here dwelt in yonder cloisters grim ;
  And oft were seen to glide
Through those old, winding galleries dim,
  Like ghosts at eventide.

Yon vaults well filled with rosy wine,
  The larder with good cheer,
Well pleased they could *the world resign,*
  To tell their aves here!

When round that stern old tower the storm
  Howled dismally and wild,
In yon refectory, bright and warm,
  The well-spread banquet smiled.

Round went the goblet, and each quaff
  Warmed each glad heart the more ; ·
Round went the song, — the jovial laugh
  Burst forth in loud uproar!

Nor died away, till from above,
  With measured, solemn peal,
The midnight hour was told, — *their love
  And self-denying zeal !*

O, where are these good Fathers now ?
  The crumbling walls ask, where ?
O'er those sepulchral pavements bow
  And ask, — THEY SLUMBER THERE !

THE GOLDEN WEDDING.

TIS fifty years! 'tis fifty years! how swiftly they
    have fled!
Since I thee, my best and dearest, to the bridal altar
    led!
In youthful grace and beauty thou wast blushing
    fresh and fair;
'Twas with pride and exultation that I stood beside
    thee there.

The hopes that then we cherished were the kindling
    hopes of youth;
The vows which then we plighted were the vows of
    love and truth;
And light before us glanced as we thought of coming
    days,
As when the summer sunbeam o'er the trembling
    water plays.

Of changeless bliss we dreamed not, for all too well
    we knew·
That athwart life's devious path many an unseen
    arrow flew;
But we trusted that when wounded, when the bitter
    tear should start,
Sweet sympathy would heal, and cheat of half its woe
    the heart.

And we thought that should kind Heaven deign to
     smile upon our lot,
Grant a home and tranquil days in some dear se-
     cluded spot,
The flowers would seem more lovely and the stars
     shed purer light,
As we gazed on them together with reciprocal delight.

Now that fifty years are passed, and we cast a look
     behind,
What speaks the quick emotion that is rushing o'er
     each mind ?
Saith it of disappointment, — of each vision empty
     found ?
Of hope's bright star declining and thick darkness
     gathered round ?

No, no, our thanks we offer to the gracious Hand
     that guides ;
'Tis a placid stream that bears us, and peacefully it
     glides.
May coming years thus greet us, till life's latest sands
     are run,
And life's close be like the twilight when has set a
     cloudless sun.

FAREWELL TO ROME.

Composed in a night ride from Rome to Civita Vecchia.

I.

IMPERIAL City! I have dreamed of thee
  Through long, long years, since when, in early
    prime,
  I traced, with heart deep stirred, thy history
  Of men heroic, and of deeds sublime:
Thy storied names, which on the scroll of time
  But gather brightness with the flight of years;
  Or, — if all stained with tyranny and crime,
  With* blood of slaughtered innocence and tears
Of bitter agony, — but blacker grow,
  As grows the detestation of mankind;
  Around thy Tiber, have availed to throw,
And o'er thy hills, where sits decay enshrined,
  A spell that warmed my soul with classic fire,
  And waked, to see thee, restless, keen desire!

II.

And I *have* seen thee! And my feet have trod
  Among thy crumbling glories; climbed the height
  Of thy famed Capitol, where erst thy god,
  Great Jupiter, enthroned in awful might,
His dwelling kept; whither old warriors came
  With pomp and triumph from the field well won,
  To bring their trophies, and to light the flame
  Upon his altar; forth, when day was done,

My steps have strayed to see the moonlight fall
  Where ivies o'er the Coliseum creep,
And mark the shadows, by the ruined wall
Where dwelt the Cæsars, dark and lonely sleep!
  Henceforth 'tis memory all, — the dream is o'er;
  Rome, fare thee well, I muse on thee no more!

THE ANGEL-CHILD.

THE seal of heaven was early set,
  Sweet child, upon thy sunny brow;
Though lost to earth thou livest yet,
  All bright and glad I see thee now!

Those glowing eyes, that gentle smile,
  Spoke thee for earth a thing too fair;
A cherub lent from heaven awhile,
  A cherub's grace 'twas thine to wear.

Oft fondly beat a father's heart,
  To see thy budding life unfold;
And oft a mother's tear did start,
  Born of deep yearnings all untold.

Hope dreamed that many a smiling year
  Should many a ripening charm display;
But, oh! a voice we could not hear
  Won thee in childhood's dawn away.

Yet but in seeming didst thou die:
   A joyous spirit, swift of wing, ·
'Twas thine to cleave yon azure sky,
   And, like the lark, to soar and sing.

Unquenched is that immortal fire!
   Dear child, thou didst not live in vain;
And Heaven shall grant our warm desire,
   To fold thee to our hearts again!

MISANTHROPY, AND RESPONSE.

O WORLD, to some so bright and fair,
   Thy charms I cannot see;
Thy joys — thy purest, choicest — are
   But hollow joys to me.

When all around look blithe and gay,
   And every heart is glad,
I turn in weariness away,
   In spirit sore and sad.

Not e'en the fireside's kindly cheer
   Can smooth my knitted brow;
In that which once I prized so dear
   I find no pleasure now.

Farewell, ye pomps of life! farewell,
   Ye pageants all untrue!
Scenes 'mid which others joy to dwell
   I bid ye glad adieu!

Where nature blooms in beauty pure
  My footsteps now I bend,
There, unmolested and secure,
  A life of peace to spend.

Be mine the hermit's lonely cot,
  Round which the wild-flowers wave;
And there, unheeded and forgot,
  Be mine his lonely grave.

RESPONSE.

AND think'st thou, fool, when thou hast fled
  The busy haunts of men,
That thou shalt find thy passions dead,
  To waken not again?

Think'st thou thy soul's deep craving, felt
  Without thy wish or will,
When thou hast by thy pallet knelt,
  Shall evermore be still?

The warm affections in thy breast,
  That keenly thirst for love,
Think'st thou that these can lie at rest,
  Content no more to rove?

The conscious power for noble deeds,
  That wakens high desire,
Think'st thou, when thou hast told thy beads,
  'Twill stir no inward fire?

The sense of duty that commands
  To do with all the might,
When thou shalt fold thy idle hands,
  Will this forswear the right?

The thought of deeds of love that thou
  Shouldst every day have done,
Will it not haunt when thou shalt bow,
  As nightly sets the sun?

The world's great agonizing cry,
  From suffering millions wrung,
Will that for thee in silence die,
  When thou hast vespers sung?

The dread of reckoning strict and stern
  For unused gifts and powers,
Will that not in thy bosom burn,
  Through all thy lonely hours?

Ah, fling thy fatal dream aside,
  Stand forth in manhood true;
Where life's great battle rages wide
  Be strong to dare and do!

In virtue's conflict stern and high,
  Thy soul shall grow divine;
In triumphs, joy shall light thine eye,
  And holy peace be thine.

With splendor then shall close the day
  That ends thy mortal strife;
Men by thy grave shall pause, and say,
  "He lived a noble life!"

SONG.

YEARS have seemed months, love,
  When passed at thy side ;
But months seem long years, love,
  When without thee they glide ;
Wearily breaketh now
  The bright dawning day,
Wearily evening falls,
  And thou far away.

What though I roam, love,
  'Mid old storied towers,
Wander through palaces,
  Gardens, and bowers ?
Or stray by sweet rivers
  Made classic in song ?
One charm still is wanting,
  One name on my tongue.

Thy smile hath cheered, love,
  Hath lighted my path,
When dark clouds have gathered,
  Or burst in their wrath ;
So long hath it blessed me,
  So dear hath it grown,
Without it my heart pines,
  All saddened and lone.

Speed, speed the hours, love,
  That bear me once more

Back to thy fond arms,
  A wanderer no more ;
Bright though the way be
  That tempts me to roam,
I'm most of all blest, love,
  With thee and at home !

PALMER'S INDIAN MAID.

I.

WONDROUS Enchanter ! at that touch of thine,
  The cold, dead marble warms and lives and
    wakes ;
The shape thy thought would give, it plastic takes,
Rises and stands in symmetry divine :
That Indian Maid seems but to wait thy call,
  To break the spell of silence, and in speech,
  With those just parting lips, our souls to teach
Truths pure as crystal drops on flowers let fall.
For not alone the outline soft as air,
  With each material grace that charms the sight,
  Thou fashionest, but settest also there
A spiritual beauty, calm, ethereal, bright ;
  As if within there glowed an angel soul,
  Whose living light serene suffused the whole !

II.

Creator of the Beautiful and True,
  What matchless shapes before thine inward eye
  For ever float ! what visions open lie
Of rarest things that science never knew !

As in the bosom of the sleeping lake·
 That no breath ruffles, of a summer morn,
 Sky, mountain, rock and tree, green slope and lawn,
 A treasury of beauty seem to make ;
Even so, methinks, dwell ever in thy mind
 Types of all fairest things, — an endless store, —
 That stay thy bidding to stand forth enshrined
In visible form, thenceforth to change no more.
 Thy pure creations bid our souls aspire
 To know the Infinite Beauty, and admire !

THOU ART UNTO MY SOUL.

THOU art unto my soul even as a rose,
 When, blooming full on the fresh morning air,
 It breathes its perfume, while in soft repose
 On its pure bosom glitter dew-drops fair :
Or thou art as the star serene that glows
 At twilight, when, dim lingering o'er the hill,
 Day's last hue fades, and night her mantle throws
 In deepening shades ; the star that sweetly fills
With tender, pensive thoughts the gazer's breast,
 Who looketh from this troubled world afar,
 And dreameth that perchance in it is rest
To weary spirits, worn with life's rude jar :
 Morn hath no flower more fair, more sweet than thou,
  No gem more radiant studs night's ebon brow !

THE NEW YEAR.

FADES soon the mystic glory
　That on fair childhood lies ;
And all too brief the story
　Its vanished dream supplies ;
And youth with heart high beating,
　With hopes that spring so fast,
Than morning mist more fleeting,
　On swift wing sweepeth past.

The pride, the strength, the beauty,
　That come with manhood's prime ;
The zeal that nerves to duty,
　And stirs to deeds sublime ;
Ambition's lofty scheming,
　And pleasure's cup run o'er,
Wealth o'er its treasures dreaming,
　Success that asks no more ;

All, all, years, swiftly flying,
　Too soon leave far behind ;
To each year, ere its dying,
　Some jewel is resigned ;
Some star that bright was glowing,
　To the strained sight is lost ;
Some flower, that fresh was blowing,
　Falls blighted by the frost.

The friends that once were treading
  Life's pathway by our side,
Their love its sweetness shedding,
  Like perfume far and wide, —
With finished years, have slumbered,
  Have vanished from our sight,
With holy angels numbered,
  Beyond the vault of night.

O Earth! thou ever growest
  Yet poorer to our thought;
Time breaks the spell thou throwest
  O'er hearts thy bribes have bought;
Beyond thy pageants ranging,
  Our souls do beauty see,
Whose charms, from thine estranging,
  Withdraw our love from thee.

Yet, life! thy years that stay not,
  Thy scenes that glide away,
Thy pleasures that delay not,
  The strifes that fill thy day;
Come not in vain to mortals,
  If faith divine they give,
And up through heaven's high portals
  Bring man with God to live.

New Year! that, with glad greeting,
  Hast come once more to me,
In whispers still repeating
  Words oft said tenderly;

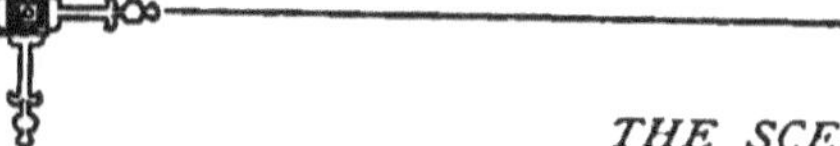

Thy voice my soul now heeding,
  To noblest aims I rise,
And on where God is leading
  Tread with uplifted eyes.

Though all is darkly hidden
  Along the path I take,
No tear shall fall unbidden,
  Nor foe my peace shall break.
Thy hand may kindly feed me,
  Give rest by waters still;
Or, if through storms it lead me,
  My soul accepts Thy will.

When years, so swiftly flying,
  Shall all have run their round;
When death itself is dying,
  And earth no more is found;
O Saviour, then behold me,
  From Thy great judgment-throne,
And let Thine arms enfold me,
  Thy lips call me Thine own!

THE SCEPTIC.

O, PITY the poor doubter, darkly driven,
  He knows not whither, o'er life's troubled main;
On sun and stars, to light the wanderer given,
  His eyes, now half bedimmed, are turned in vain.

No needle points for him the dubious way;
  No friendly chart guides o'er the trackless deep;
No lighthouse greets him with its gladsome ray;
  No haven welcomes when wild tempests sweep.

The voice divine within he heedeth not;
  The book of nature he doth all misread;
Celestial Truth denied, her words forgot,
  Illusion cheats him and false lights mislead.

In fond conceit he dreams ere long to find,
  By his own wisdom led, a region fair,
Where placid streams adown sweet valleys wind,
  And days serenely glide without a care.

Ah, no! though many a blooming realm there be,
  Where beauty smiles beneath a cloudless sun,
Yet such fair shore his eye shall never see,
  Misfortune's victim ere his course be run.

His fated bark, long tossed the ocean o'er,
  At last shall founder helpless and alone;
Or stranded on some rugged, surf-beat shore,
  O'er him, in woful dirge, the waves shall moan.

Thou that hast faith, on God's good Word hold fast;
  Thy chart and compass both His truth shall be,
Till, reached thy port and all thy perils past,
  In peace thou floatest on the crystal sea.

SONG.

GENTLY I glide, love,
　Glide o'er the deep;
Hushed are the wild winds,
　The proud billows sleep;
Soft gleams the summer moon
　On the still sea;
Yet roams my thought, love,
　It wanders to thee.

All, all is beauty,
　Around and above;
With me are kind hearts,
　And eyes beaming love;
Fair lips breathe music
　That charms the rapt ear,
But stirs not the soul, love,
　'Tis not thee I hear!

Where'er thou art, love,
　Peace fill thy breast!
Pure spirits guard thee,
　Awake or at rest;
When the morn breaketh,
　With breeze fresh and free,
O, may it bear, love,
　This fond heart to thee!

TO THE SHEPHERDS.

" Comfort ye, comfort ye my people, saith your God." — Is. xl. 1.

O COMFORT ye my people, comfort ye,
　　The Lord Jehovah saith,
The faithful souls that daily unto me,
　　As if with fainting breath,
Call for the helping hand, or lift their eyes
In calm, appealing silence to the skies.

O comfort ye my chosen.　Lo! they tread
　　As on a desert way!
Foot-sore and weary, and oft hard bested
　　Through many a toilsome day;
With heart-aches oft and tears that dim their sight,
With cares by day and fears that haunt by night.

Speak words of comfort, ye who lead the flock;
　　My well beloved, — more dear
Than priceless gems that from the rifted rock
　　Are gathered bright and clear, —
I count my jewels, and with sleepless eye
Watch o'er them ever, guard them from on high.

Tell them my changeless love, whate'er betide,
　　Shall make them safely dwell;
In my Pavilion hid they shall abide,
　　Nor dread the hosts of hell;
In weariness, with me they shall have rest
And find divine repose as on my breast.

When days are dark and earth looks bleak and
     drear,
    When sinks the lonely heart
And falters faith ; say, Be ye of good cheer,
    Nor let your trust depart ;
The Lord forgetteth never.   He, your Light,
To cloudless day shall change the darksome night.

To the green pastures lead them, where my Word
    Spreads out all pure delights ;
Where the sweet voice of grace and promise heard
    To love and hope invites ;
And distant vision of the eternal hills
Where feed the ransomed flock with rapture fills.

Bid them be mindful what the joy shall be,
    When their glad eyes, so long
Expectant waiting, their dear Lord shall see !
    When from the immortal throng
"Worthy the Lamb !" they hear, and at His feet
In grateful transport bow, their bliss complete !

Ay ! go, ye shepherds, comfort ye my flock
    With words of faithful love ;
Say I will give them water from the rock
    And manna from above ;
The stream for them divide, with mighty hand,
That parts earth's desert from the blessèd land.

Tiie following hymn should have found a place among the original hymns with
which the volume opens, but was by accident omitted.

A HYMN OF LOVE.

IN Thee, O God, the hosts above
    For ever live supremely blest ;
And I, on earth, like them would love ;
    Like them, as on Thy bosom rest.

I may not know Thee as Thou art,
    While here my darksome way I tread ;
Yet thanks that now I know in part,
    And hourly by Thy hand am led.

Unseen, Thou dost Thyself reveal,
    In Thine own ways to sense unknown ;
Thy hidden glories oft I feel
    Come flowing o'er me from Thy throne.

All sweetest tenderness and grace,
    Beauty and majesty divine,
Draw my charmed soul to Thine embrace,
    And blend my mortal love with Thine.

In Thy pure light 'tis mine to bask,
    Around me falls its noontide beam ;
In calm content no more I ask,
    While filled with Thee, my God, I seem.

The joy that through my being flows
    New gladness lends to brightest days ;
Morn fresher wakes, and evening glows
    More lovely, while I breathe Thy praise.

The wide creation spreads more fair
　　As bright o'er all Thy smile I see;
And thousand voices, soft as air,
　　Seem whispering to my heart of Thee!

Thine image on each human brow
　　To nobler beauty seems to wake;
With warm embrace I welcome now
　　Each man a brother for Thy sake!

As past me fly the swift-winged years,
　　Thy mercies all their circuits fill;
Thy goodness, like the sun, appears
　　Throughout all time resplendent still.

Since once for sin the Lord hath died,
　　No more I fear that Thou wilt frown;
Come life, come death, whate'er betide,
　　Love floods my soul and fear shall drown!

As mounts the joyous lark on high,
　　To greet with songs the purple dawn,
So would I pierce yon azure sky,
　　And hail Heaven's brightly breaking morn.

O God! the lustrous gates unfold;
　　Let Thy full glory on me fall;
Thine unveiled face I would behold,
　　And know Thee mine, — my All in All!

AN EPISTLE.

To the Rev. Dr. A. H. C., an honored Friend in a responsible
Position, but sighing for Retirement.

FLED for a time from care and toil,
　　I tread once more my native soil;
And 'mid kind friends and grateful cheer
Survey the scenes from childhood dear.
The same blue heavens are still o'erhead;
The same green fields before me spread;
The same grand ocean as of yore
Heaves its huge billows to the shore;
The same gray rocks lie piled beside,
That surf and surge have long defied;
Along the same smooth beach I walk
With genial friends, and kindly talk;
Or in the twilight stray alone,
Made pensive by the waves' dull moan;
While memories wake of distant years
That open hidden springs of tears, —
Memories of youth's bright scenes that o'er,
With their dear pleasures, come no more.

　Ah! where are they, the fair, the young,
That with me here oft sat and sung
Till faded the last lingering light,
And evening melted into night?
Alas! of these the many rest,
By the green turf their bosoms pressed;

One here, one there, life's labors done,
Its prizes lost or nobly won.
With kindling hope and purpose high,
Together we went forth to try
What years might bring of good or ill;
They rest, I wait, am toiling still!
'Twere weakness now for them to weep
Or wish to break their peaceful sleep.
Be this, — since years to me remain, —
My care that years pass not in vain.

On Sabbath morn the courts I trod
Where met the throng to worship God.
The old, the young, were gathered there,
To warm their hearts with praise and prayer.
'Twas mine to preach, as oft before,
His Word who liveth evermore;
And, while I brake the Living Bread,
And hoped the hungry sheep were fed,
And called the heedless to forsake
The husks of earth, that bread to take,
Methought that sweetly o'er us came
The Spirit once revealed in flame,
And eyes through tears were seen to shine
As if hearts burned with love divine.
O, then 'twas joy to think how long
These walls had echoed prayer and song;
How in forgotten years long gone,
A saintly host, here newly born,
Had mounted to the courts above,
Made faultless in eternal love.
'Twas joy to think how happy he
Who shepherd of this flock shall be;

AN EPISTLE.

Who here, afar from noisy strife,
Shall close in peace a useful life.
I thought of thee, my friend, wayworn,
O'erpressed with burdens bravely borne;
Recalled thy frequent wish to find
Some sweet retirement to thy mind,
Whither, from life's great contests fled,
Through quiet paths thy feet might tread.
'Tis true thy wish, in reason's light,
Might well suggest that prophet's plight
Who, sent to Nineveh, was fain
To flee to Tarshish o'er the main,
And whom at sea a fate befell
Which all wise men should ponder well.
Yet thou, perchance, on this canst stand, —
Thy Tarshish *may be reached by land !*
And so I mentioned thee as one
Who here might sink, as sinks the sun
In glory, when thy day at last
Should close, in tranquil service past.
Right glad I found thy honored name
Known well and kindly, — "such is fame."
True merit cannot lie concealed ;
Its lustre, far and wide revealed,
Attracts all eyes, and surely draws
From wondering thousands fit applause.
So now for thee an open way
Lies straight before.   Heaven speed the day
When thou, once set o'er this loved flock,
Truth's richest treasures shall unlock ;
By living streams the sheep shall lead,
And as in pleasant pastures feed.

O vision fair!   O pleasing dream!
This all unreal must I deem?
With joy these eyes thy joy shall see,
If thy long wish fulfilled shall be.
Meanwhile my fervent love I send,
With each best hope, and thus I end.

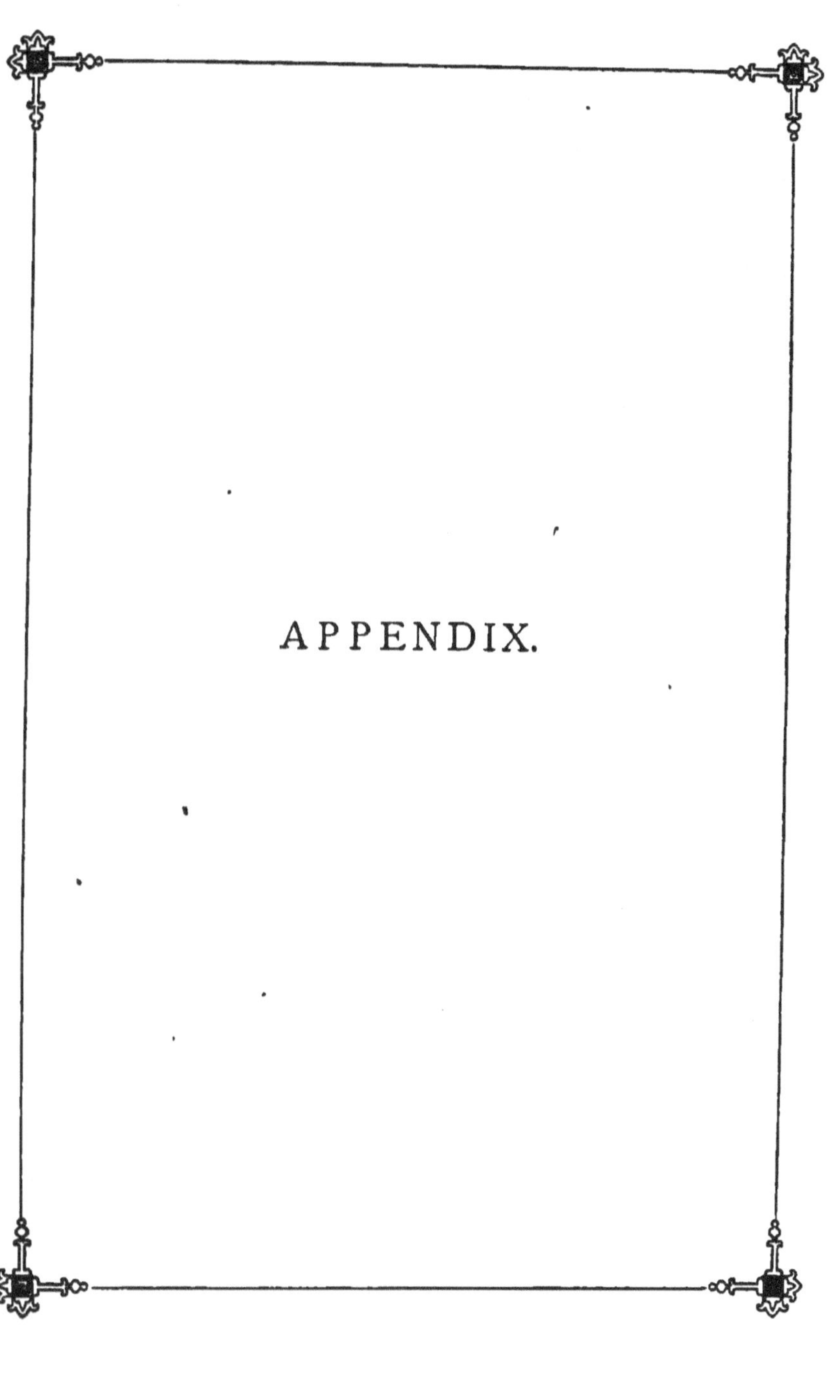

APPENDIX.

APPENDIX.

NOTE A.

"MY FAITH LOOKS UP TO THEE."

THE desire manifested by so many, to learn something in relation to the origin of this hymn, is not, perhaps, an unreasonable one. The writer, however, would feel no little delicacy in making any attempt to gratify it, were it not that in one way and another it has happened that very inaccurate, and in some instances wholly apocryphal, things have been reported concerning it. It has furnished quite a striking illustration of the difficulty of transmitting verbally, with entire accuracy, a few simple facts, from one person to another. On the whole, therefore, it has seemed best to state all there is to be stated, which is really very little, in respect to the time and circumstances of its composition.

Immediately after graduating at Yale College, in September, 1830, the writer went to the city of New York, by previous engagement, to spend a year in teaching for two or three hours each day in a select school for young ladies. This private institution, which was patronized by the best class of families, was under the direction of an excellent Christian lady, connected with St. George's Church, the rector of which was then the good Dr. James Milnor. It was in Fulton Street, west of Broadway, and a little below Church Street on the south side of the way. That whole

section of the city, now covered with immense stores and crowded with business, was then occupied by genteel residences. The writer resided in the family of the lady who kept the school, and it was there that the hymn was written.

It had no *external* occasion whatever. Having been accustomed almost from childhood, through an inherited propensity perhaps, to the occasional expression of what his heart felt in the form of verse, it was in accordance with this habit, and in an hour when Christ, in the riches of His grace and love, was so vividly apprehended as to fill the soul with deep emotion, that the piece was composed. There was not the slightest thought of writing for another eye, least of all of writing a hymn for Christian worship. Away from outward excitement, in the quiet of his chamber, and with a deep consciousness of his own needs, the writer transferred as faithfully as he could to paper what at the time was passing within him. Six stanzas were composed, and imperfectly written, first on a loose sheet, and then accurately copied into a small morocco-covered book, which for such purposes the author was accustomed to carry in his pocket. This first complete copy is still — 1875 — preserved. It is well remembered that when writing the last line, " A ransomed soul," the thought that the whole work of redemption and salvation was involved in those words, and suggested the theme of eternal praises, moved the writer to a degree of emotion that brought abundant tears.

The winter of 1830–31 was a season of memorable religious interest in the city of New York ; and, as " coming events cast their shadows before," there was doubtless among Christian people, in December of that winter, a more than ordinary degree of religious feeling, in which the writer probably shared. But the season of manifest religious revival did not commence till a month or two

later ; so that it was not true, as has been stated in some
.notices of the hymn, that it was written in the midst, and
under the impulses, of this revival. This fact, of course,
is of no particular consequence. It is only one example
of many, in which slight inaccuracies, rhetorical state-
ments, and the imaginations of writers or speakers, have
sometimes combined to form quite an unauthentic history
of its origin. It is simply for this reason that it has
seemed worth while to state the exact circumstances.

A year or two after the hymn was written, and when no
one, so far as can be recollected, had ever seen it, Dr.
Lowell Mason met the author in the street in Boston, and
requested him to furnish some hymns for a Hymn and
Tune Book which, in connection with Dr. Hastings of
New York, he was about to publish. The little book con-
taining it was shown him, and he asked a copy. We
stepped into a store together, and a copy was made and
given him, which without much notice he put in his pocket.
On sitting down at home and looking it over, he became
so much interested in it that he wrote for it the tune
"Olivet," in which it has almost universally been sung.
Two or three days afterward we met again in the street,
when, scarcely waiting to salute the writer, he earnestly
exclaimed, "Mr. Palmer, you may live many years, and do
many good things ; but I think you will be best known to
posterity as the author of ' My faith looks up to Thee.' "
Hymn and tune together soon passed into common use in
this country ; and in 1840 the hymn was introduced into
England through a collection published by Dr. Andrew
Reed, and is now found in nearly or quite all English and
Scotch manuals of worship of recent date.

It would not be ingenuous in the writer to affect indif-
ference to the fact that these brief words of his have been
found fitted to give expression to the utterance of so many
Christian hearts the world over, and that the hymn has

become a favorite among all evangelical denominations. The favor with which it has been received is doubtless to be attributed to the embodiment in it, in appropriate and simple language, of that which is most central in all true Christian experience, — the act of faith in the divine Redeemer, — the intrusting of the individual soul to Him entirely and for ever. That it has come to be so often heard in Christian assemblies, and at the sacramental table ; that in instances almost without number it has been the last earthly song of the dying saints of God, as well as their refreshment amidst the disciplines of life ; that it has been translated into many languages, and is literally sung around the world ; and finally that, in a great number of known instances, it has so brought the loving Saviour to the distinct apprehension of souls oppressed with sin as to call forth for the first time penitence and trust, — has been to the author an inexpressible joy, and of devout and, he hopes, humble thankfulness to God, from the inspiration of whose Spirit he cannot doubt it came.

It has been with much hesitation, and at the urgent request of many, that these paragraphs have been written. It is hoped that they may save the necessity of replying to letters of inquiry, which have been received in inconvenient numbers.

The text of this hymn has suffered by alteration in only two instances, to the knowledge of the writer. The compilers of a hymn-book published many years ago in Boston took the liberty of altering the hymn so as to change materially its theological significance and spirit. On the earnest remonstrance of the author, however, with the publishers, they at length agreed to publish the unaltered hymn at the end of the volume, with a reference to it as the original text, and did so in good faith. The other change was made by a compiler who substituted " distress " for " distrust " in the last stanza ; not perceiving that the whole hymn had reference to the affections of the soul, and not to the sensations of the body, to which the former word would most naturally be taken to refer ; and that it was wholly incongruous to divert the thought from the former to the latter. In the preface to the small volume entitled " Hymns of My Holy Hours," the author wrote as follows : —

" The writer feels obliged to add that, if the compilers of manuals for public worship shall desire to introduce any of these hymns into their collections, he cheerfully consents, provided always that the hymns be taken exactly as they are. 'He repeats, even with greater emphasis than in the preface to a former volume, his protest against the alteration or abridgment of the hymns of a living author, to adapt them to the uses or the tastes of others without his consent. He cannot but regard it as a breach, not of courtesy alone, but of Christian morality as well."

He adheres to this view of the matter, and hopes that those who are willing recklessly to sacrifice the unity and completeness of hymns, to make them fit the blank space they may happen to have to spare on a given page, will pass by his pieces altogether.

The request has often been made, by letter and otherwise, that the author would communicate any interesting facts that had come to his knowledge in connection with the use of this hymn. A great many such facts have been communicated to him ; but considerations of delicacy would forbid the publication of them in many cases, and the number, too, would render it impossible. He will, however, add here two or three touching incidents which may serve as examples.

During the late civil strife, and on the evening preceding one of the most terrible battles of the war, some six or eight Christian young men, who were looking forward to the deadly strife, met together in one of their tents for prayer. After spending some time in committing themselves to God, and in Christian conversation, and freely speaking together of the probability that they would not all of them survive the morrow, it was suggested by one of the number that they should draw up a paper expressive of the feelings with which they went to stand face to face with death, and all sign it ; and that this should be left as a testimony to the friends of such of them as might fall. This was unanimously agreed to ; and, after consultation, it was decided that a copy of " My faith looks up to Thee," should be written out, and that each should subscribe his name to it, so that father, mother, brother, or sister, might know in what spirit they laid down their lives. Of course they did not all meet again. The incident was related afterward by one who survived the battle.

Another interesting case was that of an active business-man, residing in the interior of the State, who was accustomed to visit the city of New York from time to time for business purposes. Before coming, on a certain occasion, he had observed a swelling slowly forming on his person, which, though not troublesome as yet, occasioned him some anxiety; and, after attending to the matters for which he came, he went to submit the case to the judgment of an eminent surgeon. He was frankly told that it would prove a malignant tumor, and would probably terminate his life by the end of six months. This was of course a stunning blow. He was an intellectual believer in Christianity, and a man of upright life, but was without a Christian hope. Before leaving the city, he called on a Christian lady, — a sister, we believe, — and told her what the surgeon had said. On parting from her, she placed in his hand a printed leaflet, which he accepted and put in his pocket. Then he took the cars on the Hudson River road, and, when seated, sunk into profound thought on his position. He recalled his past life, so filled with the divine goodness, his sinful neglect to return this with love and obedience, and his failure to receive the Saviour of the world into his heart. Some hours, perhaps, had passed in this way, and his heart had become full of tender feeling, when he remembered the leaflet and took it from his pocket. At once his eye rested on the words, —

> "My faith looks up to Thee,
> Thou Lamb of Calvary!"

He read the hymn through slowly, and many times over. His heart adopted the language, a new-born faith found full and delightful expression in it, and from that time he had a tranquil rest in God. The prediction of the surgeon was fulfilled ; and he died joyfully, having this song sung to him to the very last.

We will add but a single example more. It is contained in an extract from a letter of an excellent young lady, the daughter of a clergyman, who had been long suffering from a chronic disease : —

"One morning, long ago, I awoke with more than the usual exhaustion, and a sense of discouragement amounting to oppression. Do you know that kind of despair so like suffocation? Bitter repinings rose in my heart ; hard thoughts of God and sinful questionings. Why must it be ?. What shall I do? I heard the rain beating against the windows. I knew the day must be dreary, and I sighed aloud, 'What will there be to cheer me to-day?' And then I hastily glanced about the room, gladly discovering that I was alone, and turning again to my pillow wearily. Hark! the chords of a piano! The family must be at morning worship. Up through the register, as distinctly as if breathed at my bedside, came the strain, —

> "'My faith looks up to Thee,
> Thou Lamb of Calvary,
> Saviour divine!'

" I enjoyed it, and listened eagerly.

> " 'Now hear me while I pray,
> Take all my guilt away,
> O let me from this day
> Be wholly Thine ! '

" I felt calmed. I *would* look up for cheer. I could not say that dismal morning, 'Thou, O Christ, art all I want ; ' but I could say, ' My faith looks up to Thee.' Afterward, for several days and nights, I repeated the hymn constantly, especially the stanza, 'While life's dark maze I tread.' Maze was just the word for me. You know what a tangled wild my path of late has been."

Note B.

Nothing could well be more uncandid than the representations of a certain class of writers in their attempts to disparage the Fathers of New England. It is not wonderful that some errors of past ages and of their own age were still revealed in them. It is not strange that, having left their native land, and endured all sacrifices for the sake of enjoying their own opinions unmolested, they should have been sensitive to the intrusion of new elements of strife. That they misjudged and acted wrongly in some particulars is readily to be admitted. But that even their faults " leaned to virtue's side," only ill-nature and prejudice can deny.

" It was in self-defence," says the historian Bancroft (History United States, vol. i. p. 463), " that Puritanism in America began those transient persecutions of which the excesses shall find in me no apologist ; and which yet were no more than a train of mists hovering, of an autumn morning, over a fine river, that diffused freshness and

vitality wherever it wound. The people did not attempt
to convert others, but to protect themselves. *They never
punished opinion as such ;* they never attempted to punish
or terrify men into orthodoxy. The history of religious
persecution in New England is simply this : The Puritans
established a government in America such as natural justice warranted, and such as the statutes and common law
of England did not warrant ; and that was done by men
who still acknowledged the duty of a limited allegiance to
the parent state. The Episcopalians had declared themselves the enemies of the party, and waged against it a war
of extermination. Puritanism excluded them from its asy-
lum. Roger Williams, the apostle of ' soul-liberty,' weak-
ened the cause of civil independence by impairing its unity ;
and he was expelled, even though Massachusetts always
bore good testimony to his spotless virtues. Wheelwright
and his friends, in their zeal for strict Calvinism, forgot
their duty as citizens, and they also were exiled. The
Anabaptist, who could not be relied upon as an ally, was
guarded as a foe. The Quakers denounced the worship
of New England as an abomination and its government as
treason, and therefore they were excluded on pain of
death."

Elsewhere (vol. i. p. 454) Mr. Bancroft writes : " Some
of the Quakers were extravagant and foolish. They cried
out from the windows at the magistrates and ministers
that passed by, and mocked the civil and religious institutions of the country. *They riotously interrupted public worship ;* and women, forgetting the decorum of their sex, and
claiming a divine origin for their absurd caprices, smeared
their faces, *and even went naked through the streets."* It was
for these gross violations of public order and decency and
the rights of other people, and not for their religious opinions, that they suffered.

The historian further says : " The **effects of Puritanism** display its true character still more distinctly. . . . Puritanism was a life-giving spirit ; activity, thrift, intelligence, followed in its train ; and, as for courage, a coward and a Puritan never went together."

Again, the same pen writes : " Of all contemporary sects, the Puritans were the most free from credulity. . . . So many superstitions had been bundled up with every venerable institution of · Europe, that ages have not dislodged them all. The Puritans at once emancipated themselves from a crowd of observances. Hardly a nation of Europe has as yet made its criminal law so humane as that of early New England. A crowd of offences was at one sweep brushed from the catalogue of capital crimes." So other standard historians.

It is a sin alike against the memory of the greatly good and against truth and Christian charity, to attempt to hide beneath a few mistakes the most exalted virtues.

Note C.

The Anglo-Saxon race have everywhere exhibited strong social affections, and among them have been found, to a greater extent than among those of any other race, examples of well-ordered, intelligent, and virtuous homes. But even in England the number of such homes in proportion to the entire population is small. They are not relatively numerous beyond the circle of the aristocracy of rank and wealth. But among the Anglo-Saxon population of our older States the proportion of such homes is large. You can hardly go into any respectable-looking farm-house in Massachusetts or Connecticut without finding on the parlor table, along with the Bible, the works of Shakespeare, Milton, Addison, Johnson, Cowper, Wordsworth, and other

eminent writers, and seeing many other indications of a degree of intellectual and social culture not extensively found among the common people of any other land.

NOTE D.

THE writer believes most fully that he has not over-stated this matter in the text. The desire for the intellectual development of their children, so that they may become qualified to bear some honorable part in the great activities of life, is one of the strongest of parental instincts. Our fathers showed how powerful it was in them by founding schools and colleges almost before they had secured for themselves the ordinary comforts of life; and with patient care they began the course of education in the family. Yale, Harvard, and other institutions, not only originated in parental solicitude, and tastes and impulses nourished in the household, but are largely dependent on these to-day, and always must be.

NOTE E.

THE dissolution of the family by the going forth of its younger members one by one to the tasks of life, though it is always a sad process in itself, has yet its compensations. The happiness, the enduring welfare of the child, becomes to the thoughtful parent the paramount consideration. When, therefore, children go forth from beneath the paternal roof under favorable auspices, the pang of surrendering them is materially mitigated; and if they are seen living usefully and well, and especially if they rise to eminence among the wise and good, parents cannot but find in this a rich and abiding satisfaction that in large measure compensates for the loss of their society.

Note F.

The poet Burns, though he went to an early grave the victim of his own appetites, exhibited often an exquisite appreciation of what was morally beautiful and touching. In one of his letters he writes that he could never read without tears the following text from the New Testament : —

" The Lamb which is in the midst of the throne shall feed them, and shall lead them unto living fountains of waters ; and God shall wipe away all tears from their eyes."

Cambridge: Press of John Wilson & Son.